Someone was flying a helicopter up the
Hudson Valley of 1777 . . .

Wycliff peered through the darkness and smiled a
grim smile. The clearing was lit day-bright by the
Soviet work lights. He glanced left and right. His
Rangers crouched in the bushes, nearly invisible in
the darkness and rain. Now he brought his walkie-
talkie to his lips. "That's it, men. Go!"

Gunfire erupted from three sides of the clearing,
stabbing from the darkness as his men opened fire. A
Russian screamed and pitched forward from the helicopter's cargo door. AK fire flamed back, barking
against the night. A grenade burst near the helicopter
and the work lights died. The Russian fire abruptly
fell silent.

The victory was so sudden it was difficult to recognize. Wycliff sped across the clearing. The mortar
crates were empty! *Ambush* . . . he thought. Raw light
arced through the sky and then the deep-throated
yammer of a heavy machine gun opened up from the
woods on their flank. Bullets chopped through the
Ranger line. . . .

FREEDOM'S RANGERS

SEARCH AND DESTROY

KEITH WILLIAM ANDREWS

BERKLEY BOOKS, NEW YORK

FREEDOM'S RANGERS: SEARCH AND DESTROY

A Berkley Book/published by arrangement with
the author

PRINTING HISTORY
Berkley edition/March 1990

ISBN: 0-425-12004-X

One

The Hinds skimmed in low across the ridges at near treetop height, the roar of their engines drowning the howling wail of the emergency sirens. An Ilyushin circled high overhead as parachutes blossomed and drifted toward the airfield. Some *desantniki* were already on the ground near the northern perimeter, battling with base security forces. After the first wave of MiG-39 and Sukhoi ground-attack bombers had departed, large parts of the British installation were in charred and flaming ruin.

Lieutenant Travis Hunter checked the pulse of a British soldier sprawled near the overturned wreckage of a lorry. No . . . the man was dead, the pale blue eyes wide and staring, as though still showing shock at the snap-horror of the surprise attack. Hunter slipped his Uzi submachine gun into a more comfortable position and peered upward as the Hind gunships roared overhead. He could clearly make out the red stars painted on their sides, could see the rocket pods and missiles slung from their stubby wings. Gunfire crackled from the north.

"Lieutenant! Lieutenant! Over here!"

Hunter spotted Master Sergeant Greg King waving at him thirty yards away, near the entrance to the base command post. He waved back, then broke into the open, crouching low as he ran. None of the random fire from the Soviet paratroopers had come his way yet, but there was no sense in giving them an easy target.

"We seem to be in the middle of a war," Hunter said as he dropped to cover next to the brawny Ranger sergeant.

"It's becoming a goddamn habit," King growled. The concrete wall behind him was chipped by shrapnel from a near miss. He cradled his big FN-FAL assault rifle, eyes scanning the horizon. It was early morning, and the sun was just clearing the rolling sweep of the Blue Ridge Mountains to the east. Black smoke hung in a ragged smear against the sky to the northwest where a Sukhoi had run afoul of a British SAM.

"Where are the others?"

"The airfield. Lieutenant Taylor took them up first thing with some of the British sassmen to pick up some gear."

"Rachel . . . ?"

King's eyes were shuttered. "I . . . think she went with them. . . ."

"Oh, God . . ."

Hunter raised his head above the wall, peering past the command center toward the north. The airfield was masked by blue haze, but Hunter caught the steely glint of morning light on a helicopter canopy. It looked like a Russian helicopter transport was making a landing approach. A brilliant flash stabbed from a building visible only as a low, dark shadow beyond the field. The distant, hollow boom of the blast made the air tremble moments later.

His eyes went to a small, open-topped lorry abandoned by the side of the road. "I'm going up there, Greg."

There was worry in the way King licked his lips. "The brigadier's orders were pretty specific. . . ."

Hunter grinned suddenly. "And you know what the Brits can do with their orders! I'll be back in thirty mikes. . . ."

"Yes, sir. Begging the lieutenant's pardon, sir, but you're damn well not leaving me here!"

The pretense of military formality was a rebuke, Hunter knew, but he ignored it. "Right, then. Let's move!"

The sneak Russian attack appeared to be concentrated on Charles Field at the north end of the base, on the near side of the Shenandoah River's looping sprawl. The blue-purple bulk of the Appalachians shouldered into the sky beyond.

When the first wave of attacking aircraft roared in, the Rangers would have been at the big warehouse just off the runway, Hunter decided. They would probably still be there now. King slid into the driver's seat—placed in British fashion on the right side of the vehicle—turned the starter switch, and sprayed gravel as he gunned out onto the road, forcing

Hunter to cling to the roll bar for support. An odd-looking flag whipped from the lorry's antenna. Hunter's eyes went to it, tracing the unfamiliar design: three vertical bars laid out, red-white-red, with a Union Jack field at the hoist.

We don't belong here....

Time travel, Hunter reflected as he sped north, was a weapon as dangerous to its users as to its targets. The Chronos Project had been created by a team of scientists working in secret in a war-torn and partly occupied United States, a way for Free America to strike back against the Soviet empire. Through the Chronos Portal, a small, elite commando team could enter a specific time and place in the past in order to rewrite the pages of history. Communism might be kept from taking root, the horrors of Nazism blotted out before they occurred, dictators removed before they took power....

The world of the year 2007 might be transformed into a utopian pax instead of the devastated horror it had become.

The problem was that the Soviets had a time-travel program, too, one more advanced in many ways than the Chronos Project. Hunter's first missions to the past at the head of his Ranger team had brought him face-to-face with the VBU and plunged him headlong into the strangest war he'd ever known.

The VBU—the letters stood for *Vremya Bezopasnosti Upravlenie*, Russian for Time Security Directorate—was also attempting to alter history, instigating changes that would benefit the Soviet Union. The world of that strange flag on the lorry's antenna was the product of VBU tampering with the past...with *Hunter's* past. Raw chance had landed the Rangers here. It was the present of 2007...but it was the present of a world with a history radically different from his own, where the British had won the American Revolution and there had never been a United States of America.

The Dominion of British North America was a nation similar to the U.S. in some respects, and wildly different in others. The Dominion of this universe was as hard-pressed by the Russians as Free America was in Hunter's world, hedged in by enemies on every side. The Soviets were demanding the Dominion's absolute surrender, under the threat of all-out invasion and the nuclear devastation of BNA cities.

If not for the fact that the British had a time-travel project of their own, the Ranger team would have been stranded by the VBU tamperings in the past. There would have been no way to get home . . . because there would have been no home to return to. As it was, the Shenandoah Temporal Research Facility, nestled in among the ridges of Virginia, wasn't home, but at least here they had a fighting chance to set things straight.

If the Soviets let them have that chance.

Captain Sir David Wycliff had been in bed when the first ground-attack fighters shrieked in across the treetops from the east and loosed their air-to-surface missiles at the STRF's radar and SAM installations. The corrugated steel walls of the Nissen hut that served as his quarters rang with the blast of a nearby explosion, knocking lamps from tables and shattering the glass in the bedroom window.

He climbed out of bed and padded barefoot to the window, careful to avoid the broken glass on the floor. "Russians!" he said, watching a fireball rise above the base ammo dump. "The bloody bastards aren't waiting!"

Julie MacGregor brushed an unkempt spill of blond hair out of her eyes and sat up in the bed. "I thought their last ultimatum gave us three more days!"

"Maybe they can't count!" Wycliff began gathering parts of his uniform, which were scattered across the floor. "Maybe they just want to hurry us up! Since when have *Russians* ever kept their bloody word?"

Julie rolled out of bed and dressed hurriedly. The dull, heavy crump of distant explosions sounded from the north, mingled with the howl of jet fighters and the eerie wail of a siren. "I've got to get to Ops Center," she said. "The brigadier may want to move up the drop time after this."

Wycliff nodded as he finished knotting his boots. "Sounds like the attack is at Charles Field," he said. "I'll go across with you."

He paused in the front room of his quarters. The near miss had shaken the hut hard enough that one of his antique muskets had been jarred from the pegs on the dark brown wood paneling. He stooped to retrieve the weapon, a Brown Bess musket almost two hundred fifty years old, and set it gently back on the wall. Wycliff's passion, after the Army, was

Army history, and his antique gun collection reflected that love.

Don't know why you should bother, some analytical, detached portion of his mind rebuked him. *You won't be coming back here, you know. . . .*

The thought made him turn to Julie. The chief technician for the Shenandoah time-travel project, she was a love quite apart from the Army. Their eyes met . . . and then they were in each other's arms again. *Oh, God . . . how can I abandon . . . my world?*

Ever since Wycliff had joined the Shenandoah Project, he'd lived with the knowledge that he and his team of Special Air Service commandos were being groomed for what amounted to a suicide mission.

The plan was to send them back to intervene in history in such a way that the Communist menace would be eliminated before it could properly begin. History would be changed for the better . . . but everyone connected with the Shenandoah Project knew that the same change that eliminated the Soviets would in all probability eliminate them as well. No one could guess what the new universe would be like, but all agreed that it would be different enough that individual personalities would change beyond all recognition. If there was a David Wycliff in the new universe, it was most unlikely that he would have met and fallen in love with a blond time-travel technician named Dr. Julie MacGregor.

The execution of that strange form of suicide had been comfortably far-off until the arrival of strangers who claimed to be from an alternate reality, Rangers from something called the "United States." By unilaterally interfering in the past, Travis Hunter and his Rangers had brought all of them face-to-face with the knowledge that their universe was about to be . . . changed. Replaced by something else.

Damn Hunter, anyway. . . .

He hugged Julie as Soviet fighters howled overhead outside.

By the time they reached Wycliff's car, the helicopters had arrived, the rough thutter of their props disturbing the morning air. Wycliff spotted them low in the north. *Hind gunships . . . Hip transports*. His trained eye identified them at once, leading him to the obvious conclusions. *Army jobs . . . but they*

*must have flown in from a carrier group off the coast. They
don't have the range for a round trip. This'll be a one-way,
all-or-nothing grab, then. They're after the airfield so they
can land the big transports later on.*

Bouncing wildly across pavement split by the near miss,
the car screeched toward the base command center.

Sergeant Roy Anderson peered over a tangled barrier of
rubble spilling from the gutted control tower. Russian helicopters circled the field, machine-gunning anything that moved,
but he and the others had so far managed to stay out of sight
and out of the line of fire.

Chambering a 40mm grenade into the breech of his M-203,
Sergeant Eddie Gomez came up beside him. "Toldja not to
leave home without it," Gomez said, grinning. He'd insisted
on bringing his M-203/M-16 combo along that morning, even
though they were simply going to the airfield to pick up some
equipment.

"My daddy always told me not to carry firearms into the
host's sittin' room, Eddie," Anderson replied. He'd left his
M-16 back at the barracks, and he was regretting it now.
"Leastwise, not unless the hosts were armed and dangerous!"

SAS Trooper James Buchanan looked up as a stray bullet
shrieked off the concrete facade of the control tower twenty
feet above their heads. "Seems flamin' dangerous enough to
me, mate," he said. The Brit grinned, his eyes returning to the
darting movements of Russian troops among the hangars and
damaged airfield vehicles several hundred yards away.

Anderson tried to estimate their chances. The Soviet attack
was concentrated on the airfield, which meant more Russians
were on the way . . . probably in big Ilyushin transports. The
first wave had slipped in under the radar screen at dawn, flying nape-of-the-earth to launch blistering air strikes against
SAM sites, radar installations, and the Harrier jump jets sitting in the airstrip parking bays. Next had come the *desantniki*, the paratroopers who were moving to secure the field and
the major buildings. Now the Soviet helicopters were arriving
. . . lumbering, heavily armored Hind-D gunships and Mi-8
Hip troop transports. Each Hip could carry up to twenty-four
men. Those, Anderson reasoned, would be reinforcements
sent to hold the airfield until the Ilyushins arrived.

Against all this there was him and Gomez and a scattering of SAS troops that had accompanied them to Hangar 7 to collect their radio gear for the coming mission. Only a few of them were even armed.

And two of their people were missing. He raised himself above the rubble, peering into the smoke. "Anybody know where Lieutenant Taylor or Rachel got to?" he asked.

Gomez pointed across the airfield. "Hangar 5, Roy," he said. "They went across with a couple of the Brits to get the RS-17s."

Damn . . .

Gunfire probed from behind the shattered carcass of a Harrier as a trio of helicopters roared overhead. *We'd better find some more weapons fast,* he thought, *or we're in deep trouble.* . . .

Five hundred yards away, Lieutenant Ben Taylor grabbed Rachel's arm and tried to pull her down below the low wall. "Get down!"

She glared at him, her knuckles white as they gripped the Russian AKS-74 rifle she'd picked up on the airstrip. *"Get your hands off me* . . . *!"*

The rest of her words were smothered by the roar of the Hind as it swept overhead, searching for targets.

Taylor jabbed a thumb toward the Hind. "That thing's got too much armor!" he yelled, his mouth a few inches from Rachel's ear. The thunder of exploding rockets, the shrill clatter of the Soviet helicopter as it passed, made anything like normal conversation impossible. "You won't be able to touch it with that AK!"

Rachel nodded understanding and ducked back under the cover of the wall. The Hind hadn't seen them yet, but if they moved, they'd be in the open—easy targets for the heavily armed gunship.

Or for Russian troops. Taylor brought his H&K MP5 submachine gun to his shoulder and loosed a short, rattling burst at a pair of Soviet paratroopers racing across the tarmac a hundred yards away. One of the Russians jerked backward as though kicked in the face and collapsed on the field, writhing. The second man dove for the cover of a pile of concrete blocks.

Taylor heard the pounding of boots on the tarmac and turned to see a number of troops racing toward them. They wore the camo fatigues and desert sand berets of the SAS.

He recognized the man leading them. Sergeant John Mason, Taylor knew, didn't like the Ranger interlopers from an alternate reality, but he was a good soldier . . . and a good man to have on your side. He signaled the newcomers as the Hind swung low and wide, lining up for a strafing pass.

"Mason!" Taylor yelled. "Take cover!"

The Hind thundered down on them, cannon fire slamming among the British soldiers, spraying chips of tarmac and gravel. An SAS trooper carrying the bulky tube of a Blowpipe SAM pitched over dead. The other soldiers scattered, diving for cover as the Soviet gunship howled past, close enough, it seemed, to touch. Rachel sat up beside him, the AK bucking and kicking in her hands as she emptied a magazine into the receding helicopter.

She caught his eyes on her and lowered the weapon. Her smile held no warmth. "Hey," she said. "It couldn't hurt to try!"

Then the Hind skittered sideways in a low, flat turn, and white spears shooshed from the rocket pods hanging beneath the wings, ripping into Hangar 5 with multiple explosions that gutted the structure in flame and spinning fragments of corrugated steel.

Taylor dragged Rachel down to the ground, lying halfway across her body as the pounding, shrieking noise assaulted his ears.

"It could damned well get us killed!" he yelled in reply, but the words were lost in the roar of exploding warheads.

Two

They swung onto the airstrip tarmac, the tires of their appropriated lorry squealing as King twisted the wheel to avoid a gaping crater by the runway. A Hip transport descended nearby, its rotor wash swirling the drifting smoke that obscured much of the airfield. Hunter could see the rear clamshell doors already open, could see the ramp lowering as the troops on board prepared to rush out. He fired a burst from his Uzi, but the range was too great for any noticeable effect.

They had to get closer. He slapped King on the arm and pointed to a spill of debris near Hangar 7. "Floor it!" he yelled. A Hind-D howled low overhead, cannons rattling toward Hangar 5, a hundred yards behind them. Moments later the hangar was shredded by rockets, but Hunter kept his eyes on the Hip.

They had to get closer. . . .

"Look out!" Anderson pointed. A Hip transport was settling in for a landing. He'd flown helicopters before on his father's Texas ranch—civilian jobs like the Bell 47—and he could tell by the way it was maneuvering that it was heavily loaded.

The rattle of a heavy machine gun sounded close by. A British Land Rover pulled up close beside Hangar 7, an SAS man hanging on to the L7 machine gun rigged on a pintel mount in the back.

White contrails arced across the sky as a Hind-D made a pass. Exploding warheads punched gaping holes in the hangar's wall, sending jagged chunks of metal scything across the field. The Brit machine gunner sagged across his weapon's breech as the muzzle swung to point straight up. The Land Rover's driver slumped sideways and spilled out of the right-hand seat.

"Stay put, Eddie!" Anderson snapped. "Hit 'em with your 40s!"

Anderson scrambled to his feet and ran, keeping his body doubled over. He vaulted into the back of the Land Rover as the Hip touched ground two hundred yards away.

He shoved the body of the gunner aside, dropped the muzzle of the weapon into line with the Hip, checked that the ammo belt was free, and squinted down the sights. Soviet troops were boiling down the ramp, spreading across the airfield, firing as they ran. Anderson recognized those camouflage uniforms. *Spetsnaz!*

The *Spetsialnoye Nazhacheniye* were the Soviet equivalent of the American Special Forces, well trained and deadly masters of commando raids such as this. Anderson's finger closed on the L7's trigger and the gun roared, spraying hot brass from the ejector port as he hosed machine-gun fire into the advancing enemy. The front rank of spetsnaz troops toppled as though swept over by a broom. Bullets sparked and chipped at the tarmac. The Soviets scattered, seeking cover.

Anderson heard the thump of Eddie's M-203 grenade launcher above the racket of his machine gun. A moment later a savage blast tore at the side of the Hip, kicking the slowly spinning rotors askew and sending a fireball rumbling into the sky above the stricken helicopter. Russians tumbled from the burning aircraft, their clothing aflame. Anderson continued firing as Gomez's M-16 joined in, cutting down Russians with no place to hide.

Hunter saw the grenade go off against the Hip's side. King swung the vehicle hard to the left to avoid billowing flames and hurtling debris. Soviet troops ran out of the smoke and Hunter cut them down with short, sharp bursts from his Uzi.

Spetsnaz!

Machine-gun fire barked from the smoke near Hangar 7, and King twisted the lorry sharply to the left to avoid being hit. The targets were on the far side of the burning Hip, but rounds were howling in through the smoke, deadly in their random blindness. Hunter could hear the screams of Russians dying beyond the fire.

He tapped King again and pointed toward Hangar 5. There were more Soviets there . . . *desantniki* rushing a thin line of SAS troops close to the hangar's shell-pocked wall. The paratroopers had their backs to the runway and to the racing lorry.

Hunter snapped a fresh magazine into his Uzi and hung on as Greg accelerated. Behind them and to the right, a Hind gunship swooped in for the kill.

The *shoosh-boom* of a rocket tearing into the roof of the hangar behind him hurled Anderson from the Land Rover. He took the impact on his shoulder, managing a clumsy shoulder roll that brought him down several yards from the Land Rover as a second rocket followed the first into the shattered side of the hangar. He followed the rocket's trail back through clots of drifting smoke.

"Oh, Lord . . ." He could see the squat, ugly shape of a Hind gunship sweeping in low across the airstrip, zeroing in on the source of machine-gun fire. Anderson scrambled to his feet and ran as the third rocket struck home, spinning the Land Rover end for end, a crumpled mass of flaming metal.

An explosion of burning fuel completed the destruction of the Hip transport. The Hind raced forward, its rotor wash scattering the oily smoke as it swung its ugly, bug-faced prow to bear on Anderson. . . .

Lieutenant Taylor watched the Hind circle above the airfield. White rocket contrails speared toward Hangar 7. He saw the explosion of the Land Rover, saw cannon fire probing the ruins where the other Rangers were hiding.

Taylor had been a helicopter pilot before volunteering for Ranger training. He knew that even the rugged, heavily armored Hind gunship was vulnerable to the right kind of weapon.

His eyes fell on the Blowpipe SAM, lying beside the sprawled body of an SAS trooper. He'd worked with the Blowpipe several years before as part of a NATO cross-training exercise. That would do the trick. . . .

If he could reach it.

Taylor told Rachel to keep her head down and broke from

cover. Gunfire snapped and howled through the ruins as he ran toward the fallen trooper. His thinking was curiously detached as he ran, beyond the pulse of adrenaline in his arteries, beyond the shrieking roar of airborne death. *I'll only have one chance,* he thought. *One shot.*

He knelt by the body, scooping up the launcher and pawing at the dead soldier's gear until he found the detachable aiming unit that clipped onto the side of the missile canister. He brought the tube to his right shoulder, tracking the gunship through the monocular sight.

Gunfire erupted from his left. He was aware of paratroopers climbing over the barricades of rubble, aware of Mason's men cutting the *desantniki* down as they swarmed over the wall. Rachel was on her feet, firing short, precise bursts as the Russians advanced. A bullet plucked at Taylor's sleeve but he ignored it, concentrating on the helicopter.

The Hind slowed and steadied, barely five hundred yards away, its cannon fire tearing into the ruins of the hangar to Taylor's left. He pulled the trigger.

The round nose cap of the missile canister popped off as the booster engine ignited. Taylor held himself steady and erect, gripping the launcher to keep the Hind centered in the sight. The missile's sustainer engines kicked in with a white flare of light. Taylor's right thumb found the small joystick control, which sent course correction commands over a radio link. An infrared sensor showed him the missile's position, let him gently guide the missile up . . . up . . . over to the right . . . No! Too far! *Too far!*

The lorry screeched to a halt a dozen feet from the rubble wall. Hunter triggered his Uzi into the backs of Soviet paratroopers who staggered or spun or simply slumped into limp heaps as a storm of 9mm death swept through them. A shoulder-launched missile swished out from behind the barricade on a trail of white smoke, arrowing toward the Hind at his back.

He released the trigger and snapped the muzzle of his subgun up as SAS troops appeared at the barricade. He saw Rachel, her hair a black swirl as she ran, an AK in her hands.

"*Rachel . . . !*"

/ •   •   •

Taylor's over-correction sent the missile wide, narrowly missing the Hind's tail. At the last possible instant the proximity fuse triggered the warhead.

The blast shattered the helo's tail rotor, causing it to fragment in hurtling chunks of metal. No longer able to balance against the torque of the main rotors, the helo began a wild, wobbling spin.

It struck, the boxy, armored form crumpling under the impact as it tried to corkscrew into the tarmac. Flame gouted skyward as fuel and munitions erupted in multiple, echoing blasts.

An SAS trooper ran up. "Nice shooting, mate." Taylor, numb now as he released the joystick and let the empty tube fall to the ground, could only nod. Rachel joined him as a lorry drove in past the rubble barricade. He recognized King at the wheel . . . and Hunter. Someone clapped him on the back . . . the British soldier named Yates.

He noticed a burning at his left shoulder. Looking down, he saw the tear in his fatigues, the thin, bloody scratch where a Russian bullet had grazed him. He'd not even been aware of it.

Fresh thunder echoed from the sky and he looked up. Pent-up adrenaline shook him.

"Not to worry, mate," Yates said. "Them's our boys now. Harriers out o' Alexandria . . ."

There was no Washington, D.C., in the BNA universe, Taylor thought distantly. But there must be an air base at Alexandria. The jets hurtling overhead bore BNA markings now and not the red star of the Soviets.

"About bloody time," a trooper said. "Look at 'em go! 'Ave at 'em, mates!"

Another Hind pirouetted to earth, exploding in flames on the far bank of the Shenandoah. A pair of Harriers coasted in, hovering on shrieking jets above the broken runway. Taylor saw Russian spetsnaz and paratroops nearby, their hands raised in surrender.

"We . . . won," Taylor managed to say. The shock of the realization left him dazed. His mind was clear, but his body and his speech were dull and unresponsive.

"Yeah, we won," a voice said from nearby. It was Mason, the SAS top sergeant. "For all the good it'll do us."

"What do you mean?"

Mason turned away without answering. A moment later Hunter and King were there.

"Great shot, Ben," Hunter said with a grin. "Now, if you're through playing hero, we'd better hotfoot it back to the Ops Center. The brigadier is waiting for us, and we're already late."

The smoke from burning helicopters blackened the morning sky.

Hunter watched Brigadier C. Gordon Carruthers digest the report from his chief of staff. The British commander of the Shenandoah Temporal Research Facility was tall and lean, with a pencil-thin mustache that gave him the air of some old-time Hollywood leading man. Carruthers paced from one side of the conference room to the other, hands behind his back, head bowed, as Colonel MacAvey spoke.

"All in all, two enemy ground-attack aircraft and five helos shot down," MacAvey said. "An estimated eighty enemy troops dead, plus another hundred prisoners. Nine helos escaped, but it is our estimate that they will not have fuel to reach their carrier task force."

"No," Captain Wycliff put in. "Those Hinds wouldn't have been able to land on a carrier, anyway. It was a one-way mission, do or die."

"It'll be die, then," MacAvey said. He looked up from his report, studying the others around the table through his thick-lensed glasses. "We believe that the Russians were not expecting to find an SAS squadron here. If so, it indicates a hole in their intelligence. It all adds up to a clear win for our side."

"It's not over yet," Carruthers said. "We've had reports of another wave, much larger, already on its way. They were tracked leaving Cuban airspace less than thirty minutes ago."

"But they couldn't still mean to attack, surely," a British major across the table said. "Not after their first assault was so badly handled!"

"That doesn't seem to worry them, Major," Captain Wycliff said. "Evidently they felt the first wave hurt our defenses badly enough that they're going ahead and sending in the heavy stuff." Wycliff paused before adding, "Ilyushin transports. Ten of them, with a cloud of MiGs and Red Navy Yaks flying escort."

"Can you stop them?" Taylor asked.

MacAvey shook his head. "Not a chance. The whole country's on alert, but it looks like the buggers are going to come in over every border any time now. It seems the Reds are through waiting. We might slow them for a while . . . but we won't stop them this time."

"How long?" the major asked.

"Three hours, tops," the brigadier said. His face was drawn, the words stiff. "The radar boffins give them an ETA of 1300 hours. Then we'll be up to our eyebrows in Russians."

"And it's nearly 1015 hours now," Wycliff said. "The question, I suppose, is whether we can be ready in time."

Carruthers stopped his pacing and turned his gaze on Julie MacGregor. "Well, Doctor? Can you lock into the appropriate coordinates in two hours?"

She frowned. "I have my people working on it now, Brigadier. There's a real problem with the target date, though. We think the temporal effects of the last mission are setting up a kind of interference. It will take time to get a positive lock. . . ."

"And time is just what we don't have," Wycliff said. The SAS squadron commander's head turned sharply, nailing Hunter with a savage glare. "Dammit, Hunter! This really is your fault, you know. We shouldn't have to go back a second time!"

Wycliff's attack was so sudden, so unexpected, that Hunter didn't know how to answer. His own feelings of guilt over the current situation gave him no peace, but Wycliff's accusation was startling in its frankness.

"You can't blame him for what's happened?" Rachel said.

"I blame him for unilaterally taking on the Russians at Brandywine," Wycliff replied. "Before he knew everything he had to know! Thanks to the leftenant, we may lose both our universe and yours . . . and be stuck with something even worse. . . ."

Hunter closed his eyes, his hands hardening into white-knuckled fists. *It was right there for me to see, and I didn't even notice!* he thought. *God! How could I have been so dense?*

When the Rangers had first arrived in British North America, it had not taken them long to pinpoint the general time and place—the Temporal Nexus Point, as the engineers called it—where the VBU had changed history. In this universe the British had won the American Revolution. General George Washington died at the Battle of Brandywine, on September 11, 1777. His successor, a General Putnam, surrendered to the British at Valley Forge the following year. It had been Hunter's research in the STRF library that had pinpointed Washington's death as the critical factor responsible for changing history.

They'd been transported to 1777 Pennsylvania with orders to find proof that the VBU was indeed active at Brandywine. The Rangers had found that proof, and in the process they'd saved General Washington's life. A recon by Gomez and King located the VBU headquarters in a stone building, Leicester House, located on a hill near the battlefield. Rangers and SAS had returned to the VBU base together, found the Soviet time machine, and taken it out in a sharp, blazing firefight that had obliterated the VBU's presence in Revolutionary America. . . .

Or so they'd thought.

It wasn't until the STRF's Intelligence Section had gone over papers and records captured at Leicester House that it was discovered that the VBU was after more than General Washington.

"And how was he supposed to know the Russians had a second target?" Rachel demanded. "We found their headquarters and we destroyed their time portal downlink. I'd say it was just damn good luck that we found out they had another commando force back there . . . and what its target was!"

"And perhaps if Leftenant Hunter had done his research better, we could have taken care of the entire problem with one mission! As it is, we have to mount a second op . . . and with a bloody time limit besides! Even *you* ought to be able to see where that leaves us."

"Just a damned minute!" Hunter stood, his fist coming down hard on the conference table. "Yell all you want, but direct it at *me*, not Rachel! It was my mistake, after all!"

"It bloody well was!" Wycliff's face was dark, flushed with anger.

The brigadier held up his hands. "Gentlemen! Enough! We have less than three hours to go . . . and no time for bickering. The Russians have pretty well put paid to the two-week deadline, anyway, what?"

"And if it wasn't for Hunter," Wycliff insisted, "we might not have to go back a second time at all!"

Hunter's eyes locked with Rachel. He felt the warmth of her love there but forced himself to look away.

Saratoga! God! How could I screw up so badly?

Three

There shouldn't have been a problem at all, Hunter thought. It took time for changes initiated in the past to reconfigure the sweep of history that followed; in the case of a change in 1777, it would take about two weeks before the shape of 2007 was transformed into something new. By saving Washington's life at Brandywine, Hunter had arbitrarily doomed the time line of British North America.

The British had been working toward the same end, of course, with their own time-travel project, but Hunter had made a critical mistake in his research. The captured papers made reference to a second VBU operation in 1777, besides the assassination of Washington . . . something intended to change the Battle of Saratoga.

For all his love of history, Hunter could not remember many of the details of the battle. He knew that in *his* timeline Saratoga was a critical American victory, a campaign covering two separate battles that ended in the surrender of a British army on the banks of the Hudson River in Upstate New York. Because of that victory, the French had recognized the fledgling nation . . . and that recognition proved absolutely vital at Yorktown four years later.

According to the British North Americans, only one battle was fought at Saratoga, a short, grisly affair in which an unexpectedly fierce artillery bombardment had utterly demolished the American Army under General Horatio Gates.

But the battle had occurred on September 19, 1777, over a week after Brandywine. Hunter had noticed the discrepancy during his research before the Brandywine intervention . . . but he'd been so excited about discovering that George Washington had died in this new, altered history that he'd assumed the new version of Saratoga was the result of the change in Pennsylvania. All history after Washington's death in battle was suspect, after all, for it was from that point that the two histories diverged.

Only now it was evident that the Russians had interceded *twice*, once at Brandywine and again at Saratoga. Exactly what they'd done was unknown. It was assumed that a party of VBU agents had already left their headquarters in Pennsylvania for New York when the SAS/Ranger raid against Leicester House was launched.

So the job was half complete. By saving Washington, Hunter had introduced a change in British North America's past; but because he'd missed the VBU interference at Saratoga, a second mission would be necessary now, to stop them from turning a British defeat into an American disaster.

Normally, two weeks would have been enough time to organize that second mission. Unfortunately, now there was a second deadline, a much more immediate one. With Soviet heavy transports less than three hours away, they might well lose their chance to intervene at Saratoga.

And if they couldn't make this second change? Hunter didn't want to think about it. The world of British North America would be replaced in less than two weeks by something new . . . and utterly unpredictable. It would be a world where Washington survived the American defeat at Brandywine . . . but where Saratoga ended with the destruction of an American army. There might be no French recognition of the United States. Perhaps, under Washington's leadership, the Revolution would carry on past 1778, but without French help it was unlikely that the struggle would succeed.

And what if the analogue of British North America or the United States in this new universe never developed time travel? Then the fight would truly be over, for there would be no going back to try again . . . even assuming Hunter and the others could themselves somehow escape the effects of the change.

Hunter wrestled with the guilt of his mistake.

"It's pointless to bicker," Carruthers said sharply. "As you pointed out, Captain, there is no *time*. We're all agreed that

Saratoga is vital. We have to pull it together before we run out of options."

"Do we still have options?" Wycliff asked.

"My people are ready to go," Hunter said. *But, dammit, we don't know what we're walking into!*

"And mine," Wycliff said. "The tailor shop says our costumes are ready, but after the strike at the airfield, we're short on some stuff." He began ticking points off on his fingers. "We only have five RS-17s. We lost a lot of our radio gear at the airfield this morning and we're down to eight working sets. All the tents and camp gear were destroyed at Hangar 5. And we don't have any horses in at all."

The Russian attack that morning had badly upset the schedule the Ranger-SAS team was following. The plan worked out after their return from the Brandywine op called for one full SAS troop—sixteen men—plus Hunter, Rachel, and the rest of the Ranger team to be dropped into the area near Saratoga, New York, at some point in time just prior to September 10, 1777. All twenty-two people would be wearing clothing designed to let them blend in with the locals without exciting comment, and they'd hoped to use horses gathered from farms near the Shenandoah base to serve as pack animals for their gear. The jump-off had been scheduled for three days later.

And now they had three hours.

"I don't think the lack of gear poses that big a problem," Hunter said. His eyes shifted from one face at the conference table to another. There was open hostility on Wycliff's face, deep pain and weariness in Carruthers's. The brigadier had lost two sons within the past few days...one in the Russian nuclear destruction of Toronto, a second in the attack on Leicester House at Brandywine. "We can sleep in the open, so we don't have to mingle with the locals too much. And at least we have the period dress so we can dress like natives when mingling is necessary."

"We have a supply of gold nuggets ready, by the by," one of Carruthers's staff officers said. "That ought to serve you as money well enough."

"It would have been nice to have the horses to carry our gear, though," Anderson pointed out.

"I don't know about you Rangers," Sergeant Mason said.

"The sass can yomp cross-country with everything we need on our backs. Who needs horses?"

"If there's no time, there's no time," Hunter said. "We'll manage with our rucksacks. It's the lack of hard information that has me worried."

"What do you mean?" Carruthers asked.

"Two points, actually. We know the Russians will have someone at Saratoga . . . dispatched from Leicester House, I suppose. We don't know how many there'll be, how they're armed, or where they're going to be."

"That's why we're sending a whole troop back," Wycliff said. "Plus your lot. That'll be enough to bag them. Can't be more than six or eight of the buggers detached from the Brandywine op, if that."

Hunter nodded. "The other problem is just how the VBU made Saratoga turn out the way it did in your history. We've got to change that if we're to recover our history, and I just don't know enough about how the battle went originally to be able to make any guesses."

Wycliff's eyes narrowed. "I thought you were the bloody expert on your history."

"In general, I suppose. I know the Americans won Saratoga . . . that they won a couple of battles there, in fact, as part of a campaign over a month or so . . . and that the British under General John Burgoyne surrendered to them afterward. But that's not enough to tell us what the VBU plans to do to change that."

"I see no problem whatsoever," Wycliff said. He turned to face Carruthers. "We have radio direction finders enough to bracket the whole area, Brigadier. We are deliberately going back better than a week before the battle, in order to catch the VBU bastards when they arrive. We'll stop them before they do their mischief . . . and it won't matter a trice whether Hunter knows what's going on or not."

Carruthers's frown deepened. "It will have to do," he said after a moment. "I see no alternatives. If we don't at least try to carry out this mission at Saratoga, everything we've done so far . . . all our losses . . . will have been for nothing." He fell silent, and his hands closed into fists, the knuckles starkly white. No one at the table spoke for long moments. Finally Carruthers continued. "As I understand it, if you gentlemen can carry this off, our . . . universe, our world, will become only a . . . only a might-have been. An alternate reality that never was." A smile tugged at the corner of his mouth. "God, I welcome that now. And if you are successful, then Mr. Hunter's world will have been restored . . . with the hope that the fight against the Communists can be continued. That, I believe, is worth working for. Three hours from now we will lose even that hope if the Russians arrive and shut us down. I and my people will buy you as much time as we can, but we will have no hope of stopping them. Everything, gentlemen, depends on you."

"Then we'd best move, Brigadier," Wycliff said abruptly. "My boys have to suit up and assemble." He exchanged glances with Julie. "And the technical people had best find that lock-on, eh?"

"Dismissed, then," Carruthers said. "I'll see all of you at the Circus."

The Circus was what the STRF people called the central control area, where gateways were opened into the past. A broad stage at one end of the room was dominated by power conduits and busbars surrounding the faint blue nebulosity of an opening portal. "Eight minutes," an amplified voice announced from a speaker on one wall. "All normal."

Wycliff walked down the line of SAS troopers, inspecting each in turn.

"Hope you're not gigging us for uniform violations, Captain," someone he'd already passed by said.

"That'll be quite enough, Fitzroy," Wycliff said quietly, but he smiled. All of them wore period civilian clothing, an odd-looking mix of vests and hunting shirts, breeches and boots that looked oddly out of place with the heavy, military-issue rucksack each man carried on his back. The backpacks were already checked and rechecked. They carried camo fatigues, ballistic vests, and load harnesses, grenades and ammo, sleeping bags, and rations enough to let them operate independently of locals for a week. A few carried hand-held walkie talkies or the small RS-17 radio direction finders that would be useful for pinpointing VBU transmissions. Several men were packing extra. Trooper White lugged a L7 light machine gun, while MacNeil carried the team's recall beacon.

Except for White, each man carried one of the stubby, bullpup-loaded L85A1 assault rifles, which bureaucrats insisted on calling an Individual Weapon. They looked neither military nor authentic for 1777, and the result was amusing.

Wycliff reached the end of the line, then turned to address all of his men at once. "I have absolute confidence in this mission," he said slowly. "Dressed the way you are, you'll probably scare the Bolshies to death."

His joke was answered by a ripple of laughter. The men seemed relaxed, rested, and ready to go. *Good.*

"I'll say it again," he said. "We will keep our contact with the locals to a minimum. Stay together, stay alert, and the op will come down fine. Now . . . let's kill Russians!"

The answering roar was all he'd hoped for. The team was ready, eager for blood after the morning's clash with the Soviets. *We might just pull this thing off.*

He walked across to where he'd left his own rucksack. Sergeant Mason came up behind him. "Here, Sir David. Let me." The burly man helped Wycliff set the heavy ruck on his shoulders. "Hello . . . we're packing enough junk to start a business."

"Hope it won't come to that." His mind went to the leather pouch of gold he carried. *We want to stay clear of the locals, not trade with them*, he thought. *But if we need money . . .*

Wycliff cinched the harness tight. He was wearing a snug-waisted, long-tailed coat, the sort a businessman of the period might wear. The one unusual touch was the reproduction flintlock pistol hanging from its holster on his belt instead of a more modern concealable weapon. He'd taken the weapon from his collection with the excuse that it might serve as a trade item, should the gold not be enough.

Or was it that he was having trouble letting go of his own personal past? He looked up and caught Julie MacGregor watching him from behind her computer console. *We've said our good-byes, but . . .*

The hell of it was that success on this mission meant the loss of . . . everything. If the scientists were right, the op would change all of them into completely different people, with different pasts, different lives, different loves.

His determination to carry on with the project, Wycliff knew, was wavering, now that the time for departure was at hand. Not that he'd compromise the mission, of course, but the realization that he was sacrificing his universe to give these strangers their chance to keep fighting the Russians grated. Was continuing the fight worth the price?

As he walked toward Julie his pack felt heavier.

From across the room, Rachel watched Wycliff and Julie talking, saw the way the girl looked up into the SAS captain's eyes. She recognized the affection there and felt a pang. *Travis* . . .

She was worried about Hunter. The discovery that he'd missed the fact that Saratoga was a critical change in the new version of history seemed to have catapulted him into a bleakness of mind and heart she'd never seen in him before. Hunter, Rachel knew, tended to seesaw in his moods, from animated excitement to a self-searching worry that bordered on depression, but she'd never seen him this afflicted.

There was no denying the love she felt for him, but the man could be so exasperating! She'd fought with him before over what she thought of as his obsessive concern for details in these time-travel missions, his fear that if they missed some tiny, hard-to-spot fact, some action they took in the past could destroy their history as completely as any VBU plot.

For Rachel the choice was simpler. Action—*any* action— was preferable to doing nothing, to allowing the Russians to run roughshod over her country . . . and her people.

Her hand came up to her chest, feeling through the material of her costume for the small locket concealed there. Her mother's locket—a symbol, really, of her own past, now long lost. Rachel and her mother had been close . . . until an auto accident on the winding roads near the Mount Bannon time-travel project in Colorado had killed her. Someday the Rangers would succeed in their quest to change the past. When that happened, the Russian menace would be gone . . . and other things would be changed as well. *Someday* . . .

She heard a step behind her and turned. Hunter was there.

"Hello, Raye." He looked uncomfortable, and not entirely because of his dress. Like the British, the Rangers were outfitted in period clothing. Hunter wore a tan-colored coat over a white shirt, the same antique garb he'd worn at Brandywine. The coat concealed the automatic pistol at his hip but did not quite hide the Uzi slung from his shoulder on a leather harness.

"Hello, Travis." She struggled to find the right words. "Are you . . . okay?"

He managed a grim smile. "Fine, Raye. You . . . you're looking lovely," he said awkwardly.

She glanced down at herself, suddenly self-conscious. Her costume was loose and not uncomfortable, but there was so much of it, a floor-length skirt over a layer of petticoats over a cotton shift. She wore a long-sleeved blouse and a long scarf crossed over her breasts. The satchel in her hand was out of place, but it carried fatigues, boots, and her 9mm Beretta.

"I feel like Cinderella looking for her pumpkin."

"You'd better wear that, though." He pointed at a scrap of cloth tucked into the waistband of her apron. She looked down, puzzled, and he explained. "Your mobcap. Be sure to keep it on. Where we're going, a woman without a hat is indecent."

Her expression darkened as she adjusted the hat on her head. *That's the sort of detail he keeps worrying about. That fussiness is going to paralyze him someday. . . .*

"I'd better check the others," Hunter said. "You have everything you need?"

"I'm fine, Travis. Really." She smiled. "At least you're letting me come along without an argument."

He returned the smile ruefully. "Not much choice this time, is there?"

There wasn't, it was true. If they were successful, they would remain in the past long enough to make certain that the Battle of Saratoga ended as it should have. By the end of that time, the Transformation Wave first set in motion days before by Hunter's saving of Washington at Brandywine would reach 2007. If all went well, the changes at Saratoga and Brandywine together would restore their own universe . . . Time Square and General Thompson, the United States of America. . . .

Her hand touched the hidden locket again. *And our chance to set everything right again.*

As Hunter turned away from Rachel, a dull, rumbling boom sounded through the complex from somewhere overhead. He paused, looking up at the naked cement ceiling and its tangle of exposed wires, cables, and light fixtures, as though trying to see through to the outside.

Carruthers stood at a console nearby, holding a headset to one ear. "They're here," he said simply. He had a British L85 slung over his shoulder, a strange accessory for a brigadier. "The first Ilyushin touched down three minutes ago. Paratroopers are already on the ground. It won't be long now."

"We're ready, Brigadier," Hunter said. "You'll . . . make sure they don't follow us through?"

He read the anguish behind Carruthers's quiet eyes. "They won't follow you. Charges have been planted at the key power leads. Five minutes after you go through, the Circus will become a very expensive scrap heap. You'll be on your own then . . . with a vengeance."

"We'll handle it, sir. I wish we could help you here somehow."

"I suppose you will be." He cocked his head to one side. "I wonder if there's a me in the universe you're trying to restore?" He smiled. "If there is, look him up and get him to buy you a drink."

"I'll see what I can do. He . . . uh . . . might not believe the story."

"I daresay that's so."

The thunder sounded closer. White dust sifted down from the ceiling with the heavy, thumping concussions.

"Pardon me, Brigadier. I want to see to my men."

"Quite right."

Hunter walked to where his men were standing, a little apart from the SAS team. He glanced over toward Wycliff, who was talking with Julie MacGregor, then watched the SAS captain straighten, turn, and walk back to his men.

He's more concerned about our working with the SAS than I am, Hunter thought. The worry was not entirely reasonable. They'd pulled off the Leicester House strike at Brandywine by working together smoothly . . . or smoothly enough, at least, though there'd been problems. Hunter knew the SAS commander was concerned about the Rangers'—especially Hunter's—willingness to follow orders. That had been a sore point at Brandywine, and Wycliff's worries seemed sharper now.

He wished he could understand the man's thinking better. *Why does he have it in for us?*

He approached the other Rangers: Gomez, grinning as he slung his M-16/M-203 combo over his shoulder; Anderson resting his L7 machine gun butt down on the floor and snugging his rucksack tight; Taylor shrugging into his period coat and adjusting its hang to hide his holstered automatic pistol.

"I feel like a damned walking supply depot," King said, coming up beside them. His backpack was stuffed full of additional belts for Anderson's L7, as well as ammo for his FN-FAL. "I haven't hauled this much junk since I was a recruit!"

"You know the old Boy Scout bit, Greg." Anderson said. He had drawn the British MG from the base stores and had his own M-16 strapped to his pack. "Be prepared!"

King grinned at Hunter. "Hell, Lieutenant, I thought we were just after the VBU . . . not out to fight the whole damned war!"

Hunter nodded, turning away. He didn't feel much like joining the usual pre-mission banter.

It was true they were heavily loaded. Their first task, once they arrived, would be to find a place to set up camp, somewhere out in the woods and well away from the comings and goings of the Continental Army. They'd need to reconnoiter the country, try to get an idea about how the Russians might strike. They would make their final plans then.

"Full power in a couple minutes," Carruthers announced. "Ready to go?"

Hunter surveyed the four men in his command as they shouldered packs and weapons. "Yessir. All set."

Julie MacGregor looked up from her control console nearby. "We have a positive lock, Brigadier. We're still getting some interference from the earlier portal links in that time period."

"Do the best you can, then, Doctor. Will you be able to hold the gateway open long enough for all of them to pass through?"

Julie's gaze passed Carruthers, seeking the SAS Captain. "No problem, sir."

Hunter felt extremely uncomfortable as he watched Julie's eyes shift over to Wycliff, who was still talking to his men.

He wondered if she blamed the Rangers for setting in motion the events that were separating them.

There would be no reunions for Julie and Wycliff. If they succeeded, Julie and British North America would be gone. If they failed . . .

No, there would be no reunions.

Hunter stepped closer to Julie's console. "I'm . . . sorry," he said softly. "I know how you must feel."

She managed a smile. "Not to worry, Leftenant. We'll hold them . . . at least long enough for you to do your part . . . back there." The smile faded then, and she reached out to touch Hunter's arm. "Only one thing, Mr. Hunter. You will stop them, won't you? There won't be another . . . Toronto?"

Julie had lost her entire family in the same firestorm that had claimed Carruthers's son.

"I'll do all I can. All *we* can."

"Then . . . then thank you." She turned and hurried away, back toward her control console.

"Full power," a voice announced over a loudspeaker. "Positive lock, holding steady."

"Time," Carruthers said.

"Brigadier . . ."

He shook his head. "Smash the buggers, Leftenant. For King and Country, eh?"

The phrase seemed wildly inappropriate for an attempt to ensure that the British *lost* the American Revolution, but Hunter grinned and accepted the brigadier's outstretched hand. "Yes, sir. For King and Country."

The thunder sounded closer. . . .

Four

The blue glow shimmered and swirled above the portal platform. Power throbbed, charging the air with the sharp tang of ozone. Hunter shrugged against his pack and swung into the end of the double line waiting to file through, next to King and just behind Gomez.

Wycliff stood to the side of the line, his eyes sweeping across the group. "Right, then! Forward!"

The first pair of men vanished into the blue light, followed by the second . . . the third. The line moved forward, stepping up the ramp and onto the platform. Hunter heard the swish of Rachel's dress and petticoat as she walked, just ahead of Gomez. There were only two pairs of SAS men left now, just ahead of Rachel and Taylor.

Wycliff stepped close to Hunter. "You'll do well to remember who's in charge here," he said, his voice low. "I'll stand for no wild stunts like you pulled in the Brandywine op."

"Yes, sir," Hunter replied. "Listen, Captain, I . . ."

The explosion rang through the portal chamber with the force of an earthquake, shattering light fixtures and staggering the men and women technicians working at the consoles. The double doors at the far end of the room leading to the outside corridor dissolved in smoke and flame, leaving a gaping opening through which struggling men moved.

Hunter spun, bringing his Uzi up and snapping off the safety in a quick motion. BNA troopers spilled backward into the room, barely visible through billowing smoke. The harsh chatter of automatic fire sounded from the passageway, matching the flickering, stabbing flashes of auto weapons visi-

31

ble through the smoke and half-darkness. British troopers screamed and fell, cut down by the withering fire. A technician reared up from his chair, clutching his back. As he turned and slumped to the floor, Hunter saw the line of spreading red patches up the back of his white coat.

Then the attacking Russians were fully visible, spetsnaz mingled with Soviet paratroopers. They must have rushed the Ops Center, blasting their way in so quickly that no coordinated defense was possible. They spread out into the room now, their AKs seeking unarmed targets.

Hunter's Uzi barked as he loosed a full-auto barrage into the advancing mass of camouflaged uniforms. Russians pitched backward or doubled over, grasping at red, blossoming wounds.

From the side of the room, Brigadier Carruthers raised his L85. The stubby, bullpup weapon barked in precise, single-shot cadence. Another spetsnaz trooper went down . . . and another . . .

The other Rangers spread out behind Hunter, seeking clear fields of fire. Gomez yelled something unrecognizable and loosed a 40mm grenade at the corridor through the shattered doors. Light flashed, and a pair of Russian bodies catapulted forward into the room, sprawling wetly across the floor. Anderson had the big L7 braced on his hip, and its deep, hollow-voiced thunder filled the chamber in a ponderous *thud-thud-thud* that swept through the Russians and chopped them down in bloody, kicking heaps.

Against the background of swirling smoke, Hunter saw Julie standing at her console. "Go through!" she yelled. "There's damage! I can't hold the lock much longer!"

"Julie!" Wycliff started forward.

Hunter grabbed his arm. "Come on, man! We've got to go!"

The captain twisted with a snarled curse, jerking his arm free. At the same moment more Soviets ran into the room, spraying the technicians with random sweeps of autofire.

Julie staggered as though kicked in the back.

"*Julie . . . !*" Wycliff yelled again.

Anderson's machine gun chopped into spetsnaz. "Greg!" Hunter bellowed above the din. "Get everybody through! Double time!"

The room was momentarily clear of Russians . . . of living ones, at least. But they would be back in greater numbers at any second. It would be only moments before some vital piece of equipment was destroyed in the firefight, before some power cable was broken, and the portal into the past would vanish. He dashed down the ramp to where Wycliff was stooping over Julie's still form. "Come on, man! We can't stay here!"

Rachel was there next to him, awkward in the long dress. "The field won't hold much longer," she said. Hunter didn't know if she was talking to him or to Wycliff.

The SAS captain appeared dazed. He reached down as if to pick the girl up. "Leave her, Captain! She's dead!"

Carruthers joined them, clutching the British rifle. "Get out of here," he said with a snarl. He showed Hunter a radio detonator in his hand. "I'm going to blow the place as soon as you're gone. Move out!"

Hunter and Rachel took Wycliff's arms, turning him away from the body on the floor and hurrying him back up the ramp. The platform was empty now, except for Greg King's husky form silhouetted against the blue haze, his FAL battle rifle at the ready.

Gunfire snapped behind them. Hunter gave Rachel a hard shove, which sent her hurtling forward into the glow. Wycliff followed, unresisting now, almost passive. Hunter turned and saw the Russians coming through from the outside again. Carruthers stood in their path, a lone and tiny figure.

"Run!" Hunter heard him yell.

The two Rangers dove headlong through the blue glow.

Behind them, Carruthers's thumb came down on the remote control.

There was a much greater sense of isolation here, Hunter thought, than there had been among the open, rolling hills of southeastern Pennsylvania during the Brandywine op. The forest that covered much of Upstate New York was tangled and in many places impassable. The scenery was spectacular —an explosion of yellow, orange, and red fall colors approaching their peak—but visibility was limited by the surrounding woods to a few dozen yards and an occasionally glimpsed patch of blue sky.

Their destination lay on the west bank of the Hudson River some forty miles north of Albany, New York. There was no way to know exactly where their Temporal Landing Zone was in relation to their target at first. The difficulty Julie had been having in holding a solid lock for the BNA portal raised the question of whether they were within a few miles of their target . . . or much farther.

On the theory that any streams they encountered in the region would ultimately lead them to the Hudson, the party forged its way east across the rugged terrain.

It wasn't until the sun was well down toward the hills in the west that they came upon what passed for a major highway, a hard-packed dirt road running north along the west bank of a broad, sluggish, steep-banked gray river that could only be the Hudson. Another hour's reconnoitering allowed them to pinpoint their position.

Hunter watched in silence as Sergeant Mason laid the topographical map provided by the STRF's library section on the ground.

"Right here," Mason said. He probed the map with his finger. "The Albany Road runs north-south along the river here . . . and we're about a mile west of it. We're isolated from the main highway by the woods, but the terrain is gentle."

"There is plenty of water," the corporal they called Dark Walker volunteered. "And excellent cover. This should be an ideal base site."

"The date is good," Trooper Buchanan said. "September tenth, on the nose. But I did get me some queer looks from that tavern owner when I went in and asked for the date and time!"

There was a chorus of chuckles around the ring of SAS men and Rangers studying the map. Hunter glanced across at Wycliff, sitting somewhat apart from the rest, his back against a tree. He was not laughing, not even joining in the discussion. It had been Mason who suggested this clearing in the woods as a campsite for the team, Mason, more than any of the others, who'd been leading the group since their arrival in 1777.

He's in shock over Julie's death, Hunter thought. He stole a look at Rachel, who was leaning across Mason's shoulder to get a look at the map with the others. *I suppose I'd be the same way. But is he leading this bunch, or isn't he? And what part do I play . . . or any of us?*

Wycliff's head came up, as though he felt Hunter's gaze, and his eyes locked with Hunter's. There was an indefinable emotion there—hostility . . . and something more. Hunter could feel the struggle in the man as he worked to pull himself together, to take command once more.

The SAS commander stood up slowly, brushing dirt and twigs from his blue coat, dragging his hands across his eyes and cheeks as though waking from a restless sleep. "Jul— Our people did good by us," Wycliff said. His voice cracked. "Despite the . . . trouble. But we're totally on our own now."

There was murmured assent around the circle. Hunter knew what Wycliff was reaching for. The blue glow had snapped off an instant after he and King dove through. When the light vanished, Hunter had felt a moment's desolation like nothing he'd known before. The chance that any of them might see the year 2007 again depended totally and absolutely on their ability to carry out their mission here, with the equipment they carried with them or with what they could improvise. There would be no help from British North America, and no returning . . . ever.

"We'll want to split the troop up," Wycliff continued. "Four-man teams. Use the RS-17s to listen for Russian activity."

"What about the Rangers, Captain?" Hunter asked quietly.

"They'll obey orders, Leftenant. I'll decide later. Let me see the map."

The site of the Battle of Saratoga lay to the north of their camp. The Hudson River described a flattened S-curve to the east, beyond which lay a long, low, north-south ridge. On the near bank, the Albany Road crossed a rickety wooden bridge, then forked at the site of a two-storied log building displaying a sign with the legend BEMIS TAVERN. Other buildings—a barn, an outhouse, some sheds—were scattered about the crossroads. Judging from the number of horses by the stables, the inn appeared to be the hub of local social life.

North of the tavern, the land rose in an imposing, bare-topped hill, dropping off sharply toward the river and identified on the map as Bemis Heights. There were plowed fields up there, and the buildings of a small and somewhat shabby-looking farm.

Beyond the Heights were twisting ravines and round-topped hills. The land was mostly wooded, with occasional cleared patches marking other, scattered farms. It was peaceful . . . suffused with the stillness of a complete absence of cars, trucks, or the mechanized rush of a later century.

There would be noise enough soon, Hunter thought. In another nine days, if history went as it should, those thickets and ravines would tremble with the thunder of gunfire and the shrieks of dying men.

"I see no problems," Wycliff said after a moment's study. "We have enough RDFs to cover the field pretty well. We're assuming a small party of Russians coming up from Pennsylvania. The only road they can use is the Albany Road here, along the river. We can assume, I think, that they're not here yet."

"They might be, Captain," Trooper White observed. He grinned. "Maybe they've already checked in at that inn, while we're out here sleeping on the ground!"

"I doubt that," Wycliff replied. "We have deliberately returned to 1777 just before the Brandywine op. Hunter's . . . excursion at that battle will actually be taking place tomorrow. If the VBU dispatched somebody from their time portal base at Leicester House, oh . . . even a day or two ago, it'll still take them a few more days to reach Saratoga."

The thought that they'd returned to 1777 a day before their previous operation here was still a strange one. Certain as yet poorly understood physical laws appeared to prevent a person from entering the present of 2007 from a trip to the past if he already occupied that present. However, there seemed to be no reason why one time traveler couldn't return to the same moment in the *past* as often as he wanted. Not that Hunter would be meeting himself this time around, two hundred fifty miles from Brandywine, but it was still an intriguing idea.

"Are we certain that they're coming from Pennsylvania, Captain?" Hunter asked suddenly. "They had a local base at Brandywine. Perhaps they have another here."

"Unlikely, Leftenant." The voice was cold, remote. Wycliff paused, then continued addressing the entire group. "The VBU time machine was at Brandywine. Everything suggests that was their operational headquarters in the past. I'm sure our Russian friends will set up a base of some sort here once they arrive, but they have to get here with their equipment first. I suspect the VBU must be hauling modern heavy weapons to change the outcome of the battle here . . . probably mortars."

"That's a long way to haul those things without trucks," someone observed.

"Precisely. Horses, coaches, and wagons are the only forms of overland transport available in this era. My guess is they've loaded some mortars on a wagon and departed Pennsylvania within the last day or two . . . and that they will reach this area in another three or four days at the earliest. Travel time in this era is painfully slow, gentlemen, over uncertain roads. We should have plenty of time to set our little surprise for them."

It made sense, Hunter thought. He'd been kicking himself ever since his discovery that he'd missed Saratoga as part of the total VBU plan to change the outcome of the American Revolution. A large part of his anguish revolved around the fact that he didn't remember anything about the Battle of Saratoga itself. Brandywine was easy; no feat of memory was necessary to know that George Washington had *not* died there, as the BNA history books claimed. But what had happened at Saratoga?

He knew the broad sweep of the campaign. The British General John Burgoyne had evolved a plan to divide the rebellious New England colonies from the rest of America, an overland invasion south from Canada down the Hudson Valley. A smaller force would come in from the west, down the Mohawk Valley, and a major force under General Howe would march north from New York. The vastly outnumbered American Army, under General Horatio Gates, would be trapped between three British forces somewhere near Albany and destroyed. Even if Gates escaped the trap, the British would control the Hudson Valley, and the Americans would have to attack them if they wanted to reopen communication between the sundered halves of the country.

Burgoyne's strategy had not gone entirely according to plan. The Mohawk Valley force was defeated earlier in the summer and turned back. The British commander in New

York, General William Howe, with plans of his own already
in motion, had sailed south to invade Pennsylvania. It was that
invasion which resulted in the clash at Brandywine, and, ultimately, in the British occupation of the young nation's capital
at Philadelphia.

Still, Burgoyne's army alone should have been sufficient to
defeat the ragged and divided American force that stood in its
way. After a painfully slow march south through the wilderness near Lake Champlain, Burgoyne had crossed the Hudson, moved south along the west bank until he encountered
Gates in position at Bemis Heights, and . . . what?

Hunter couldn't remember. In the BNA version of history,
a portion of Gates's army had become bogged down in fierce
fighting amid the ravines and clearings north of Bemis
Heights. A British column under General Fraser managed to
plant Burgoyne's artillery on a hill overlooking Bemis Heights
from the west. At some point during the afternoon of the battle a merciless artillery bombardment shattered Gates's camp
on Bemis Heights, routing the American Army and sending
the survivors fleeing south in complete disorder. Burgoyne
had occupied Albany a week later.

It was the effectiveness of the British bombardment that
made Wycliff suspicious, Hunter knew. Certainly the SAS
commander possessed a keen understanding of the tactics and
weapons of this period . . . an understanding reflected by the
collection of antique firearms at his home at the STRF base.
"Eighteenth-century artillery simply did not possess that kind
of killing power," Wycliff had declared during one of their
planning sessions before their departure. "If the VBU changed
the outcome of Saratoga, it must have been because they introduced something extra . . . like modern mortars."

It was all the Ranger–SAS team had to go on.

Their operational plan called for setting up camp near
Bemis Heights well before the arrival of either the British or
the American armies. From here they could survey the land,
find likely places the VBU might use to set up their attack on
Gates's camp, and use their scanners to track possible Russian
radio communications. It was a good plan.

And yet something nagged at the back of Hunter's mind.
As Wycliff continued to address the group, going over patrol

assignments, Hunter leaned back, eyes closed, teasing at the unformed thought in an attempt to draw it out. The grand VBU strategy embraced two battles, occurring eight days and two hundred fifty miles apart . . . Brandywine on the eleventh, Saratoga on the nineteenth. The Russians at Brandywine had planned to assassinate George Washington by planting a sniper team a few hundred yards from his headquarters. That had not been the only Russian presence at the battle, of course. The VBU headquarters was only a mile or two from the field, and there had been a small group of VBU agents disguised as local farmers and acting as guides for the main British army. . . .

Hunter's eyes shot open, and he sat bolt upright. That was it!

"A problem, Leftenant?" Wycliff's lips twisted in what might have been amusement.

"Sir, something just occurred to me. We may be missing an important point."

"Such as . . . ?"

"My people have come up against the VBU before—twice in Germany and again at Brandywine. Every time they've gone about their plan in the same way, by infiltrating their people in among the locals."

"I don't see your point."

"Munich, 1923," Hunter said sharply. "The VBU agents were disguised as Nazi SA troops. At Hitler's villa in 1938, they were there disguised as SS. At Brandywine, some were with Washington's army, disguised as Continental soldiers. Others were with Howe's army, dressed like locals and acting as guides."

"Well?"

"Don't you see, sir? Why should they be doing it different *this* time?"

Wycliff frowned. "You're saying the VBU might be disguised as Americans?"

"It's possible. I'm even more concerned that they might be with the British. The other day you mentioned the British artillery . . . and said that it was the effectiveness of the bombardment of Gates's camp that made you suspicious. Well? What if the VBU has already infiltrated Burgoyne's army?

They might be planning on helping him carry out that bombardment with their own weapons!"

"Is that likely, Trav?" Taylor said from across the circle of listening men. "It'd be hard to disguise a Russian mortar as an eighteenth-century fieldpiece."

"It does seem farfetched, Leftenant," Wycliff agreed. "Easier to imagine them positioning themselves somewhere clear of both armies. This terrain would make it simple, actually. A Soviet 120mm mortar has a range of over five thousand meters."

"Maybe." The new thought nagged at Hunter. *What else did we miss? What else did I miss?*

"Where is the British army now, Captain?" Sergeant Mason asked.

"Not on this map. Something like thirty . . . forty kilometers north. They're probably still on the east side of the Hudson, though I'm not sure when they're due to cross over."

"Then it's not likely that a wagon loaded with Russian mortars could have reached them yet from Pennsylvania."

Wycliff's smile became open. "Not at all."

"We ought to check it out," Hunter insisted. "I'm just not sure the VBU has changed its way of doing business overnight."

The SAS commander appeared to study the map for a moment. Then, surprisingly, he nodded. "Very well, Leftenant. I do not happen to agree with your reasoning, but it would be useful to know just where the British are. As they march south, I will want to know their progress so that I can keep my own patrols clear. I suggest you take your people out on a recce."

"Very well, Captain." It was not an unappealing thought. It would give him and his men a chance to operate apart from Wycliff . . . perhaps give the air a chance to clear.

"You will depart tomorrow morning, first light," Wycliff said. He pointed on the map. "Proceed north, along the Hudson. Your primary mission will be to locate Burgoyne's army and ascertain whether it has crossed the river yet. On your own time you can look for the VBU." There was a chuckle at that from the SAS men. "Well, gentlemen. I believe that about covers it. In good time too. It's getting too dark to read the bloody map."

That raised another chuckle. Wycliff seemed to be recovering, but Hunter wondered what he was really thinking.

Hours later Rachel lay in her sleeping bag, her face a few inches from Hunter's, speaking with him in whispers, their hands touching. Around them lay the bundled forms of the others, while here and there, glimpsed by the light of a carefully tended fire, sentries moved among the trees. Dinner had been packaged rations and water, and bed a precious time to be close to Hunter . . . and as private as the situation was likely to allow for the next week or so.

She studied his face carefully by the uncertain, flickering light. He was no longer brooding, she decided. Perhaps the thought of getting out and doing things had chased some of the inner questionings.

Or had it? There were still shadows there. . . .

"Are you still worried, Travis? About what we don't know?"

"Yeah," he admitted. "This hike tomorrow will help fill in some of the gaps. But there's a lot we're guessing at. How much more have we missed?"

"You'd damn well better stop dwelling on it, Travis!" The words were sharper than she'd intended, but Rachel forged ahead. "We didn't have time to study it to death."

He looked into her eyes for a long moment. "It's not that I have a passion for research, Raye. You know that. But one of these days some damned little insignificant detail of history is going to trip us up. Back here, it's what we don't know that could hurt us. Hell, what we don't know could get us killed . . . and wipe out our own world and history forever!"

"And someday you're going to get so paralyzed wondering if you have enough data to work on, the VBU will come in and do the wiping for you! Dammit, Travis, sometimes you just can't stop and think things through! You have to act!"

Rachel was immediately sorry she'd opened her mouth. Travis lay back, his eyes closed, and it was a long time before he spoke again. "I think we'd better get some sleep, Raye. Early reveille tomorrow."

"Travis . . . I'm sorry . . ."

"Nothing to be sorry for." His voice was dead, empty of emotion.

She reached out, touching his face. "I shouldn't have said that. Please . . ."

Then they were in each other's arms, clumsily embracing with their sleeping bags between them. They kissed.

Twenty yards away Wycliff stood in the night just beyond the circle of the campfire's light. Unable to sleep, he'd gone from sentry to sentry, talking with the men, encouraging them.

He'd heard nothing of the whispered conversation between Hunter and the girl, but he saw their embrace, and the sight brought a rush of memories. *Julie* . . .

It wasn't that he blamed Hunter and the others for her death, but there was a lingering pain there, the realization that these strangers from another reality had started events moving that would end Wycliff's world within the next few weeks. That he had been working toward precisely the same goal didn't matter.

It was Julie's death, and his own helplessness. The Ranger was responsible for Wycliff's presence here in this black wilderness, instead of where he belonged . . . dead at Julie's side.

Five

Rachel lay in the bushes near the Albany Road, watching the horsemen at the crest of the hill.

"Americans, almost certainly," Jimmy Buchanan said beside her as he studied the distant activity through his binoculars. "Probably laying out their defenses."

"Huh," Pete Yates said from behind a nearby bush. "Might be our Bolshie friends, too, lookin' over tha' killin' ground."

"Hmm. Maybe." Buchanan studied the horsemen a moment longer.

Roger White lowered his own binoculars. "I'd like a closer look."

Rachel looked at the SAS trooper. "Shouldn't you guys wait for the captain?"

Buchanan set his tricorn hat more firmly on his head. "God only knows when Sir David'll be back, luv. Won't take a moment. You stay and mind the store. Ready, Pete? Rog?"

"Let's suss it out, mate," Yates said cheerfully.

Rachel watched the three vanish soundlessly into the underbrush. *Mind the store. Right.*

"The store" was Bemis Tavern, squatting on a bare patch of ground at the forking of the Albany Road, perhaps a hundred yards west of the slippery clay banks of the Hudson. Several horses were visible in the stable in the back, evidence that there were patrons inside.

The road was heavily traveled. Most of the traffic seemed to be associated with the activity on the Heights, south of the tavern. They'd seen army officers and lumbering wagons hauling picks and shovels and other digging gear, small bands of ragged men in Continental uniforms, and larger numbers of

43

rough-looking men in frontier garb, their long muskets balanced across brawny leather- or buckskin-clad shoulders.

There'd been coming and going along the road all morning, ever since Hunter and the other Rangers packed up their rucksacks and melted off into the woods to the north. It was nearly midday now, and Wycliff and his SAS troopers were scattered across the landscape on patrols and surveys, with orders to rendezvous back at the camp that afternoon. The log-walled inn at the crossroads was the natural focus of much of the activity.

She had accompanied one of the four-man SAS teams and Captain Wycliff to watch the activity. Wycliff had taken one of the men with him to have a closer look at the river. Now the other three were gone, checking what looked like digging on Bemis Heights.

Leaving her to sit and "mind the store." *I don't mind being a fifth wheel,* she thought, *as much as being treated like one.*

The *clop-scrape-clop* of approaching horses brought Rachel's head around. Two more riders were coming from the south, wearing the blue-and-buff uniforms of Continental Army officers. Both were young men, though one was little more than a boy—an aide, perhaps. She ducked farther back behind the bushes and listened to their passing.

"*Htseh mee s'eh pteetsh, Polkovnik,*" the younger man was saying. "*Chi neh zehtshahwahbi pahnee nahpteesh s'eh chehgos?*"

Rachel froze in cold horror. The horsemen rode past, oblivious to her presence a few feet away. The language was incomprehensible to her, but she'd heard enough Russian spoken to recognize the gooey Slavic cant to the words. And one of the words she thought she recognized—*Polkovnik* was Russian for "colonel."

Russians! she thought, horror mounting. *The VBU! They're already here . . . and disguised as American officers!*

She rose slowly, following the riders' progress down the road. Their horses' hooves boomed hollowly on the planks of a wooden bridge fifty yards away. The riders walked their mounts up to the front of the tavern, still talking, though Rachel could no longer hear them. The junior officer gave a casual salute, dismounted, and handed the reins of his horse to a boy who came out of the tavern to meet them. The other officer, the *Polkovnik*, brought his mount's head around and took the left-hand fork in the road, walking up Bemis Heights toward the other officers visible at the crest of the hill.

Okay, Rachel thought, fighting to control her breathing, which had gone suddenly shallow. Her heart pounded hard in her chest. *Okay, it's the VBU. I'll have to tell the others.*

What more could she do? She fixed her eyes on the tavern door where the younger of the two Russians had vanished. *What was he doing in there . . . who was he talking to? I could go in*, she thought. *Maybe ask someone who the Continental lieutenant is.*

If the VBU was already here, already infiltrated into the Continental Army, it would be important to know what their position with the locals was, who they were talking to, what they were doing. This might be an opportunity to learn some of the answers.

Rachel stood, brushing twigs and dead leaves from her bodice and long skirt. Remembering Hunter's warning back at the Circus, she checked her mobcap. Her arms itched where her cuffs gathered at her wrists, so she rolled both sleeves up above her elbows. Dressed this way, she felt very much the proper eighteenth-century lady.

I'll "mind the store" for them . . . and maybe find out what the hell the Russians are up to.

Making certain that no one was visible on the road, she stepped out from cover and started down the road toward the tavern.

The interior of the inn was dark and smoky. The innkeeper's jovial grin vanished as Rachel stepped across the stone threshold and looked inside. "What do *you* want?" The man's tone was less than cordial.

"Excuse me, sir," she said. "I . . . thought I saw someone come in here that I knew."

"Haw! Lookee here, Sam!" Laughter sounded from half-seen shapes at low tables around the room. Suddenly she felt much less sure of herself.

Frowning, the innkeeper wiped his hands on his apron. "This is a decent establishment. We don't want the likes o' you here."

"Haw! C'mon, Jotham, let her stay! Liven the place up a little!" Voices chatted and chuckled in the darkness. She looked around wildly, unable to make out faces or details but aware that the attention in the room was focused on her.

Jotham stepped between Rachel and the laughter. "There's nothing for you here, miss. You'd better go."

Rachel felt her face flush. She had the feeling she had just done something terribly wrong, terribly embarrassing, and she still wasn't certain what her mistake had been.

A meaty hand closed on Jotham's shoulder, shoving the innkeeper aside. A grinning, bearded face leered at her out of the darkness. "Mind yer own damned business, Bemis!" The hand closed over Rachel's wrist. "C'mon, girl!" Other hands grabbed Rachel, snatching at her clothing. Men, most of them large and bearded, ringed her in.

"Hey, wench! Who ya want to be with first!"

"Haw! I seen her first, Nathan! What's yer name, girl?"

Rachel brought her foot down on an instep, eliciting a bellow of pain and surprise. "Let me go!"

Someone shoved her. "Hey, th' wench has spirit!"

Jotham Bemis shook his fist. "I run a decent establishment here! Out! All of you . . . out!"

Other men stood around the floor as spectators, grinning at the struggle. "Aw, let 'em have their fun, Jotham," one of them said. "Lucas an' his boys ha' been workin' hard. Only right they play hard too!"

"Not in my place they don't."

Rachel knew a moment of stark terror. She was helpless, hemmed in by groping men. Someone plucked her scarf from her shoulders.

She screamed, thrashing in their grip.

"'Ere now . . . what's all the fuss about, woman?" A voice bellowed in her ear. She screamed again.

"Shut that racket, slut," someone else said.

Rachel worked her right hand free of a sweaty hand and drove her fist as hard as she could into something soft. The something *oofed* and backed away. There was a loud clatter as someone swept tin cups and pewterware from a table, shrill laughter as she was picked up and lowered onto wood sticky with the spilled accumulations of past meals and drinks. Her skirts were shoved up, and she felt questing fingers running up her leg, under her shift.

The fingers drew back. The abrupt silence was startling,

emphasizing one man's muttered "What in the devil . . . ?"

Suddenly free, Rachel twisted off the table, landing on her feet, her hands poised in front of her as she assumed a karate stance. She was no expert, and her long skirts were a hindrance. She had no illusions about her ability to fight them all, but she was going to try. . . .

Captain Sir David Wycliff was not feeling the part of the gallant knight arriving to rescue the damsel in distress. He felt, rather, an unreasoning fury at the girl who had wandered off against orders, and anger at the American Ranger who had saddled him with her. He and Corporal Walker had returned from their recce along the west bank of the Hudson to the spot where they'd left the others, and found all four missing.

Then they heard the scream from Bemis Tavern.

He burst through the open doorway of the inn. The tableau there made him pause . . . six men gathered around Rachel, who was lying on a table with her skirts up about her waist, her long legs bare below the white slash of her panties. Other men clustered near the innkeeper, who was screaming threats and imprecations. There was a sudden silence as Wycliff plunged forward into the dimly lit dining hall.

Rachel's captors appeared to have drawn back from her momentarily. The girl twisted away then, rolling to the floor and coming up in a clumsy martial-arts stance. Wycliff saw a ruffian reaching for her and snapped his foot up in a roundhouse kick at an unprotected kidney.

The man grunted and fell, writhing. Wycliff spun to face a second local but saw him go down as another local, this one in the uniform of a Continental Army lieutenant, swung a chair over his head and smashed it across the local's back.

Then it was a free-for-all as Rachel's attackers turned and fought back. Walker stepped past Wycliff, an open hand chopping into the base of another ruffian's neck. One bearded thug slashed out with a knife. Wycliff expertly disarmed the man, sending the knife thudding onto the floor, then brought an elbow up into his nose. Blood splattered and the man collapsed in a heap. Wycliff stepped across him and grabbed the next target in line, a trim, dark-haired man in frontier clothing and a wiry mustache.

The man held up his hands as Wycliff clenched his fist. "Not me! I'm not with them!"

Wycliff shoved the man aside in disgust and turned to face the fighting.

But the fight was over. Six locals lay scattered in various sprawling positions across the dirty plank floor. Rachel's eyes met his as she leaned back against the edge of a table. "Oh, God, Captain . . ."

"What in the *hell* are you doing here?" It took all of Wycliff's self-control to keep from shouting the words. Of all the stupid, lame-brained . . .

"I . . . I wanted . . ." Her wide eyes went from face to face, locking at last with those of the blue-uniformed lieutenant. Her mouth snapped shut.

Wycliff spun on his heel to face the innkeeper. The man had stepped into a back room and was returning now, a long-barreled musket in his hands. "I'm sorry for the trouble, sir," he said softly. "We'll pay for any damages, of course."

"Who is that woman?" the man replied. His voice was shaking. "Why did she come *here*?"

"Ah . . . she's had some problems," he said improvising. He tapped his forefinger to his temple. "Not quite right, you know?" He read the man's disbelieving expression and decided to spin the story out further.

The SAS trooper at his side gave him inspiration. Corporal Dark Walker was an Indian, a native of the autonomous Dakota Territory in the midwestern reaches of British North America. In 1777, this part of New York was at the fringes of the wilderness. The people here would understand. . . .

"Actually," Wycliff said, "she was captured by Indians when she was a child. They raised her. Twenty years she's been with them. I'm her brother. My . . . ah . . . Indian friend here helped me find her. I bought her back from the tribe that had her, and we're taking her home to . . . to New England."

The innkeeper's suspicious expression had softened as he listened. He squinted at Rachel in the half-light. "Huh. Raised by Indians, eh? Mohawks?" He peered at Dark Walker's features. "What tribe'r you, brother? You don't look Mohawk. . . ."

"I doubt that you've heard of us." Walker grinned easily, his words slow and cultured. "My people are civilized. It was a tragic crime what the Mohawks did to . . . Miss Wycliff."

"That's right. You can see, she . . . uh . . . doesn't understand some things." He turned to Walker. "Better take her
outside. Stay with her."

"Yes, sir."

The man laughed as the Indian led her outside into the
light. "Don't understand some things? You got that right, mister!" He set the musket aside, extending a hand. "I'm Jotham
Bemis."

"David Wycliff." He took the hand. "What do we owe you
for the damages?"

Bemis made a shooing gesture. "Nothin' busted that can't
be fixed." He nodded toward the unconscious patrons on the
floor. "That was a rough lot, anyhow. Here with them sappers
from Gates's army. They was gettin' rowdy. Appreciate your
quietin' them down. You, too, Lieutenant," he said, turning to
the Continental officer.

"My pleasure, sir. Sorry about chair."

Wycliff's eyes narrowed. The man spoke with a heavy
accent . . . an obviously Slavic one. "Can I buy you a drink,
Lieutenant?"

"Dzhenkuyeh!" The boy's eyes brightened. "Is good!"

The meaning of the word was obvious, but it was not *spa-
seebah*, the Russian for "thank you."

Wycliff ordered drinks for himself and the foreigner.

"Never did see such fightin' in all my days!" Bemis chor-
tled. "That pal of your'n's civilized, huh?"

"Well . . . more or less." He reached inside his vest and
pulled out the pouch of gold. "Just one thing more. I do insist
on paying for the damages here. Now, we don't have much
paper currency with us—not traveling, you know—but perhaps you'd settle for this?" He spilled some small nuggets into
his palm.

Bemis winked. "Beats the paper New York has been issuing lately. Sure I'll take gold."

"Good." He turned and hoisted his drink toward the Continental officer. "So, Lieutenant. Tell me about yourself!"

An hour later Rachel still felt as though she were trembling, although her voice and thoughts were again more or
less under control. The terror of her helplessness at the tavern

had left her weak and shaken. She welcomed the chance to escape outdoors. Another moment inside that tavern . . .

"I will thank you in future to pay strict attention to my orders," Wycliff said stiffly. They walked side by side, south along the Albany Road. The skies were leaden, and a fine drizzle was falling. "What you did this morning could very easily have cost us the success of this mission."

"That American army officer in the tavern," she said. "I heard him speaking Russian with another guy!"

He smiled. "You speak Russian?"

"No. But I've heard it spoken, and I recognized a word I heard . . . their word for *colonel*."

"*Polkovnik*, yes." He chuckled.

"What are you laughing at?"

"The gentleman you suspect is *Podpouruznik* Stanislas Paszkiewicz. He is aide to Colonel Tadeusz Kosciuszko. They're Polish."

"Polish?"

"A great many Polish words are identical to Russian, my dear. *Polkovnik* is one. They're written differently, of course, but they sound the same."

"But what are Polish troops doing *here*?"

"Not helping the VBU, I assure you. Colonel Kosciuszko is an engineer. I gather from his aide that they came over in 1776, to offer their services to the American Congress. It seems the colonel is helping the American general erect fortifications up on Bemis Heights."

"You mean he belongs here? He's not a time traveler?"

Wycliff grinned. "Certainly not. I gather from his rather talkative lieutenant that the colonel left Poland in a bit of a hurry. Something about a beautiful daughter and an irate father . . ."

"Oh, God," she said. "I'm sorry. I just thought . . ."

"You thought." Wycliff's smile darkened. "Young lady, you don't really understand where you are, do you?"

His gibing tone ruffled her, put her on the defensive. "What do you mean?"

"I know something of this time," Wycliff continued. "My hobby, you know . . ."

"Military history . . ."

"And the history of *people*. You can't understand the one without the other."

She looked at him sharply. "I had the impression you didn't think individuals counted for much." Several times she'd heard Wycliff state his views that in the sweep of history individuals were relatively unimportant in the grand drama of clashing armies and historical imperatives. He had actually argued against the necessity of saving George Washington's life, since, as he put it, "they'd find someone else just as good."

"Individuals, no. People, yes. Cultures ... societies ... customs ... morals. These are the things that make up the *fabric* of history." He jerked his thumb back over his shoulder. "That tavern back there is not one of our modern-day hotels, you understand. Frontier travel was something proper ladies simply did not undertake!"

Rachel looked puzzled. "How did they get around, then?"

"They didn't. Or they stayed with relatives along the way. Frontier inns like Bemis Tavern ... a man paid his money, a few shillings, probably, for a bed where he could sleep stacked up with six or eight other men. Or he could pay less and find a spot on the floor of the bar, after it closed up. There were no such things as 'private rooms.'"

"Oh ..."

He glanced at her dress. "You're wearing only one layer of petticoats under your skirt. That means you're not particularly well-to-do. And ..." He reached out and tugged at the material of her sleeves, bunched up high on her arm. "When you're back here, never, *never* expose your elbows!"

"My ... elbows?"

"Different people, different customs ... and morals. These people wouldn't find it especially shocking if you bared your breasts in public, not if you had a baby with you. Breasts are for suckling children, after all. But your *elbows* ..."

The revelation brought a hot flush to Rachel's face. She tugged her sleeves down to her wrists. "Then they thought ..."

"That you were a prostitute. Or an army camp follower, which was often much the same thing."

Small stones crunched beneath their feet as they walked

along the clay-surfaced road. "That's why you shouldn't have gone into a public inn."

"No," Rachel said. After a thoughtful moment she added, "I really messed it up, didn't I?"

Her sudden agreement seemed to surprise him. "Well... offhand, I would say yes. But it seems to have worked out well. They believed my story about you and the Indians, so no harm was done, after all."

"Except to my pride."

"There is that." Wycliff hesitated and looked embarrassed. "There is one other thing."

"What?"

"I... ah... noticed back there that you were wearing knickers."

"Knickers?"

"Undergarments. Your briefs... under your shift."

She glared at him.

"They shouldn't be any of my business, of course... but you ought to get rid of them. At least refrain from letting the locals see them again."

"Dammit, Captain, I hadn't intended to show them off!"

"Yes, well... you see, the shift is the only undergarment a woman of this period ever wore. She slept in it... made love in it... gave birth in it... and rarely removed it."

Rachel wrinkled her nose. "And the men all tried to stand upwind of her."

He smiled. "People were not all that concerned with hygiene, true."

She was silent for several more paces. "I'll be more careful, Captain."

He hesitated for a moment longer. "As I see it, no one is the wiser. Just don't let it happen again."

"No," she said. She let out a long, slow breath. "I certainly won't."

Colonel Ilya Ilych Yakushenko replaced the radio's handset and removed his earphones. His pale eyes shifted to his second-in-command. "That was Comrade Captain Salekhov," he said, his voice cold and even. "There are American agents at Bemis Tavern."

"What... now? But how, Comrade Colonel?"

The Soviet colonel shrugged. "'How' does not particularly bother me now, Comrade Major. The fact that the Americans seem to have discovered our operation does."

There was silence for a moment, sharpened by the faint rattle of a drizzling rain on the canvas of their tent. "Is Comrade Salekhov certain?"

"*Da*. The Americans were rather obvious about it, he says. He referred to them as 'white crows.'"

The major nodded. "White crow" was a KGB spy term meaning an agent who gave himself away in a spectacular way, someone who stood out in a crowd rather than blending in as a good covert operative should.

"What are we to do, then, Comrade Colonel?" the major asked.

The colonel's lip twisted, an open sneer. "We shall act, of course. Boldly. Salekhov would have us find a hole and pull it in on top of ourselves. That, possibly, is the way the KGB does things. We, of course, operate differently."

"But Comrade Colonel! VBU policy states—"

"VBU policy be damned, Petrov! Soon it will be the GRU that dictates VBU policy, not the damned KGB!"

"*Da*, Comrade Colonel."

"For now we must deal with these Americans. Assemble the men. This is what we shall do. . . ."

Six

Hunter held up his hand and the Rangers went to ground, weapons probing the riot of fall colors surrounding them.

"Whadja hear, Trav?" Taylor asked at his side.

"Shh! Listen!"

Far off, beyond the rustle of rain-dripping leaves, they heard the thuttering hammer of gunfire. Autofire . . . in an age of single-shot muzzle loaders.

"Russkies?" King asked.

"Has to be," Roy Anderson said. "It's comin' from up north. None of Wycliff's people are up that way."

Hunter watched Ben Taylor work the bolt on his H&K subgun, chambering a round. *His hands are shaking,* Hunter thought. "Are you okay, Ben?"

"Huh? Me? Yeah, Trav, fine!" The words were a little too sharp, a little too urgent.

He shoved his rising unease aside. "Right. Let's move, people. If that's the VBU, we'd better find out what they're up to!"

The Rangers set out at an easy, ground-eating jog. The battle sounds grew louder as they ran, autofire mingled with the crack of muskets, then died away. *Who the hell are they shooting at?* Hunter wondered. As Anderson had pointed out, none of the SAS troopers should be this far north. The musket fire suggested locals. . . .

The possibility that locals, people who belonged in this time and place, might die because of Hunter's actions was one of the worries that plagued him constantly. You didn't have to be George Washington to have a profound effect on history.

And the Russians had just killed someone who might not have died otherwise.

Hunter checked to make certain a round was chambered in his Uzi, and increased the pace.

Taylor was having difficulty controlling the shaking that threatened to overpower him as they spread out along the crest of a low, heavily wooded ridge. The sound of voices had attracted them, voices speaking in Russian.

Below them, glimpsed through the yellow-and-orange splendor of the leaves, was a narrow dirt path. There was a wagon there, a pair of horses in the traces, and others behind on a lead. Men moved by the buckboard.

Bodies sprawled in random, bloody heaps on the rain-slick clay. Taylor saw muskets on the ground, heard the gurgling moan of someone in gut-shot agony.

He counted five men up and moving. They wore long-tailed green coats and tricorn hats, with their hair gathered in back and tied in a queue in the fashion of the period. Only the deadly AKM assault rifles slung across their shoulders gave them away as something other than soldiers who belonged in the American Revolutionary War. One man was trying to calm horses spooked by the gunfire. Another checked the back of the low, open wagon, rooting through bundles of picks, shovels, axes, and other tools.

Taylor's hands shook harder, and his breath began coming in short, hard bursts. The terrain, the colored leaves, the details of the green uniforms took on an unnatural clarity.

My God, what am I doing here? He glanced left and right, watching the other Rangers train their weapons on the tableau at the base of the hill.

Ben Taylor had been wrestling with the problem ever since his return from Brandywine a few days before. This was a strange kind of war he found himself fighting, this struggle with the Russians to reshape the past. Its strangeness had been hammered home in that other battle when he had very nearly opened fire on an advancing line of British soldiers . . . had very nearly violated the very history he was trying to restore.

The thought, the *responsibility*, still made him shake.

It wasn't the same for the others. Hunter, King, Gomez, Anderson . . . even Rachel had all been to the past before, knew what it was like, what to expect. Taylor had just begun training for time ops when they'd found themselves catapulted into the altered universe of British North America.

He strained to make out details of the scene below. Were all those men carrying modern weapons? Could the Rangers be certain they weren't locals who had somehow come across the weapons in a VBU cache? They were speaking what sounded like Russian, but . . .

The staccato snap of Hunter's Uzi shattered the stillness. An instant later the others opened up, raking the clearing around the wagon with auto fire.

A man's face vanished in a fine red spray. Another groped for his AKM, then twisted backward. A horse shrilled and reared as the man by its head folded over, his chest exploding in bloody gouts.

Taylor froze, squinting over the barrel of his H&K, unable to fire.

The entire skirmish lasted three seconds. Horses stamped and snorted and shied against their leads. Five new corpses lay mingled with the others.

"Ben! Greg! Overwatch!" Hunter rapped out. "Eddie and Roy with me!"

The three men rose from hiding and made their way down the slope, their weapons raised cautiously. It was possible that other enemies still lay hidden in the woods.

No fresh gunfire greeted the Rangers as they stepped into the open. Taylor looked away as they began to check the bodies. His eyes met King's.

"Problem, Lieutenant? You look white as a sheet."

"No." He turned back to the scene on the road below, his hands twisting on the grips of his unfired subgun. "No problem . . ."

Hunter checked through the tools in the wagon: picks and shovels; rope and axes; a pair of heavy, glass-paneled lanterns with candles inside. The wagon must have belonged to the party ambushed by the VBU. Lines of bullet holes pocked and pierced the rough wood, and there was a crimson splash across the plank that served as a seat. Horses snorted nervously. There were two hitched to the front of the wagon, and three more in a string behind it. None of the animals had been injured, but bloody human bodies lay everywhere.

"This one's wounded, LT!" Anderson called from nearby.

Hunter turned. At first he thought Anderson had found a wounded VBU agent, but the lanky Ranger was stooping beside a man in dirty buckskins, one of the victims of the Russian attack.

"Multiple abdominal wounds," Anderson continued. He made a face at the odor and at what the odor meant. "Bowels pierced."

"Here's another," Gomez said. "Chest wound."

"First aid," Hunter said. His eyes went to the surrounding trees. He'd waited a long time before beginning the attack on the Russians, in case more of them joined the five on the road. It was still possible they were being watched, but they couldn't stand by, doing nothing while these men bled to death.

There were four other men in rough, frontier dress, sprawled among the five Russian bodies. There was no help for them; they'd been killed outright in the VBU attack.

And what does that do to our history? Hunter wondered. *Damn the Russians! They don't care . . . except where it helps their plot.*

Hunter swung at a rustle from the trees, his Uzi leveled. Something moved, across the road from where he'd left Taylor and King. As his gun came around he heard a frightened sob.

Step by step, Hunter advanced, leaving the road and making his way through the underbrush. He swept branches aside with his arm and found himself looking into the filthy face of a boy.

He was twelve, maybe fourteen, and looked scared, but the eyes that blinked back at Hunter from under an unruly tangle of blond hair were not blanked by shock or wild with panic.

"Easy, son," Hunter said. He lowered the Uzi. "We won't hurt you."

"Was that . . . was that you what killed the Tories, mister?"

"Tories?"

"Them that's in them green coats. Tory militia!"

The American Revolution had been as much civil war as war against England. The Tories, Hunter knew, were those Americans who remained loyal to the king, often taking up arms and joining homegrown militia regiments to fight against their patriot neighbors.

VBU troops, disguised as Tories . . .

"What's your name, son? What are you doing here?"

"Ephraim Parson, sir." He pointed south. "I live twelve, mebbe fifteen miles off that way. Near t' Bemis Heights."

"What happened?"

"I j'ined up with the engineers!" The fear vanished, at least for the moment. "Cap'n Parker, he needed a scout, someone that knew these woods. I told him I knew 'em like't th' back of my hand. Ma, she wouldn't let me come, only I snuck out yesterday an' came, anyway. We been checking out the roads up this way an' pullin' down bridges to slow up Burgoyne's army!" His face darkened and the fear returned. "Only Cap'n Parker's face went all bloody."

"He's dead, son." Hunter had seen the tall, buckskin-clad man with his face missing, lying near the wagon. He extended a hand. "Come on out of there. The . . . Tories are gone."

"Whatcha got there, LT?" Anderson asked as Hunter and the boy stepped out of the bushes.

"Scout for the American army, Roy." Hunter put his hand on the boy's shoulder. "Ephraim, how about seeing to the horses? Make sure they're not hurt, and keep them calm."

"Yes, sir!"

Hunter and Anderson watched the teenager depart. "Report," Hunter said.

"Two wounded. Americans, I think."

"Engineers. Destroying bridges and blocking roads." He explained what he had learned from the Parson boy. Then he nodded toward where Gomez was helping one of the wounded men. "What are their chances?"

"Not good, LT. You think this'll screw up our timeline?"

"I don't know, Roy. If one of those guys is supposed to have a famous son, yeah, it might." He shrugged. "Or else none of them was supposed to have a famous son because all this was supposed to happen . . . in our history."

It was a common problem in dealing with time tampering. Important events—the death of George Washington in battle, say—became part of the history books and showed where things had changed. But the death of a handful of army engineers along a muddy forest road . . .

Maybe it had happened in Hunter's history. There was no way to know.

"We can't worry about it now, though," Hunter continued. He looked up at the sky, barely glimpsed through the leaves. "We've got three, maybe four hours of daylight left. I wonder if we can get them back to their own lines?"

"You're not planning on carrying them?"

"We've got that." He jerked a thumb over his shoulder toward the wagon. He nodded to the east. "Off that way somewhere is the Albany Road. If we find it, it'll be an easy drive south to Bemis Tavern."

"Like you say," Anderson said slowly. "There's no way to know . . . but what if those two are supposed to die? In our history?"

"You'd rather leave them here to bleed to death?" he said sharply. He saw the pain in Anderson's eyes and immediately regretted the words. "Sorry, Roy. But I'm not going to leave them."

"What about our recce?"

"We've found Burgoyne's army, haven't we?" He gestured toward one of the "Tory" bodies. "Better yet, we know there are VBU with him."

"Five of 'em, anyway. You think that could be the lot?"

"Can't bet on it. Not until we know what the VBU was up to. My guess is we get this intel back to Wycliff . . . fast."

"Right you are, LT." Anderson looked up at the sky. "I just hope we can make it before nightfall, though. Driving a wagon at night in these woods won't be fun."

Wycliff raised his binoculars to his eyes. A broad grin spread across his face as he tracked the slowly moving object in the eastern sky. "We've got the buggers!"

It was not yet dark, but the late-afternoon sun had already been blocked out by the hills and woods to the west. In the east a brilliant star—it might have been Venus—hung above the ridge line on the far side of the Hudson.

But the light was not Venus, or any other natural object. It was moving, drifting slowly from south to north above the ridge line. When the men strained to listen against the early-evening stillness, they could make out the faint, pulsing throb of an engine.

In that place and time, what Mason and Wycliff were witnessing could easily have been called a UFO, something flying above the wilderness long before aircraft existed or balloons were commonplace. But Wycliff knew exactly what that light was.

Someone was flying a helicopter up the Hudson Valley of 1777.

"What's the make?" Mason asked at Wycliff's side.

"Can't quite make it out. Transport, I'd say, by the way it's moving."

"How in the bloody hell did the Bolshies get a helicopter back here?"

"We'll sort that out later. Right now . . . look! They're setting down!"

Mason looked down at the map spread out on his lap. "Got it! That'll be four, maybe five kilometers from Bemis Heights." The sergeant looked at Wycliff as the realization struck him. "God, Sir David! It fits!"

"That it does, Sergeant." Wycliff grinned wolfishly. "That it does."

The two men were squatting on the side of a hill south of Bemis Heights, not far from the tavern and the Albany Road. Proof that the Russians were already in the neighborhood had come earlier that afternoon when one of the SAS patrols had picked up a brief radio transmission from the woods north of the Heights, followed by an acknowledgment so brief that they'd been unable to get a line on it.

Knowing that the Russians were already in the area had led Wycliff to further disperse his teams, watching for any sign at all of VBU activity or presence. He'd not expected that sign to be as blatantly anachronistic as a helicopter. The brilliant light was settling to earth now in a clearing on the ridge across the river and opposite Bemis Heights. That clearing would be an ideal spot from which Russian mortars or other modern artillery could be directed at the Continental Army, once it took up residence on the hill north of the tavern.

And it'll be the spot where I can get back a bit of my own . . . and Julie's . . .

"What're we going to do about it, Sir David?" Mason asked.

"Back to camp, Sergeant. The lads'll be coming in and

we'll brief them then. I think we've got a good chance of wrapping this show tonight."

Across the river, the brilliant light winked out.

"Shouldn't we wait for Travis?" Rachel asked. She sat with the others, sixteen men gathered around Wycliff and his map. All of the SAS men had taken off their period costumes in favor of camouflage fatigues and battle harness, and their faces were blacked out with makeup, leaving their eyes startlingly white and solemn in the gathering gloom of evening. Rachel felt out of place, still in her eighteenth-century dress.

"Your friends may not be back for days, Miss Stein," Wycliff replied. "Besides, the operation is quite straightforward. I see no reason to wait at all."

"Don't you worry, luv," Trooper Buchanan reassured her from across the circle. "We'll have things all wrapped up here and save the Rangers all the work!"

She smiled a reply but felt a terrible unease.

Wycliff used a flashlight to illuminate the map. "Very well. We can assume the Russians are using this clearing as an L-Zed for their helicopter. We'll infiltrate by teams, meet . . . here, and suss the place out. If possible, we capture the helicopter in order to look for plans, maps, orders, or other intelligence, but our mission priority is the elimination of VBU personnel. Understood? Good."

"What about me?" Rachel asked.

"You're not coming with us, certainly," Wycliff said with a sniff. He indicated a point on the map, close by the river, a mile north of Bemis Tavern. "But we can do this. There is a creek just here . . . Mill Creek, where it's bridged by the Albany Road. We will designate that as our rally point. Meet there after the mission, whatever happens." He scanned the blackened faces around him. "Clear?"

There was murmured assent. Wycliff looked at Rachel. "You, Miss Stein, will wait at the bridge. We will leave you one of the radios, and you can warn us off if there's trouble. You have a pistol? Good. Just don't go panicking and blowing away any of my people in the dark."

Rachel controlled her voice. "I believe I can manage without panicking."

"I have complete confidence in you." He looked at the

others. "That about covers it, gentlemen. Any questions? Excellent. Look to your watches. It is 1915 hours on my mark . . . now. We will move out at 1930 and plan to assemble at the ambush site at 2200 hours." His teeth showed stark against his darkened face. "Gentlemen, the VBU are going to wish they'd stayed in 2007!"

Rachel's disquiet grew sharper. *God, I wish Travis were here now.*

Seven

Wycliff peered through the darkness and smiled a grim smile. *You have to admire the bastards for sheer pluck,* he thought. Work lights illuminated the grounded helicopter under a misty, hissing drizzle. The aircraft was an old Mi-8 Hip with its usual weaponry removed and replaced by extra fuel tanks. Scarred clamshell cargo doors stood open at the rear, where men in camouflaged uniforms passed crates to others on the ground. They looked like the crates the Russians used for transporting mortar rounds.

Mortars! That confirmed his thinking. From this ridge top the Russians would be able to sight in on the American camp atop Bemis Heights with pinpoint accuracy. A rain of high-explosive shells in a day when artillery was inaccurate, short-ranged, and—with a few exceptions—nonexplosive solid shot would be more than enough to send Horatio Gates's ragged army fleeing in every direction.

His eyes swept the clearing, searching for sentries. The clearing was lit day-bright by those work lights. He glanced left and right. Other commandos crouched there in the bushes, nearly invisible in the darkness and rain, their assault rifles loaded and ready. They'd been careful to maintain radio silence as they deployed. Now, however, he brought his walkie-talkie to his lips. "That's it, men. Go!"

Gunfire erupted from three sides of the clearing, stabbing from the darkness as his men opened fire. A Russian screamed and pitched forward from the helicopter's cargo door. Others dove for cover behind stacked crates. AK fire flamed back, barking against the night.

A grenade burst near the helicopter and the work lights

died. The Russian fire abruptly fell silent. Wycliff brought the
radio to his mouth again. "That's it, lads! Now! Second and
third teams, move up. Eyes sharp. Don't let 'em scatter!"

The victory was so sudden, it was difficult to recognize.
Black-faced men in commando garb darted forward into the
clearing. Flame spat once or twice, seeking targets flitting
among the trees.

Wycliff started toward the Hip. His men spread across the
clearing, probing dead bodies. "What th' hell!" MacNeil
shouted. "These bomb crates are empty!"

Ambush! The thought was a harsh, stomach-wrenching accusation. Raw light arced hissing through the sky.

"Flare!" Callaghan yelled, then the deep-throated yammer
of a heavy machine gun opened up from the woods on their
flank. Bullets chopped through leaves and dirt, sending up
geysers of dust walking through the SAS line. Trooper
Thompkins screamed and clutched his midsection, doing a
slow and bloody spin as he sank to the ground. Ferguson
jerked back, blood exploding in violent splatters from his face
and throat.

The commandos went to ground, returning fire. A deeper,
heavier sound throbbed above the hammering gunfire. Wycliff
looked up. Light blazed from the sky in stark, white brilliance, wildly distorted in the rain. The squat, insect-snouted
shape of an Mi-24 Hind-A rose above the trees, drowning the
battle in the thunderous *whup-whup-whup* of its rotors. By the
dying light of the flare Wycliff could see that this helicopter,
too, lacked external weapons pods.

But the ugly snout of a 12.7mm machine gun was swinging
to bear on the SAS troopers in the clearing. The aircraft's
searchlight stabbed down, pinning them in its merciless glare.

"Scatter! Scatter!" Wycliff screamed, but no one could
hear him above the roar. Trooper Bromwell clawed at his face
as new terror exploded around them. The Hind sprayed the
clearing with sweeping, deadly patterns of high-speed autofire.

Then the Hind was gone, swinging low above the trees to
the north. Wycliff pulled out his radio. "Abort!" he yelled.
"All teams, E and E to the rally point! Good luck!"

The armored helicopter gunship returned, exploding out of

the night in flame and thunder. Wycliff brought his assault
rifle to his shoulder and opened fire.

Rachel stood on the riverbank, her long dress heavy and
soggy from the intermittent drizzle, staring into the darkness.
The Albany Road bridge lay out of sight a few yards behind
her up a muddy bank.

The distant sounds of battle were gone now. It was strange,
Rachel thought, that a modern battle could pass unnoticed
against an eighteenth-century night. The sounds of gunfire had
seemed faint and flat, like far-off thunder, the flashes no more
obvious than the wink of fireflies in the woods. She'd heard
Wycliff's orders to Escape and Evade over her radio and realized then that the hilltop clearing across the river was an ambush, a Russian trap, and that the SAS had fallen into it.

A sound made her whirl, a splash and the scrape of rock on
rock. She brought her Beretta up. "King!" she snapped, her
voice low but penetrating.

The word had nothing to do with Greg King, though she
couldn't help thinking about the big American Ranger as she
spoke. With what Rachel thought was a rather bizarre twist of
irony, Wycliff had set the sign and countersign for the rendezvous tonight as "King" answered by—

"Country!" She recognized Trooper Buchanan's voice,
ragged with fatigue.

"Jimmy!" she gasped. She lowered the Beretta as a flashlight beam snapped on. Behind the light, she saw a black form
shambling toward her, water streaming from sodden clothing,
an L85 rifle dangling by its sling from one hand. "What happened?"

"They were waiting for us," Buchanan said. He sounded as
though he still didn't quite believe what had happened. His
eyes blinked against the black smear of camo paint on his
face. "The damned Russians were waiting for us! *Two* helicopters!"

More splashes sounded from nearby. This time Buchanan
gave the sign, and the "Country" countersign announced the
arrival of another SAS trooper.

"Pete!" Buchanan said. "Glad you made it! How about the
rest?"

"Didn't see 'em none after we scarpered, mate." Pete Yates

limped into the glow of Buchanan's light. "Didn't see *anybody* after that damned Hind fell on us."

"But where did they *come* from?" Rachel asked. "Not from Pennsylvania . . ."

Leicester House had been the VBU headquarters in 1777, the location of their time portal. *Think it through, girl,* she told herself. *Keep the dates straight.*

The date now was September 11, the same day as the Battle of Brandywine, fought earlier that afternoon two hundred fifty miles to the south. By this time Travis and the others had already left Brandywine to return to 2007. The raid on Leicester House would occur tomorrow night, on the twelfth, when the Ranger–SAS commando team returned from the future to attack the VBU headquarters.

There'd been no Russian helicopters at Brandywine. So where were they coming from? Their presence suggested another base of some kind . . . and more VBU troopers than any of them had been expecting here.

"We've got to warn Travis," she said suddenly. "He's still out there and doesn't know about this. He's got to know!"

"Not a lot we can do about it, luv," Buchanan replied. "He's probably way out of range."

She caught her lower lip between her teeth and stared into the darkness. *We've got to do something!*

"Not sure it's a bright idea usin' that thing, miss," Yates said. He shook his head. "The Bolshies must 'ave a whole bleedin' army back here. I'd 'ate t' call 'em down on us!"

Of course, Rachel thought. *If we can track them by radio, they can track us. But dammit! How do we let him know?*

The communications officer shouted above the thunderous roar of the main rotors. "Nothing, Comrade Colonel! They must be maintaining radio silence!"

Yakushenko twisted in the copilot's seat to reply. "It does not matter. Their base must be on the west side of the river. We will catch them as they cross." He tapped the pilot's shoulder, pointing. "Sweep the west bank, Volnov! Along the Albany Road!"

"Immediately, Comrade Colonel!" The Hind banked sharply. Outside, there was only darkness, obscured by the reflections of instrument-panel lights on the large, rectangular cockpit windows.

The communications officer touched Yakushenko's sleeve. "Message from Captain Salekhov, Comrade Colonel! He reports his men are on the ground and moving into position now!"

"Very good. Order him to take prisoners, if possible."

"*Da*, Comrade Colonel!"

Yakushenko caught a glimpse of his own reflection in the eerie green light and grinned. The trap had worked perfectly. Many of the enemy time commandos lay dead on the ridge top, and the rest were scattered through the forest, prey to be hunted down and killed or captured at his leisure. The Mi-8 had been the perfect bait. The loss of a couple of uninformed KGB workers used as a diversion in front of the grounded transport was insignificant compared to what their sacrifice had achieved. The victory would take Yakushenko far in the VBU hierarchy. A prisoner or two would make his success complete.

The Hind stooped from the darkness, seeking its prey.

She heard something, a rustling off to the south, a sound that began as little more than a quaver in the wet air. Yates had vanished into the darkness, following another set of feeble splashings that might be another of the sassmen coming across the river. Rachel and Buchanan were seated in the almost dry shelter of the Albany Road bridge, a black hole sheltered from the rain and stinking of rotting vegetation and sour, wet clay.

Rachel turned and strained, listening to the night for the almost sound. "Jimmy?" she asked. "Do you hear . . . ?"

Fresh splashing sounded from somewhere behind her. Yates called from the darkness. "It's MacNeil! Hey, Mac! Over here!"

"I hear that," Buchanan said. He unclipped a flashlight from his combat harness and crawled out from under the bridge, slipping his rifle over his shoulder. Rachel followed. The sound was louder now.

The helicopter appeared out of nowhere, thundering, a monstrously huge black-on-black shape. Its searchlight snapped on, turning the air above the river frosty blue around searing white. The beam illuminated in the drizzling rain seemed solid, a shaft of radiance sweeping across water and beach in a broad swath.

Buchanan froze, silhouetted against the light. "Down!" he screamed.

The thunder roared past, the rotor wash whipping the air and mist in a minor windstorm that stung Rachel's eyes and whipped her hair around her face. Buchanan dropped to the ground, invisible in the terror of light and noise.

Then the huge machine was gone, lumbering north along the riverbank, its searchlight stabbing and probing the dark places along woods and water.

"Pete!" Buchanan rose and raced forward. Rachel blinked at a darkness now far more complete than before. The searchlight had momentarily dazzled her, ruining her night vision completely. She stumbled as an exposed root caught at her ankle.

The thunder returned, the light exploding out of the sky with doomsday brilliance. The body of the helicopter was invisible behind the rain and the light, but the searchlight was a living thing, setting the black terrain on fire and painting the misty air blue.

Machine-gun fire hammered from behind the light, and Rachel heard Yates scream. Buchanan froze, silhouetted against the light. "Pete! No!"

The helicopter made the night tremble, whipping the branches of trees to a frenzy as it raced overhead. Rachel pressed herself facedown into the wet earth, praying that those airborne eyes would not see her.

Then light and thunder were gone again, dwindled off beyond the forest. She heard its roar, distant now, off above the woods to the northwest. A low, bubbling moan came from the darkness down toward the river.

Rachel's grip tightened on her Beretta. It was silly, she knew, to think of challenging a helicopter with a 9mm pistol, but the slick weight was reassuring. She hurried along the embankment until it opened onto a broad, pebble-layered shelf.

A flashlight lay on the beach, its beam giving enough scattered light to see dim shapes by the river. MacNeil lay on his back, very still, his legs in the water. When she touched him, her hand came away slick with blood. The gurgling sounds came from Yates, who was doubled up on the beach, his body opened from chest to crotch. Before she could reach him, he gave a last, wrenching convulsion, vomited blood, and lay still.

Buchanan lay nearby, both hands cradling his right knee. "No, luv! Get out of here! They know where we are now. The woods'll be thick with the bastards!"

"I'm not leaving you here!"

"Not much choice, luv. Leg's busted, I think. How's Pete?"

She shuddered. "Dead . . ."

"God damn . . ."

Rachel levered Buchanan up and tried to move him. He gasped and clutched at the leg. "It's no use—"

"Dammit, shut up! I'm rescuing you!"

There was a lot of blood. Exploring the wound by touch, her fingers dragged across something hard and ragged.

"Ah! Easy, luv. That's a bit of the bone showing."

There was nothing Rachel could do about setting the leg, not here, not now. Following Buchanan's instructions, she opened his first-aid kit and covered the gaping wound with a sterile dressing. She found a fairly straight branch, then used Buchanan's knife to tear a narrow strip off the hem of her skirt. It took only a few moments to apply a splint.

Voices called to one another from the woods above them. *"Anton! Edet' yeh s' youdah! Skaryehyeh!"*

"Come on!" She helped him up again. This time he was able to stand, holding his injured leg off the ground and leaning heavily against Rachel's shoulder.

"Leave me here." His voice was fuzzy with shock.

"No way." She guided him back up the slope toward the bridge.

"I'm fine! I'm fine! Get out of here!" he insisted as she laid him back in the mud. He tugged at the holstered pistol on his belt. "Dammit! Get away!"

She fled into the night.

Beyond the shelter of the bridge, the night was filled with crunching, rustling noise, the sounds of many men moving through the brush. She heard laughter once, and an order barked in Russian: *"Etee darogah! Tahm!"*

Dim gray shapes moved slowly through the woods and

onto the Albany Road. With horror Rachel realized that some of them were sure to descend into the Mill Creek gully . . . and they would certainly look under the bridge. The Russian line was past her now and only a few yards from Buchanan's hiding place.

She thumbed the Beretta's safety off and chambered a round. At the slight, metallic sound, several Russians turned. *"Pasmahtreet'yeh!"*

Gripping the pistol in both hands, she held the weapon at arm's length and squeezed the trigger. Orange flame blossomed in the night once . . . twice . . .

One of the soldiers toppled backward into the underbrush. An AK spoke sharply, stinging her face with chips of wood as bullets smashed into a tree a foot away. She scrambled up the slope. Loose dirt gave way beneath her feet.

"Ahstanahveet'yeh yehvoh!" Autofire rattled after her. *"Nyet! Zheevoy! Zheevoy!"* She kept running.

Minutes later Rachel sank to the ground, her back against a tree. Pursuit sounded on all sides. They were closing in.

Light exploded from the night. Hands shaking, she raised the Beretta.

"Nyet!" Something cold and hard smashed down across her wrist, sending the pistol spinning. She twisted to the side. The silhouette of the man loomed above her. Then something struck her from behind, and she plunged forward, her face in the dirt.

A darkness rose within, deeper and more complete than the midnight of the woods.

Eight

Wycliff rose dripping from the water. The retreat from the enemy camp and the swim across the sluggish river had left him stumbling with exhaustion. He crouched, trying to penetrate the darkness. The Hind was no longer in the area, at least, and the sounds of men thrashing through the undergrowth were gone.

It looked safe.

Got to keep moving. He checked his 9mm Browning High Power, then started south. It was something less than three miles to the clearing where the SAS had their camp. The bridge that marked their rally point was nearby, but after the repeated Russian air attacks, the surviving SAS troopers must be scattered far and wide by now.

He stumbled over something soft and heavy.

Taking care to keep the light shielded under his cupped hand, he switched on a pocket torch. The red beam only added to the body's disemboweled horror.

"God, no . . ." Yates had been a good soldier, a good friend.

MacNeil lay at the water's edge nearby.

The low moan brought Wycliff around, pistol ready. Advancing slowly, he climbed a shallow rise and made out the shape of the Mill Creek Bridge, the space underneath a blacker shadow against the night.

Buchanan lay under the shelter of the bridge, half conscious, his leg splinted. "Well, old man," Wycliff said, holstering his pistol, "it's good to see a friendly face."

The trooper moaned as Wycliff checked the wound. It was a nasty one. The break had not been set, only immobilized for

73

later treatment. If Buchanan could be carried back to the campsite, the injury could be taken care of there.

He slapped the man's face. "Buchanan! Wake up! Buchanan! Where's the girl?"

"Gone . . ." Shock blurred the words. "She . . . led them off. Captured."

"Captured? They captured the girl?"

"Heard them . . . take her . . ."

Wycliff swore bitterly as he snapped off the torch. He knew nothing about the VBU beyond what Hunter had told him, but he was quite familiar with its KGB parent and the methods they used for extracting information. It would not take them long to tear from Rachel everything they wanted to know about both the SAS and Ranger teams. The clearing in the woods would no longer be safe.

At the snick of metal he whirled about, his Browning out once more. He saw nothing, heard nothing more. Still . . .

Light stabbed from the darkness as he stepped from the shelter of the bridge. The sharp, chopping hiss of a silenced automatic weapon followed. Wycliff lurched back out of the beam, then gasped as fire seared his side.

The explosion of his High Power startled the night. He squeezed off another round, and a hand torch clattered onto rocks. He saw a black shape against the light.

For an instant the figure was illuminated by the torch. Wycliff saw the uniform, a long-tailed green coat cut in eighteenth-century style, with a tricorn hat. The man clenched a Skorpion machine pistol in one hand. Wycliff recognized the face . . . the small, dark man he'd seen at Bemis Tavern only hours before.

Wycliff fired again from the ground, but it was an awkward angle. The shot buried itself in a tree behind the man's head.

The Skorpion swung up . . .

Gunfire erupted from upriver. The man ducked and rolled, escaping the telltale glow of the torch. The Skorpion spoke softly, the sound abruptly cut short by an empty magazine. The VBU agent cursed, then crashed off through the brush up the hill.

"It's me, Sir David," John Mason was at Wycliff's side. "I heard your shot. Where'd they get you?"

Wycliff touched his side. His fingers came away slick with blood. Breathing was a shallow burning. "It's not bad," he said. "Busted a rib or two, I think."

"I'll get you back to the camp, Sir David." He reached to pick Wycliff up.

"No . . . no. I can make it . . . on my own. Just need time to rest. Maybe when it's light. Buchanan . . . under the bridge. You'll have to carry him." Wycliff hesitated. "We'll have to find another camp."

But the recall beacon was at the campsite in the woods south of Bemis Heights, hidden with the satchels and clothing they'd not needed for the raid.

Where could they go? They would have to move elsewhere, and quickly. The Russians knew now that they'd not gotten all of the SAS troopers, and they would start working on the girl as soon as they got her back to their camp . . . wherever that was.

The VBU agent at the tavern, he decided, must have noted Rachel's behavior . . . must have seen her anachronistic underwear, reasoned she was a time traveler, and set up the ambush.

He felt an almost overwhelming despair. The mission was an utter failure.

Hunter sat on the wagon's driver's seat next to Gomez and tried in vain to pierce the darkness beyond the pale yellow radiance of Anderson's hand-held lantern. It had taken them longer then they'd expected to make their way along the twisting, sometimes nonexistent trail, and it was long past dark by the time they reached the Albany Road. The horses that drew the wagon refused to move until Anderson—who had grown up on a ranch in Texas—got one of the candle lanterns lit, took the right-hand horse's bridle, and led the team step by step down the muddy lane.

It seemed like they'd been traveling for an eternity, though Hunter's watch showed it was only just past 0430 hours. It was still drizzling, a steady, annoying mist that pattered from the leaves of the forest and drenched them all to the bone. The two wounded men had long since died and been left at the side of the road. They continued ahead in the wagon, the string of extra horses trailing behind, because it was easier than walking. Each Ranger took turns guiding the horses. The Parson boy lay asleep under a soggy scrap of leather in the back. No one said anything. Gomez, the reins in his hands, appeared to be nodding off, as water dripped into his lap from the brim of his three-cornered hat.

The night was quiet, with a kind of wet, dark foreboding that pressed in on Hunter's exhaustion-numbed brain. He was looking forward to getting back to the SAS campsite . . . and to Rachel.

Movement on the road ahead brought Hunter wide awake, his hand moving toward the Uzi, half sheltered under his coat. A tall man stepped into the light of Anderson's lantern, hand upraised.

"Walker . . . !"

Corporal Dark Walker was the product of the alternate British North American history, a Dakota Indian who had joined the British army in much the same way as the Nepalese of Hunter's world became Gurkhas. From the little the other SAS men had said in Hunter's hearing, the Dakotas were among the best guerilla fighters the British had. Walker himself spoke rarely, and when he did, it was with a soft, precise English that suggested New England schools and cultured formality.

There was nothing of Boston about the man now, however, his black facial makeup smeared by the rain, his L85 rifle challenging the slow approach of the wagon.

"Leftenant Hunter!" Walker said. The relief—and the exhaustion—were clear in his voice. "Thank heavens you've come!"

The party continued its slow pace south as Walker sat in the back of the wagon and described the disaster. Hunter's horror grew as he listened to the account of helicopter attacks and machine-gun death from the sky. The battle had ended over five hours earlier; rain and distance had prevented the Rangers from hearing it. It would be hours, Walker said, before the survivors could be assembled again. Some would meet, no doubt, at the Mill Creek Bridge. By now, others would have given up on the rally point as a free-fire zone and be making their way back toward the camp.

But Hunter was most concerned about Walker's account of the Soviet helicopters. The Dakota was succinct and precise in his identification of an Mi-8 Hip transport and a stripped-down Mi-24 Hind.

"My God!" Taylor said as he sat next to Hunter, listening to Walker's story. "We're facing helicopters!"

"It's worse than that, Ben." Hunter frowned into the darkness. "Those helos have to have a base someplace." His thoughts touched at each of the logistical necessities. Two Soviet helicopters needed a place to land, a place where they would be out of sight. They would need a great deal of av gas, plus the equipment for refueling them.

Even more disturbing was a further realization. "A portal," Hunter said suddenly. "The Russians must have another portal!"

"Why?" Taylor asked. "Their time portal was in Pennsylvania. *Is* in Pennsylvania," he said, correcting himself. The Ranger–SAS raid to destroy the VBU Leicester House HQ wouldn't be under way for another sixteen hours. "Anyway, they wouldn't need a second one, would they?"

"I don't know what they need it for," Hunter said carefully. "But I do know they never dragged two helicopters through the portal at Leicester House!"

All of them had been in the portal chamber at the stone Colonial house near Brandywine. The room had a single double door leading into the house, but nothing large enough to accommodate something as large as a helicopter.

Besides, there'd been no sign of helicopters at the Soviet base . . . no fuel dump, no maintenance facilities, nothing at all but the house and the portal itself, a handful of men, and the forms and documents that had led them here.

The situation was beginning to look daunting now. The SAS force had been shattered by a Soviet ambush. Somewhere out there, location unknown, was another VBU base with a temporal downlink and, in all probability, a small army to guard it.

The first traces of dawn were lightening the low overcast over the ridge beyond the Hudson when they reached the bridge. As Walker had predicted, several SAS troopers were there, challenging the wagon from positions off the road. Sergeant Mason was there . . . and Trooper White.

"You've missed the show," Mason said. "But we can bloody well use that wagon."

"What's the problem?"

"Two wounded men." Mason's face contorted as he gestured over his shoulder toward the shelter of the bridge, barely visible now in the gray, predawn light. "One of 'em's the captain."

Wycliff's wound had already been dressed by one of his men. The SAS captain was in considerable pain and was having difficulty moving, but aside from the pain and the danger of infection, the wound did not appear too serious. Buchanan was worse, unconscious from the shock, though his leg was already splinted and dressed.

Taylor and King helped lift Wycliff into the back as the Parson boy, awake now, scrambled clear and watched with wide, grave eyes. These men were dressed strangely to his way of thinking, Hunter knew, but there would be time for explanations—for plausible lies—later.

"Back to the campsite, Captain?" Hunter asked as he hauled himself up into the wagon. Anderson and Gomez struggled to lift Buchanan's unconscious bulk into the back without further injuring the man's leg.

"Negative!" Wycliff grimaced and tried to sit up. Hunter wadded up the leather wrapping as a pillow and made Wycliff lie back on it. "Negative," he said again. "Compromised."

"Compromised? How?" Hunter knew the answer as he spoke. One of the SAS men must have been captured, someone who would tell the VBU where the campsite was. The Russians, Hunter knew, were very good at extracting information from their prisoners.

Wycliff's eyes focused on Hunter. "Your girl, Hunter," the man said after a moment. "The VBU has her."

The revelation left Hunter stunned, a cold, choking horror rising in his throat. Rachel . . . captured! *Oh God, no! No!*

"What happened?" His throat was tight, the words harsh and rasping.

"Your Rachel Stein happened!" Wycliff snapped. He struggled for a few seconds, working to control his breathing. After a moment he continued, speaking deliberately. "She gave us away by going into the tavern. She thought she was helping. But her actions attracted attention."

Hunter glared at the wounded man. "How do you know it was her fault?"

"There was someone at the tavern. Small man . . . black hair. Mustache. He was with a bunch of civilians who'd been helping some men from Gates's army survey Bemis Heights for the fortifications they're building. I saw him . . . later."

"During the fight?"

Wycliff nodded. "I figure he was helping the Russians sight in on Gates's camp. Measuring ranges, that sort of thing."

"And he pegged Rachel? Knew she was a time traveler?"

"Had to be. She rather gave herself away."

If the VBU knew Rachel was from the future . . .

Pain gnawed at Hunter's mind, and a wild, desperate fury. He had to find her! There was no hope for Rachel at all if they were certain she was a time traveler.

"Where . . . is she?" he managed to ask. His voice cracked. A throbbing behind his eyes threatened to drown out Wycliff's words with its insistent, hammering pain.

Wycliff shook his head. "No idea. But . . . you know about the helos?"

Hunter nodded.

"And you realize what they mean? That the Soviets have another base hidden back here, something a hell of a lot bigger than Leicester House?"

Hunter nodded again.

"She's gone, Leftenant," Wycliff continued. "If they have her, she'll tell them what she knows. You know that."

Hunter felt numb. His tiredness, and the pain of this fresh horror, threatened to overwhelm him, to drag him down. *Raye . . . !*

"We've got to find her," Hunter said finally.

"How?" The single word was a rebuke, a sharp slap across his face. "Even without being stripped, those helos have a range of four, maybe five hundred kilometers. With weapons removed and fuel tanks added . . ." Wycliff shrugged against the improvised pillow. "There's no way to know where their base is, and no way to track her. She's gone, Hunter. She's . . . dead. As dead as Julie."

Dead . . .

Except that the filthy, gut-wrenching horror of it was that she wasn't dead . . . would *not* be dead until the Russians had torn from her everything they wanted to know about the

Rangers, about the mission. The interrogation might be at a camp or hidden base here in 1777, or it might be at the VBU's home base in 2007, somewhere in the Soviet Union.

Hunter looked up, his eyes sweeping the cold, wet shadows of the early-morning woods. She might as well be dead, perhaps, but right now she was alive. Somewhere . . .

But there was no way of finding out where . . . of even discovering whether or not she was still in 1777. He sagged back against the side of the buckboard, his eyes shut.

And if you'd let her come with you yesterday . . . The voice was a taunt, a sneering torture echoing behind the pain and the shock.

Rachel . . .

Rachel lay on the dirt floor of a canvas tent, groggy, her head throbbing. Her hands were tied behind her back, her ankles crossed and tied as well. Morning light filtered through the open tent flap, and she heard the sounds of people moving and talking outside. She wondered how long she'd been unconscious and decided from the light that it must be mid-morning now. That meant eight, maybe ten hours since the fight in the woods.

She wondered if they'd found Buchanan . . . if he was still lying in the mud under the Mill Creek Bridge.

Rachel tried to sit up, but pain and weakness dragged her back to the ground. Terror rose then, closing on her. She fought and pulled against the ropes.

A shadow blotted out the light. "It is useless to struggle," a voice said.

She looked up. The man standing there wore a uniform of some kind, a green coat with crossed white belts and a cocked hat. His left forearm was tightly bandaged.

Rachel tried to remember where she'd seen the man before. There was something about his face . . . the mustache . . .

"You were at Bemis Tavern!"

"Guilty." The man's smile lacked humor. His English was perfect, but she had no doubt that he was VBU. Her eyes strayed to the oddly shaped machine pistol visible in its holster at his belt as he removed his coat. No . . . no doubt at all.

A second man stepped through the tent flap. He was dressed much like the first, with more frills on his uniform.

"Ah!" the newcomer said. "Our guest is awake."

The first man smiled. "She remembers me from the tavern, Comrade Major."

An icy chill ran through Rachel. She struggled again to sit up, as pain stabbed at her temples and her eyes.

"Gently, now," the first man said. "I am Captain Salekhov. This is Major Andryanov... better known hereabouts as Captain Selby, of Selby's Legion."

"Selby's... what?"

"A Tory unit," Andryanov said easily. "General Burgoyne finds us indispensable. Frontier scouts, probing through the wilderness, and all that." The smile burned a raging horror into her brain. "We are very, very good at getting information...."

Andryanov squatted next to her. He let one hand linger on her leg, caressing.

"You gave it all away last night, you know. We weren't really expecting you Americans here, but that was rather a spectacular show you put on at the inn. We were fully briefed about the Ranger unit that interfered with our plans for 1923, of course."

She tried to pull away from his touch, but he continued stroking her leg under her petticoat and shift. "Not many of your Ranger friends got away last night," he continued. "A few escaped across the river... but not many. What I want from you is exact information on their numbers and weapons ... and where we can find them."

"I won't tell you anything." She could hardly hear her own voice. Nightmare fear pounded behind her ribs, shrieked in her brain.

"Oh... I think you will. It might take time, but we have lots of that, don't we?"

Andryanov must have read the fear in her eyes, for he chuckled and drew his hand away. "You needn't worry, just yet, *devoshka*. You have a ride ahead of you first."

Captain Salekhov looked at his superior. "We're not rendezvousing with a helicopter, Comrade Major?"

Andryanov shook his head. "I think not." He stooped next to Rachel's head, extending one hand to lightly stroke her hair. "We have a prize here, Captain. We should handle it with great care. I for one do not intend to turn it over to that GRU pig and see him get the glory. We will take this one through to Uralskiy ourselves . . . when we go to present our case before the council."

Rachel saw understanding light the captain's eyes. "Very good, Comrade Major."

"Prepare the horses," Andryanov said. "If we leave at once, we will be at the Fort Edward camp before dark." His fingers dragged across Rachel's cheek and she tried to twist away from them. The Soviet major laughed and stroked her face again. "Tonight, perhaps, *devoshka*, we will have the opportunity to get better acquainted. Captain Salekhov and I have a great many questions we would like to put to you."

He stood suddenly and snapped an order to Salekhov in Russian. The captain saluted and went outside.

Andryanov grinned at her from the entrance. "I trust you feel up to a short ride?"

Nine

The Widow Parson was a tall woman of perhaps forty, with worn hands and plain clothing and a face that came alive when she saw her son Ephraim jump from the buckboard. Her home, a two-story log structure near the Albany Road a mile south of Bemis Tavern, was immediately thrown open to the men she assumed were Continental soldiers.

"You found my son!" she cried. "I didn't know what to think when he didn't come home last night."

"I'm sure he'll tell you all about it, ma'am," Hunter said. His voice sounded faraway in his own ears, as though he were listening to a stranger speak. *Raye . . .*

"You'll come in, won't you, and have some tea?"

"Can't, Mrs. Parson. We have wounded in the wagon."

The woman's face went white when she learned that her son had been in a skirmish, but the realization that these men had saved Ephraim from Tory raiders settled any questions about Wycliff and Buchanan, so far as she was concerned.

"You'd turn those poor men over to the army surgeons?" she said. "My poor husband died in an army camp hospital, rest his soul, after nary more'n a ball passing through his shoulder! White Plains, that was, just a year ago! I'll not have those men laying in some filthy camp hospital! I have extra rooms here, and here is where they can stay!"

"We don't want to trouble you—"

"Nonsense. Ephraim! We'll put them in the upstairs bedroom."

An hour later Hunter sat in the tiny, windowless room at the top of the stairs. Wycliff lay on his back in a massive four-poster bed, his bare chest taped and bandaged. Buchanan was next to him, dopey with the morphine Anderson had given him. Anderson and Mason had set Buchanan's leg, resplinting it with a broom handle broken into several convenient lengths and wrapped up in yard upon yard of strips torn from a sheet. Taylor and King crowded in at the room's door.

"The helicopters change everything, Leftenant," Wycliff said. His eyes were restless, moving about the room, but never resting squarely on Hunter. *Does he feel guilty about Rachel?* Hunter wondered. *Or is he just remembering his own grief?* Somehow, in some strange way, Hunter felt closer to the SAS captain now. He'd known that the two of them shared an interest in history. Now they shared much more.

Hunter nodded, responding to Wycliff's blunt statement. He was so tired, the effort required to move his head hurt. "So does the fact that the Soviets have a base somewhere back here," he said. "How many effectives do you have now . . . after last night?"

A bitter grimace twisted the man's face. "Seven . . . not counting Buchanan here and myself. Sergeant Mason has them in hand. Two are wounded . . . but fit for duty."

Seven SAS troopers, five Rangers, and two invalids. It wasn't much of an army to take against an unknown but large number of VBU soldiers and two helicopters at an unknown base, probably with a time portal of its own and access to reinforcements from the future . . . and all dedicated to changing the past.

"Then you lost eight killed?"

Wycliff nodded. His expression darkened. "They were waiting for us," he said softly. Then, louder, "Dammit, Hunter! They were waiting for us! Waiting for *me*!"

"It wasn't your fault," Hunter said softly. He wondered if Wycliff was blaming Rachel for betraying herself. Whatever she did, it must have been something small. Any of them, SAS or Rangers, could have given things away just as easily, through some tiny slip that proved to watchers they did not belong in this time. It could be a lapse as insignificant as looking at an empty wrist for a wristwatch . . . in a year when wristwatches had not yet been invented.

"I'm not blaming Rachel," Wycliff said, as though reading Hunter's mind. "The fault was mine. I underestimated them . . . the VBU. Once they found out we were here, it was so easy to lure us with that helo. They set the trap, and I led my people straight into it!"

The intensity of his words startled Hunter. "What else could you have done?"

"I don't know. God help me, I don't know." Wycliff hesitated, then plunged ahead. "It's your problem now, Leftenant. You've had the experience fighting the VBU. And you're senior now." He paused as a fit of coughing racked him. After a moment he continued. "Laid up like this, I'm no good at all."

"Will your people follow me?" Hunter asked. *What can I do with twelve men?*

"They damned well better. I'll pass the order to Sergeant Mason. You'll be able to rely on that one. He's a good man."

"Seems to me, the Russkies'll be coming out again, Lieutenant," King said. "They know they didn't get all of the captain's people. Maybe they know by now about the bunch we caught up north. They're bound to come looking . . . and we can be waiting for them."

"Yes . . ." Hunter thought for a moment. He had to fight the dull, throbbing ache that centered about his memories of Rachel, forcing it to some remote corner of his mind as he struggled to assess the situation.

A new thought occurred, and his head snapped up. "Oh, *shit!*"

"What?" Wycliff asked.

"I've just thought of something else," Hunter said. "Washington!"

"What about him, Lieutenant?" King said. "Yesterday was when the Russians were gunning for him . . . and we had that covered."

Time travel, Hunter thought, required a new set of grammatical tenses. While he had been fighting the green-coated "Tories" yesterday and saving Ephraim Parson, he—or at least an earlier version of himself—had also been engaged in his last mission, saving George Washington from VBU snipers at the Battle of Brandywine.

"We wrapped up the Brandywine op," Hunter said slowly. "We thought we'd got them all when we raided Leicester House. But these helicopters change everything."

Shock showed on King's face. "Good God, Lieutenant! I

didn't think of that! A Hind could be in southern Pennsylvania in a couple of hours!"

Taylor shook his head. "There's nothing we can do about it, is there, Trav? I mean, short of stealing a Russian helicopter..."

"If I could, I would," Hunter said. He looked back at Wycliff. "Our mission is the same, no matter what our losses, Captain." *No matter what our losses! Rachel...*

"The Battle of Saratoga won't happen for another week," Wycliff said. "But if you're thinking what I believe you're thinking..."

"George Washington's survival is necessary to history, Captain. To my history. If the Soviets have helicopters, they could land another sniper team down there in a couple of hours. God, they might already be there, after mopping up on your people last night!"

"There's not much we can do about it," Wycliff replied. "As your man says, not unless you can steal a helicopter."

"We have the wagon we picked up yesterday."

Wycliff laughed, then gasped as the motion stabbed at his wounded side, making him cough. "This is not 2007, Captain," he said when he recovered. "Traveling by wagon, over the sorts of roads they have back here, hell, you'd be lucky to get to Philadelphia in five or six days. And a Hind can be there with those snipers in two hours. No, I think you'd better concentrate on the situation at hand."

Hunter stood suddenly and paced the narrow space at the end of the room. The snug-waisted coat he wore pinched under his arms, tight and uncomfortable.

"With all due respect, Captain," Hunter said at last. "If you put me in command here, then I'm in command! It won't do us a damned bit of good to stop the VBU from screwing us at Saratoga... if they manage to pop Washington, anyway!"

"What can you do about it, dammit? You can't race helos with a bloody wagon!"

"Maybe not." Hunter shoved his hands behind his back, his fists clenched fiercely one in the other. "Maybe not! But we have some things going for us. I'm betting the Russians won't dispatch troops and helicopters to Pennsylvania until they have things under control here... and so long as we still have twelve men running around loose, they don't have things under control! Even after what happened last night, Captain, it'll take them time to organize, to figure out how many of us there are, and what we're doing here. They'll be looking for our camp, trying to run us down. No, they won't bother with Pennsylvania until they know they've got us."

"Then why—"

"To stay a jump ahead of them," Hunter interrupted. "We can have people in Pennsylvania in five or six days. When the VBU goes after Washington, they won't realize we're down there waiting for them. It'll lower our profile up here too."

"How many are you planning on sending?" Taylor asked.

Hunter dragged a hand over his face. *I'm tired . . . tired . . .*

How many to send? How many to keep? If he had any chance at all of finding Rachel, Washington could look after himself, but Wycliff was right. There was no chance at all of going after her now.

But Hunter's taking command of the British survivors was not as simple as it seemed when Wycliff proposed it. The SAS and the Rangers got along well on the whole, but there would be problems enough getting them to accept Hunter as their new CO without trying to blend the two units together.

"Four," Hunter said finally. "Ben . . . you're in charge. Take Roy, Eddie, and Greg. I don't remember the details, but Washington was playing tag with the British outside of Philadelphia for at least a week after Brandywine. You'll be able to find him easy enough."

Taylor blanched. "Trav! You can't mean it! We have no shortwave radios, no way to stay in touch."

"We'll arrange a rendezvous . . . and a schedule. We'll hide the recall beacon up here. If something happens to all of us, then once it's clear Washington is safe, you can come back and get it. Otherwise, I'll come meet you. The Leicester House ruins might be a good place . . . say on a certain day of the week, at a certain time."

"I don't think it'll fly, Trav! I mean, what can we *do*?"

Hunter looked at his old friend sharply. *Is he scared? Well, hell, I would be too. I* am *scared . . . or I would be if my head was on straight.*

"Travis," King said quietly. He was leaning against the door frame, his arms crossed, his expression neutral. "You're not doing this . . . because you think you can track down Rachel, are you?"

He thinks I'm trying to get them out of the way, Hunter thought. *And in a way, maybe I am. I look at them and remember her.*

"No, Greg. We have got to cover Washington . . . and we've also got to cover the Russians up here. This is the best plan I can think of."

"If you say so."

"I do."

"You'll need money," Wycliff said.

"We have the gold."

"Good. They'll need to stay at inns along the way."

"Hell," King said. "We've got sleeping bags."

"He's right, Greg. You'll need to stop for directions, if nothing else, and you'll want to buy meals and drink if only to keep from attracting attention." He frowned in thought. They'd not brought enough hard currency back to cover an expedition like this.

Wycliff sighed. "When you go back to the campsite to recover our gear, look in my ruck," he said. "You'll find a reproduction pistol. I left it there when I changed to my camies. You should be able to sell that at Bemis Tavern."

"A reproduction?"

"Oh, it's real," Wycliff said, smiling faintly. "It works. It just wasn't crafted in the eighteenth century. Funny. I always wanted to get a genuine antique black powder pistol for my collection. Now my reproduction is going to *be* an antique."

"I'll take care of gathering our stuff," King said.

Hunter nodded. He hadn't thought of that. Once they began questioning Rachel, the campsite would soon be dangerous. They would have to get the rest of their clothing, supplies, and gear quickly.

The thought reopened the wound, causing the room to swim around Hunter's head. *Oh, Raye. I'm sorry!*

King left the room. Hunter fixed his eyes on Taylor. "Go find Eddie and Roy, Ben. Let 'em know what's up. I'll want you to leave as soon as possible."

"I still think this is a bad idea, Trav."

"Goddammit, Ben! I don't care what you think!" He

caught himself, regretting the words, the rage that threatened to consume him. *It's not Ben's fault.*

"Just be ready to leave as soon as Greg gets back," he said.

"Yes, sir." Taylor executed a stiff salute, ridiculous in his period costume, turned on his heel, and left.

Black pain crowded Hunter's thoughts as he followed.

They tied Rachel's hands to the pommel of her saddle, then led her horse by a lead line, traveling north after striking their camp in the wooded hollow they called the Great Ravine. There were twenty of them, lean, quiet men wearing green like their leaders, strange only in the selection of modern weapons they carried strapped to their saddles or slung across their backs. The party made good time, traveling at a steady pace that alternated walking with trotting. At first they stuck to forest paths and trails that were scarcely visible, but by mid-morning they'd descended to the River Road some ten miles north of Bemis Heights and were clattering along at a respectable pace.

At four in the afternoon they came within sight of the bridge of boats. Rachel could make out the white pinpoints of tents on the far side of the river.

"That's Burgoyne's army," Andryanov explained, bringing his horse up alongside hers and pointing. Rachel refused to answer, refused even to look at the man. She had an idea of what was coming and was unwilling to pretend otherwise. "They've been camped there for over a month. The pontoon bridge has been up for several days, but the British have been afraid to cross until they know what the rain's going to do to the river. Burgoyne's been using us to scout ahead for him, looking for signs of Gates's army."

They turned away into the woods instead of approaching the bridge. The camp of Selby's Rangers was an untidy clutter of canvas tents and firepits. Several men waited there, some in green coats, others wearing ragged-looking civilian attire. An effort had been made, Rachel realized, to keep anachronistic elements such as AKM assault rifles out of sight.

Andryanov cut her hands loose and steadied her horse as she slid out of the saddle. There had been few stops for rest that day, and none for food. Her legs threatened to give out under her as she tried to stand, and she felt dizzy, barely able to stand. She clutched at her horse's saddle as the ground swayed under her.

Salekhov caught her elbow. "Easy, *devoshka* . . ."

All of Rachel's fear and horror and revulsion surged to the surface in that instant. She had been held prisoner by VBU agents before, and she knew now a wild desperation not to be held by them again. She whirled, the heel of her free hand driving hard and sharp up into Salekhov's nose.

Blood splattered from the VBU officer's face. Rachel's hand struck downward, catching Salekhov squarely on his bandaged arm. He screamed.

Rachel ran. Most of the VBU troopers were still mounted, and her sudden move caught them by surprise. She was past the tents and into the woods in a flash, gathering her long skirt and petticoat up around her waist as she ran, her bare legs flashing as she ducked and wove through branches that snagged at her hair and clothing.

"*Ahstanahveet' yeh!*" someone yelled at her back. The flat, cracking rattle of an AKM followed her, snapping at the branches above her head.

Rachel kept running. The ground was low here, wet with rain. Mud sucked at her shoes, slowing her, but she kept her skirt tightly gathered and pushed ahead. Sounds of pursuit echoed among the trees behind her.

She was not going back . . . not going to let them take her alive, not again. *Which way?* She stopped, her lip caught between her teeth. *There!*

The woods gave way to open sky and flat, marshy ground. Rachel saw the river ahead, saw the pontoon bridge. Her foot twisted on a clump of marsh grass and she stumbled, pitching forward.

Someone shouted in the distance and she looked around. Several of Andryanov's men were clear of the woods, some on foot, some mounted.

No . . . !

Rachel levered herself out of the mud. If she could reach the British camp, if she could just get close enough to attract someone's attention! She could see red-coated sentries, but they were so far away.

"Give up, girl!" Andryanov's voice yelled just behind her. Rachel risked a glance back. He had dismounted, the ground too uncertain for horses. The Skorpion machine pistol gleamed in his hand.

The worst he could do was shoot her. She lowered her head and kept going. But Rachel's shoes were designed to look like period footwear, not for running, and every step dragged at her, like a nightmare where the sleeper runs and runs and finds he's getting nowhere.

But this was no dream.

Something metal clipped across the side of her head—the barrel of the machine pistol, she realized—and sent her tumbling forward. She fell in a muddy sprawl, looking up as Andryanov loomed above her, the Skorpion raised for another blow.

Rachel screamed. The Russian's hand swept down, smashing the weapon into her head with an explosion of pain and red-tinged blackness.

Far off, Rachel heard the crack of a gun being fired. "Hold!" someone yelled.

She struggled to free herself from the mud, pulling her knees under her, holding her arm up as Andryanov's hand hovered, ready for another blow.

"Selby! Good God, man . . . hold!"

Rachel slumped on her side, her vision blurred as waves of pain swept over her. She sensed boots moving near her face as the new voice continued.

"What the bloody hell do you think you're doing, man?"

"She is a rebel spy, General!" the VBU major said. "She was trying to escape!"

General . . . ?

"God's teeth, man, we are not barbarians! Clarke! Petersham! Help the lady!"

Dimly Rachel was aware of someone lifting her from the ground.

"General Burgoyne . . . you don't understand! The woman should be left with us! She has information."

"No! God strike you, Selby, I will not tolerate the mistreatment of women! Bring her, Lieutenant Clarke."

Rachel felt herself being carried over the uneven ground. She tried to open her eyes and had a blurred impression of men in red uniforms, of horses gathered by the road, of earnest-faced youngsters with readied muskets, bayonets fixed.

"I will deal with this outrage personally at a later date, Captain Selby!" Burgoyne's voice continued. "It happens I need your loyalists now . . . but rest assured that you have not heard the last of this! Bring her, gentlemen. We will return to headquarters!"

The pain receded. Only then did Rachel realize that she was being rescued.

Ten

Hunter watched from a wooded bluff, his binoculars pressed against weary eyes. Rank upon rank upon red-coated rank of British troops passed along the riverside road, marching south in endless columns.

He'd seen a British army on the march once before, at Brandywine, in Pennsylvania. This army was not as large . . . nor was it as freshly dressed. Many of the troops wore patched breeches, and the red coats were tattered and frayed. Burgoyne's army had covered well over one hundred and fifty miles during the summer and early fall of 1777, most of those miles through swamp and forest and wilderness . . . and the miles and months were showing in the men's uniforms.

In the distance, a stone mansion brooded over unharvested crops. Black smoke clawed the sky, where local patriots had tried unsuccessfully to set fire to fields wet from days of rain and drizzle. Burgoyne's men were completing the harvest now, as the army set out on the final leg of its march to find the American army.

Gates's Continentals had arrived at Bemis Heights on September 12, the same day that Taylor, King, Anderson, and Gomez set out in the wagon for Pennsylvania. Gates's scouts infested the surrounding woods, clashing occasionally with British foraging parties. Despite the fleabites of snipers and raids, the British advance continued. It was slowed to a crawl by the size of its baggage train and by the fact that American engineers continued to drop trees across roads and pull down bridges across streams and ravines.

But there was no stopping it now.

Hunter lowered the binoculars and cursed softly.

"A problem, Leftenant?" Dark Walker lay on his belly at Hunter's side.

"The VBU problem, Corporal," Hunter replied. "They're out there . . . but how in the hell do we find them?"

"The loyalists . . ."

"Tories. I've seen plenty of units that are probably legitimate Tory bands. We can't just wade in indiscriminately, killing everyone with a green coat . . ."

"Wasteful," Walker agreed. "What do you plan?"

"I don't know." He studied the marching columns a moment more. "We've been all over both sides of the river in the last three days. No sign of a VBU base anywhere. There was that encampment in the Great Ravine . . ."

"Abandoned at least two days."

"Yeah." The knowledge was a dull ache. The marks Dark Walker had found suggested a number of men and horses had been there . . . and the cigarette butts—a Russian brand—identified the campers. Had Rachel been kept there after her capture?

He pushed the thought of Rachel from his mind. *She's dead by now . . . or I pray God she's dead. Oh, Raye . . .*

"Let's head back," Hunter said at last. "If the VBU are down there, there's not a damned thing we can do about it. We'll have to wait for them to come to us."

"Sometimes, Leftenant, it is the waiting which is the hardest thing."

"Right. Let's do our waiting with others."

The two men melted back into the forest.

Treetops lashed back and forth as the rotor wash swirled clouds of dust and leaves across the clearing. The Mi-8 Hip transport passed low over the line of corrugated steel barracks, settling in for a landing in the field at the center of the base. Soviet spetsnaz troops in camouflaged uniforms snapped to attention as Colonel Yakushenko stepped from his headquarters.

The helicopter's turbine whine dwindled, the rotors slowing. Nearby, the Hind squatted near the fuel dump, where workers were completing their preflight checks and fueling on the gunship.

A side access door swung open, and Major Andryanov

leapt from the transport. He hurried through the settling dust, stooping under the still turning rotors, one hand clutching the tricorn hat to his head as his green coattails fluttered in the wind.

"Welcome back to *D'vighnoy Boor'yah*, Comrade," Yakushenko called, smiling.

His answer was a scowl. "Your orders left me no choice, Comrade Colonel," Andryanov replied. He threw a glance over his shoulder, to where VBU troops in Tory green were disembarking through the Hip's rear clamshell doors. He turned to face Yakushenko. "May I ask, Comrade, why we were ordered to abandon our post with Burgoyne? The plan, as *originally* conceived, is threatened!"

Yakushenko's smile vanished. "Come inside."

Within the headquarters, Yakushenko offered his subordinate vodka and waved toward a chair. "We are faced with a small problem, Major," he said. "Our operation in the south has been . . . eliminated."

Andryanov shot a hard glance at the older man. "Eliminated! How? By whom?"

Yakushenko shrugged expansively. "Uralskiy lost contact with Baratov . . . it would have been on the evening of September twelfth. We sent *Sasha* to investigate it yesterday," he said, using the pet name by which the operation's Hind was known. "The headquarters was destroyed, burned to the ground. There were no survivors."

"The American commandos?"

Again the expressive shrug. "Presumably. The *vashti* . . ." He gestured toward the ceiling, indicating the VBU directors who controlled the project from 2007. "The *vashti* believe it is at least possible that we have tapped another reality, one where the American Rangers do not exist but where another capitalist power developed its own time-travel program. For our purposes, we may as well assume it was the Americans."

Andryanov leaned back in the chair, his eyes closed. "It sounds, Comrade, as though you have a *proval* on your hands."

Yakushenko frowned. *Proval* was a Russian word meaning calamity. Coming from a KGB officer like Andryanov, it meant more . . . a political or military disaster that usually ended with someone being shot or reassigned to a post in

Siberia. By placing the responsibility at Yakushenko's feet, the major was issuing a not-so-subtle rebuke.

"You needn't take that tone with me, Sergei Sergeivich." Yakushenko kept his voice fatherly and low. "I realize that you do not approve of my policies, but Operation *D'vighnoy Boor'yah* is threatened, and we must work together on this."

"*Da*, Comrade Colonel," Andryanov said. Sarcasm twisted the words unpleasantly. "Perhaps the GRU needs the KGB after all."

The Soviet time operations directorate known as the VBU was a joint effort between the two largest intelligence agencies in the world: the *Komitet Gosudarstvennoy Bezopasnosti*, or KGB; and the *Glavnoe Razvedyvatelnoe Upravlenie*, the GRU, or Military Intelligence. Theoretically, the KGB's purpose within the organization was to provide intelligence on potential targets in the past, while the GRU directed the spetsnaz commandos in their operations.

There was a long and bitter tradition of rivalry between the two branches, however, and at times the political problems within the VBU seemed to outweigh the merely technical, tactical, and strategic considerations of carrying out a war in time.

Operation *D'vighnoy Boor'yah*—the code phrase meant "Double Storm"—had been conceived as a decisive blow against the United States and the West. By simultaneously assassinating the Americans' revered General Washington and guaranteeing that Saratoga would not end in a French alliance with the young United States, the Soviet Union's single greatest enemy would be eliminated. The U.S.S.R. would have no trouble dominating a world in which the United States had never appeared.

Yakushenko decided that the fatherly approach was not going to work with Andryanov. He'd feared as much. The KGB major had a reputation for independent action that frequently distressed his superiors. That reputation, in fact, had led to Yakushenko's assignment to Double Storm as mission commander over Andryanov.

"I do need your people, Major," Yakushenko said curtly. "And you. You will depart for the Philadelphia area immediately."

"Why do you think the Americans are still there? You are

saying that the Pennsylvania headquarters was destroyed on the twelfth . . . that was four days ago. If the Americans were responsible, they would have returned to 2007 by now."

"Perhaps. Even probably. But until we know just what happened, we will take no chances. I want you to establish a new headquarters. The safehouse already secured in Philadelphia should meet your purpose. You will use every means at your disposal to determine whether American time travelers are still operating in Pennsylvania, seek them out, and destroy them."

"My men and I were fulfilling an important mission with Burgoyne's army, Comrade Colonel. A vital mission . . ."

"This *proval*, as you call it, is more vital. Our forces here can handle the Saratoga campaign without your help."

"*Your* forces, you mean. Army thugs and blunderers who have no regard for the importance of secrecy here."

"I have some understanding of security matters," Yakushenko said stiffly.

"And I refer to the need not to let the natives realize that we do not belong here." He indicated his own costume. "The KGB has been operating successfully with Burgoyne for a month now. He believes us to be loyalist militia and depends on us for scouting reports on American activities. He has been moving slowly. Without us, he may stop moving altogether . . . and where would that leave the Saratoga end of Double Storm then?"

"Your reports do not indicate universal success, Major," Yakushenko said ominously. "You lost a prisoner, in fact, after *my* success in luring and destroying the enemy time commandos there!"

"That is true, Comrade Colonel." Andryanov's voice was in no way conciliatory. "I have people watching her. As I indicated in my report, I recommend against taking action to free her. An armed clash might spook Burgoyne's troops . . . could even lead to their retreating to Canada."

"Agreed, I suppose," Yakushenko said. He tugged at his ear. He was not as convinced as the KGB major that concealing modern technology from the natives was important to the overall success of the mission. What did it really matter how many locals saw a helicopter or two? What could they do . . . report a UFO?

"The situation with Burgoyne is delicate just now," Andryanov continued. "The girl is safe where she is . . . at least until the American army is destroyed. Once Burgoyne is victorious, we may be able to pick her up."

"Then there is no good reason to keep your entire force operating at Saratoga, is there, Major? I need you and your twenty men in Pennsylvania more than in the Hudson Valley forests."

"The enemy commandos remain a threat at Saratoga. Your trap did not net them all. Only five of my men remain with Burgoyne now."

"An insignificant threat," Yakushenko replied. "Your Captain Salekhov can handle them. Indeed, that threat is another reason for withdrawing all but five of your people. The Americans have no idea that we are here. Oh, they may suspect we have this base, if only because they know we need a place to park *Sasha* and *Misha*. But they cannot possibly locate us . . . and they would be unable to reach us if they could. Let the survivors search for us at Saratoga. They will find nothing . . . until it is too late!"

Andryanov appeared to consider this and finally nodded. "As you command, Comrade Colonel."

"Your orders in Pennsylvania are threefold, Major. Reestablish a local headquarters. Determine if the Americans are still there and destroy them. Locate Washington and kill him. His death is still necessary to Double Storm's success."

"*Da*, Colonel."

"The fact that our attempt to kill Washington at the Battle of Brandywine failed is of no great consequence. I believe . . ." His eyes narrowed. "I believe that, historically, another major battle in the region is due within the next few weeks. Our histories should give you the lead you need to pinpoint his movements and prepare your ambush."

"*Da*, Comrade Colonel."

Yakushenko allowed his tone to soften. "I am depending on you, Sergei Sergeivich. I know that you will not fail me. That you will not fail the *rodina*!"

Andryanov nodded. He looked tired. "For the *rodina*, then . . . for the motherland."

"Good." Yakushenko reached for the vodka bottle again.

"A toast then, Sergei Sergeivich: to the destruction of the United States of America!"

They drank.

Ben Taylor pressed the radio against his ear. "Say again, Yankee Two."

"Washington's main body isn't here, Yankee One," Anderson's voice replied. *"They had a run-in with the British on the sixteenth . . . but a rainstorm soaked their gunpowder. According to the people I've talked with, Washington is at Warwick Furnace now getting fresh powder."*

Taylor sighed. "Understood, Yankee Two. Where is that?"

"About twenty miles west of here on the main road." Anderson paused, then added, *"Yankee One . . . it wouldn't take me long to head up that way and see if I can get a lead on where they're headed."*

Taylor thought for a moment. "Okay, Two. Go ahead. But whatever happens, rendezvous back here no later than tomorrow evening."

"Roger that, Yankee One. Where and when?"

"We're in camp near Paoli Tavern," Taylor replied. "It doesn't look like Wayne is going to move for another forty-eight hours or so. Plan to meet us here."

"Roger, Yankee One. Two, out!"

Taylor lowered the radio, feeling very much alone. King and Gomez watched him silently from the wagon, parked a few yards away.

Despite a broken axle and a wrong turn or two along the rugged and often deceitful roads of New Jersey, Taylor's party had arrived in southeastern Pennsylvania after six days of travel, good time considering that they didn't have a helicopter. They'd reached Chester early that afternoon, only to discover that Washington's army was long gone from where they'd left it after the Battle of Brandywine a week before.

After Anderson had set off on horseback toward the northwest, looking for news, the others had fallen in with a detachment of American dragoons who led them to a detachment of Washington's army . . . fifteen hundred men under General Anthony Wayne, encamped not far from the main British force near Paoli. In their period civilian disguises, the three Rangers had been taken for sutlers and recruited to carry supplies to Wayne's camp. There was no easy way to refuse the order, not if the alternative was having their wagon and horses requisitioned. The wagon was piled high now with blankets, broadcloth, lead, and a few precious casks of gunpowder.

Taylor hid the radio under his coat and returned to the others. A pair of Continental dragoons watched him impassively from horseback.

But who are they . . . really? Taylor worked to steady the tremor he felt in his hands. The sight of those dragoons was reawakening his own inner doubts . . . and his fear.

Once, Travis Hunter had commented to Taylor about the strangeness of this war in time. It was a war like Vietnam, faced by an earlier generation of American soldiers, where civilians, even children, might not be what they seemed, where anyone you talked to might be a VBU agent disguised as a local.

At Brandywine, a number of the VBU troops had been disguised as locals. Taylor could still remember facing one during the wild room-to-room fight in Leicester House. For one horrible, fear-frozen instant, he'd stood above the body of a man dressed in the uniform and boots of an American dragoon of 1777, convinced that he'd just irretrievably altered the course of history. It would be so easy to kill someone who history decreed was *not* supposed to die. . . .

The VBU knew that, of course. That was why they were so careful with their disguises, why they seemed to favor slipping their men into the camps of local armies, disguised as Tories or patriots or soldiers of the period.

Taylor's experiences at Brandywine had left him with the chill horror that he would kill the wrong person . . . that *he* would be the one responsible for changing history. It would be so easy to make the wrong decision, to screw up just when it counted most. When your mistake could destroy the United States, could alter the shape of over two hundred years of history—that was more responsibility than he could handle.

His hands shook harder.

"Roy's continuing his recon," he said softly so that the dragoons would not hear. They thought he'd gone into the bushes to relieve himself. "He'll be back tomorrow."

"I don't like having the team split up," King said slowly. "We're hanging in the breeze here."

"Don't you think I know that?" He saw King's sharp glance and worked to control the surge of frustration, of fear. "Just damned bad luck Washington wasn't here," he said. "But Roy'll find him . . . and then maybe we can fall in with his force."

"Yes, sir."

He doesn't agree with the way I'm handling things, Taylor told himself. *Tough. It wasn't our fault Washington's already gone! If Trav were here . . . but he's not. I wonder how things are going back at Saratoga. Not knowing is the worst part of all.*

"Anything on the RS-17?" Taylor asked Gomez.

"Not a peep, Lieutenant. If the Russians are around, they're not using radio."

Maybe it'll be okay, then, he thought. *If we can just last out until after Saratoga. Maybe the VBU's given up down here. . . .*

But Taylor had a terrible feeling that it wasn't going to be that simple.

In a grassy clearing north of the Schuylkill River, the Soviet radio technician drew a line on a map. "We have them, Comrade Major," he said. "They must be with this small force under General Wayne."

Andryanov studied the map. "Paoli. And the one they were talking to?"

"I could not get a clear fix, Comrade Major. But it was within a few miles of the first. A scouting party, I would say."

Andryanov was surprised . . . and pleased. Quite frankly, he'd not expected to track the American time travelers down so quickly.

He smiled. Perhaps that GRU idiot Yakushenko knew what he was doing, after all. In any case, the operation here would soon be concluded, and he could return to his proper post with Burgoyne's army at Saratoga.

"We have them, then," Andryanov said. He turned to one of his aides. "Vasili! Assemble the men! We have them!"

Eleven

The ringing chirrup of crickets and cicadas made an excellent cover for their approach through the night. The ground was rugged and heavily wooded, the path nearly invisible underfoot. The previous night's drizzle had given way to a clinging fog through which the black-clad SAS force moved like silent ghosts.

Hunter snugged his Uzi into a more comfortable position and listened to the sounds of the woods. After a week the sassmen appeared to have accepted him as a leader, were willing to follow him. But the payoff was coming within the next few minutes. Everything depended on whether or not he'd guessed right.

It was still dark, an hour before dawn on the morning of September 19.

A shape materialized soundlessly. Hunter recognized Dark Walker.

"What'd you find, Corporal?"

Walker's grin was a gleam of teeth from a camo-blackened face. "You were right, Lieutenant. They are there."

Hunter felt an inward surge of relief. So much had depended on the gamble.

While Hunter and Wycliff both had been certain that the Soviets planned to do something at the Battle of Saratoga, there was no way to learn what their targets and timetables were until the VBU chose to make their move. Hunter had sent SAS teams on patrols throughout the area day after day, hoping to find a campsite, a base, someone they could take prisoner, *something* that would give them the clue they

needed, but without success. They'd set an ambush around
their former campsite: again, nothing.

It was the very lack of VBU activity that led Hunter to
make his gamble. If they could find no trace of VBU activity,
it might be because the VBU was gone... pulled back into
some base within range of their helicopters but out of the SAS
troop's reach. That suggested they planned to return just before the battle began... and that meant a helicopter LZ and
airmobile deployment.

Most of the terrain in this part of the Hudson Valley was
wooded. There were clearings everywhere, farmland mostly,
like the top of Bemis Heights or Freeman's farm farther north,
but those places were too open, too public for something as
utterly foreign to this age as a Soviet helicopter.

There was a hill west of Bemis Heights that was clear
enough for a helicopter landing, though it was uncomfortably
close to the American camp and Gates's headquarters. According to Wycliff, that was the hill occupied by General
Fraser during the battle—during *Wycliff's* version of the battle, Hunter corrected himself. As far as he could remember,
the initial fight at Saratoga had been a confused series of
clashes in the woods north of Bemis Heights, with the British
never coming close to Gates's camp.

The fact that Burgoyne's army might be trying to reach that
hilltop argued that the Soviets would not be there. Surely
whoever was in command of the VBU forces here would not
want to risk scaring the British soldiers so badly that they lost
the battle!

Which left the long, north-south ridge on the east side of
the Hudson, across the river from the Bemis Heights positions, the same place where the SAS had been ambushed on
the night of September 11. There was a long, broad, grassy
clearing up there, with a clear view of Gates's camp. It was
within mortar range of the American fortifications, and an
attack from the spot could easily be coordinated with the British attack on the nineteenth. The Russians had already landed
helicopters up there, which meant they knew the ground...
and might even risk a nighttime landing.

So Hunter took his gamble and concentrated on patrolling
that ridge, giving up surveillance of the approach of Burgoyne's army.

Late on the night of September 18, an SAS sentry on the east bank of the Hudson heard the distant clatter of an approaching helicopter. His report had caused Hunter to gather the entire team, what was left of it, and climb through the wet morning dark to this point, in hopes of finding the Russians already in place.

And he'd guessed right.

"Sentries?" he whispered. The Dakota pointed up the slope there . . . there . . . indicating Russian pickets. There were twelve in all.

Wordlessly Hunter passed orders to Sergeant Mason, deploying the team. With scarcely more than a windblown rustle of branches, seven British soldiers slipped into the night. Hunter pulled his combat knife from its sheath and crept up the slope.

A sentry stood at the edge of the clearing, an AKM slung across his shoulder. He wore woodland camouflage garb, and the outline of his head was strange under netting and strips of cloth.

Hunter's arm swept across the sentry's mouth. There was a muffled grunt. Then the Sykes-Fairbairn descended, slicing jugular and carotid. The Ranger gently guided the body to the ground. He wiped the blade clean and looked into the clearing. By now the others should be in position.

Hunter could see the Russian camp clearly now. The fog was thinning, the overcast sky above growing light with the dawn. Beyond the clearing, he could make out the broad sweep of the Hudson Valley. Bemis Heights shouldered above the surrounding fog like a dark island. Campfires winked through the drizzle from the American lines there, sending slender curls of smoke into the morning sky.

Closer, squat, and black and ugly against the panorama, three Soviet 120mm mortars leaned against their bipods. Soldiers stood here and there, talking in small groups or studying Gates's camp through binoculars. Some were still rolled up in sleeping bags near the shallow pits dug for the mortar baseplates. The helicopter was gone. That was disappointing. Capturing one might have given them a lead on the Russian's base.

Seconds crawled. Russians were stacking crates near the

mortars. Hunter decided they were waiting for the start of the battle across the river before opening fire.

There was a short, sharp *click-click* from the radio on Hunter's belt. A moment later, the sound came again, *click-click-click*.

Two SAS men to the left, three to the right. Dark Walker and Mason crouched nearby, in position. Hunter brought his Uzi up.

He squeezed the trigger and the stubby SMG screamed, hosing autofire into the Soviet camp. Two Russians crumpled, their backs ragged as 9mm rounds chopped into them. Gunfire erupted from the trees on either side as the commandos opened up. From the left, the deep-throated hammer of White's L7 machine gun joined in, splintering crates and punching gory red holes in surprised Russians. A camouflaged soldier with an AKM got off one burst before his face exploded. Walker's L85 spat flame in savage bursts, knocking down a Russian sprinting toward the woods. Hunter shifted his fire to the right, where soldiers scrambled from their sleeping bags, shouting and dying.

The firefight was over seven seconds after it began.

"We got 'em!" one SAS man said, sounding surprised. Hunter remembered his name was Lawrence Shute. "We got 'em all!"

"Mason!" Hunter snapped. "You and Shute circle down the hill. Make sure it's a clean sweep."

"We got 'em all ... sir." Mason's reply was reluctant. Hunter knew the SAS sergeant resented an outsider taking charge. So far there'd been no problem, but ...

"We don't know that, do we? Move, soldier!"

"Yes." There was a long and deliberate pause. "Sir."

So long as he follows orders, I'll worry about his attitude later. "The rest of you, check those bodies. Look for maps ... orders ... anything that looks like intel."

Walker gestured from beside the mortars. "A wounded man here, Leftenant!"

Hunter hurried across the clearing, stooping at Walker's side. The Russian lay on his back, chest heaving in pain and fear, his eyes staring. The front of his camouflage uniform was soaked in blood.

Walker pointed to the man's collar tabs. "A major," he said. "Spetsnaz."

His eyes locked with the Russian's. Cold, unreasoning fury welled up inside Hunter as he drew his Sykes-Fairbairn with the soft *snick* of metal on leather and showed the ebony blade to the major.

"This one is mine," he said in Russian. The man's eyes widened in horror.

It was all Hunter could do to fight the unrelenting anger and hatred that had driven him like wildfire since Rachel's capture. A more rational part of his mind could step back, however, and decide that the hatred showing in his eyes might well be sufficient in itself to convince the Russian prisoner that he'd been captured by a madman.

"Pahzhahl'stah!" Blood trickled from the major's mouth. "Please! No . . ."

"Now, Comrade," Hunter said. He kept the ice-cold edge of fury behind the control of his words. He was aware of Dark Walker's shuttered gaze beside him. "One week ago, your people captured a friend of mine. I expect that by now your interrogation experts have wrung her out, trying to find out what she knew. I tell you this so that you will know, without any doubt whatsoever, that right now I don't care whether you live or die."

The major twisted, as though trying to escape Hunter's knife. *"Nyet! Nyet!* You are mistake! We do not have her! *She is alive!"*

For an instant, time seemed to stand still. Carefully he brought the point of the knife down to within an inch of the major's right eye. "Explain."

"We captured a girl, yes! But she escaped! We never hurt her, I swear."

Rachel . . . escaped? Alive? Hunter kept his face immobile. It was all he could do to keep from grabbing the man by his collar and shaking him, demanding further details.

"Comrade Major, I have absolutely no reason to believe you," he said. Hunter's voice was thick with barely suppressed emotion. The knife moved, betraying the slightest of tremors in his hand. "I do not believe you. You are going to tell me about the VBU plan, however, and you are going to tell me the truth."

An hour later Hunter sat back, shaken and exhausted. Major Petrov had been most cooperative. Hunter now knew the name of the VBU commander—Colonel Yakushenko—and he knew there was a power struggle between Yakushenko's GRU and Major Andryanov's KGB. He knew that the KGB contingent that had been positioned with Burgoyne's army as part of Andryanov's original plan had been pulled out just three days before and sent south to Philadelphia to search for Americans. He knew that a Captain Salekhov and four KGB agents remained with the British army. Disguised as Tories of Selby's militia, Salekhov was leading the British artillery train, under General Fraser, to the hilltop west of Bemis Heights. Once in position, Fraser's cannon would open fire on Gates's camp . . . and at the same time Petrov was to have launched his mortar barrage. The unexpected and devastating high-explosive barrage would shatter the American defenders on Bemis Heights and send them fleeing, leaving Burgoyne with a clear and decisive victory.

And it would have worked, Hunter thought. *It did work, in the BNA universe.*

Before he died of his wounds, Petrov confirmed that there was a Russian base, but he didn't know where it was. "Someplace south" was all he could say. He confirmed that a large number of Russian troops remained in 1777, but he didn't know how many, and he didn't know where they were. Only Colonel Yakushenko, Petrov insisted, knew the entire plan.

And Rachel was alive. *Alive!*

Hunter stood and crossed to the east face of the clearing. The land across the Hudson appeared flat, though the flatness was illusory. The highlands between Bemis Heights and the steeper hills to the north had been cut deeply by myriad streams, forming a patchwork of ravines and gullies through heavily forested terrain. Fog still covered most of the terrain, though trees were showing now as the drizzle lifted, revealing the blaze of autumn leaves. Here and there clearings were visible, and the tiny shapes of houses and barns. One of those plowed fields would be the one belonging to a Tory farmer who had escaped to Canada early in the war. His name would be given to the battle later that day—the Battle of Freeman's Farm.

North, up the river, a collection of buildings sprawled near the river. That was the Sword Farm, Hunter knew, chosen by General Burgoyne as his headquarters.

Rachel must be there. *What happened?* he wondered. *Petrov said she was with Burgoyne. Is she a prisoner? Or hiding from the VBU?*

First things first. There were five VBU agents still at large. "Gather the men," Hunter told Mason. "Have them blow the mortar tubes and dump them over the ridge. And tell White and Walker I want to see them."

Rachel stepped out of the tent, squinting in the brilliant morning sunlight. The earlier fog and rain were lifted now, and the sky was a glorious crystal blue. General John Burgoyne towered above her, astride his horse. She shielded her eyes against the sun and caught the warmth of his smile.

Burgoyne was tall and devastatingly handsome, dazzling in scarlet, lace, and gold braid. He doffed his hat. "Good day, madam. I trust you slept well?"

She smiled. "Thank you, General. Yes."

Beyond him, red-coated columns marched past, the rattle of their drums shocking the air. The British army was on the march.

Burgoyne reached down and gentled his horse, still smiling. "I wanted to know that you were well," he said. "Your head is feeling better?"

Rachel touched her head where Andryanov had struck her. "Much better."

"That is good." A shadow crossed his face. "That scoundrel Selby . . . You must understand, miss, that we are not animals."

It had been seven days since her rescue from the VBU. In that time Burgoyne had led his army across the Hudson some distance upriver, then marched it south to the fields and pastures of the Sword Farm.

"At any rate, m'dear, I can't truly believe Selby's story that you are a rebel spy. Unfortunately we simply cannot ignore the man completely. Civilians do pass information to the enemy from time to time, y'know."

"I understand, General." She shuddered. "And I can't thank you enough for getting me away from . . . that man. You've been very kind."

It was true. Her captivity was as comfortable as could be expected in an eighteenth-century military camp. She had reasonable privacy and the companionship of a number of women traveling with Burgoyne's army.

"Not at all, miss," Burgoyne said. "Tell me. Do you like the dress?"

She looked down at it, a long, full blue gown from London, and smoothed the pleats of her skirt. Burgoyne had ordered it unpacked from one of the thirty baggage wagons carrying his personal belongings. It had belonged to his mistress, but he'd given it to Rachel as a present, replacing the muddy rags she'd been wearing when she was rescued.

"Yes, General, thank you. It's beautiful. You've been so very kind."

"Nonsense," he said. "Ah . . . m'dear, I do most sincerely regret having been forced to deprive you of your liberty. Perhaps in two or three days we can remedy the situation." Grandly he gestured toward the marching troops, where regimental colors fluttered grandly in the breeze. "One way or the other, today the die is cast!"

The marching soldiers, seeing the sweep of their general's arm, raised a thunderous, repeated *huzzah!*

"There's going to be a battle, then?"

"Indeed! Gates is encamped on the heights to the south." He set his hat back on his head. "It's all or nothing on the toss, m'dear."

Rachel touched the neck of Burgoyne's horse. "Please be careful, General. I wouldn't want anything to happen to you."

He reached down, took her hand, and lowered his lips to kiss it. *No wonder his men call him "Gentleman Johnny."* He cut a dashing figure . . . all the more for having rescued her from Andryanov.

"Heaven and the rebel hosts willing, I shall return to your side, m'dear. *Au revoir!*" Then he was off, to the cheers and shouts of his troops.

Free! she thought. *He's going to let me go!*

Rachel had thought about escape. It would have meant getting past the sentry . . . then making her way through unknown woods in the darkness. She'd tried running in one of these ponderous eighteenth-century dresses before and was not eager to try it again. With the VBU out there somewhere, she'd even been afraid to try sending a message. There had been a VBU spy that day at the tavern. Attempts to pass letters across the lines might well attract the wrong kind of attention.

But if Gentleman Johnny let her go . . .

She would have to avoid "Selby" and his disguised commandos. But if she could find the American lines . . . Travis must be somewhere out across those woods.

Or was he? Could the VBU and their helicopters have already won? Did he think she was dead . . . or was *he* dead?

Tramping in perfect step through the billowing dust, rank upon rank of troops marched along the road. Rachel thought about death and battle and shuddered.

Twelve

"Lieutenant Hunter is not the fool you think him, Top," Dark Walker said.

Sergeant Mason scowled and looked across the clearing to where Hunter was studying the American camp. "Oh? He gets a lead on five VBU bastards over there, and he tells you and White to go with him. Not the rest of us . . . just you two. Three-to-five odds aren't smart. We should take the whole troop over there and kick arse."

"Someone has to stay and sanitize the ridge."

Mason made a face. The American leftenant had given his orders moments before. Each mortar was to receive a grenade down the tube to render it useless, before being dismantled and dragged down the slope and dumped in the river.

"Shit. Sanitize the ridge. All this work dumping weapons, burying bodies . . . Hell, Corp . . . we're sass, not bloody sappers!"

"He seems to know what he's doing. It would be unwise to leave clues here for the VBU commander if he returns. No, Top. The more I see of this Ranger, the more impressed I am." He shifted the bullpup Individual Weapon in his grasp. "In any case, he is in command now . . . and it is not our place to question him."

Hunter pulled the radio out of its case and looked at it suspiciously. It was not one of the heavy SAS walkie-talkies but a Soviet model, sleek and small, no larger than a fountain pen, with an accompanying earpiece.

They'd found several of the radios on the ridge top, two-channel jobs with a range that Hunter estimated to be several

113

miles. This one was from Major Petrov's pocket.

Hunter, Walker, and White had left Mason with the rest of the SAS troopers and returned to the Parson House. Hurriedly he'd conferred with Wycliff, explaining what he had in mind.

Wycliff's historical knowledge of the unfolding battle was invaluable, even if it did come by way of an alternate timeline. The captain pointed out a clearing on the topographical map and identified it as Freeman's Farm, where the sharpest clash of the battle took place. General Fraser would pass to the west of that clearing, he explained, heading toward the hill overlooking Bemis Heights. Petrov's information suggested that the remaining VBU agents were with that column.

Now Hunter was a few hundred yards west of Freeman's Farm, fingering the Russian radio. Walker and White, close by, watched him silently. Gunfire cracked and blammed among the trees to the east. The battle had begun only moments before, as American woodsmen hurrying north from Bemis Heights collided with the British main body at the Freeman Farm. They'd seen nothing of that clash, but it sounded close by. Fraser's column should be more to the northwest, not engaged in the fighting yet, but not very far away.

"Well . . ." Hunter moistened his lips. "Here goes."

He thumbed the transmit switch on the radio. "Captain Salekhov!" Hunter said, speaking Russian, roughening his voice in an attempt to disguise it, to imitate the dead major. "Captain Salekhov! This is Major Petrov! Come in!"

For a long, trembling moment he listened to the hiss of static in the earpiece. This was as much a gamble as his betting on the ridge top as the Soviet LZ. There could be a call sign or other form of radio security that Petrov had not told them about . . . or he could make a monumental slip that would give everything away.

For that matter, Hunter still didn't know if Petrov was telling the truth. He didn't want to dwell on the possibility that the man was lying, not when that meant that Rachel . . .

"Captain Salekhov! Come in! This is Petrov!"

A crackle interrupted the steady hiss of static. *"Da, Comrade Major,"* a voice replied. *"This is Salekhov! Why are you breaking radio silence?"*

"There has been a change of plan!" Hunter replied. "Colonel Yakushenko has returned and has ordered me to meet with you . . . personally!" There was a long pause, and Hunter felt the sweat beading above his eyebrows.

"The battle has already begun, Comrade. Movement in these woods is dangerous. However, we could rendezvous at V-33. Are you close by?"

"Very close," Hunter said. That was true, judging by the strength of Salekhov's signal. "We will be there in twenty minutes. Keep your radio on. We will call again if we have trouble." He broke the connection.

His eyes met Walker's, and the Dakota nodded. The corporal held one of the radio direction finders and was studying its face. "That way," Walker said, pointing. "A clear line . . . and not very far."

"Right," Hunter said. "Let's go."

Ten minutes later Hunter gave a sharp hand signal and the three commandos went to ground. Movement betrayed itself, fifty yards ahead through the woods.

Hunter had seen those green uniforms, the crossed white belts, the cocked hats before. Four men hurried forward along a clay road. Hunter could not see their weapons through the thick foliage. They appeared to be carrying . . . something. Bundles, perhaps, weapons wrapped in leather strips . . .

Hunter exchanged glances with the others. Walker peered across the top of his L85, while White snapped the bolt back on his L7 machine gun. Both men glanced at Hunter and nodded their readiness.

But Hunter was uneasy. Unless he could get a clear identification . . .

The VBU agents might be wearing Tory uniforms, but there were real loyalists with Burgoyne's army too. They were people who belonged here, people whose deaths could alter history in ways no one could predict.

Were those men VBU . . . or were they real Tories? Hunter had to find out before he gave the order to open fire.

Walker, squinting through the sight on his rifle, stiffened. "Leftenant!" he hissed. "I think that's the man from the tavern!"

But there was supposed to be five of them. Where . . . there! A fifth man trailed the others, acting as overwatch in a decidedly anachronistic display of modern tactics.

Hunter jerked his Uzi to his shoulder. *"Take them down!"*

Autofire rattled among the autumn leaves, drowning the crack of musketry in the east. A green-coated man screamed and pitched backward, clawing at his chest. Hunter heard the distinctive cracking of an AKM firing full-auto. Those bundles were assault rifles wrapped in leather.

The return fire was wild, blindly hurled against the woods. Hunter and the two SAS men poured round after round into the VBU position. Another Soviet trooper lay dead, while a third clutched at the gaping horror of his open belly.

Hunter saw movement, a green-clad shape sprinting through the trees, already too far for a certain shot. "Keep on 'em!" he shouted at the others. "I'll nail that one!"

Then he was up and running, ducking low to avoid the whiplash of low branches as he raced through the woods. The sound of autofire continued behind him as White and Walker dueled with the surviving Russians. The fifth VBU agent must be somewhere ahead.

Hunter burst from the woods into an unexpected clearing and nearly fell in his effort to stop. A lone man stood there, twenty feet away, a pair of richly ornate dueling pistols clenched in his hands and leveled at Hunter's face.

He felt suspended in time, his attention focused on the hexagonal barrels of the two heavy black-powder muzzle-loading pistols. Hunter's first thought was that he'd made a mistake, that this man in front of him was a genuine Tory . . . a guide, perhaps, traveling with the Russians and now terrified by weapons that would seem like magic to him.

At the same time Hunter took in the man's dark features, his black mustache, and remembered Wycliff's description of the VBU agent in the tavern.

There was no time to make a decision, no time to think. The man's hands were already tightening around his pistol grips as Hunter's finger closed on his Uzi's trigger. The Uzi was pointed barrel low, aimed at the ground near the man's feet. He let the autofire burst drag his muzzle up, sweeping across the standing man.

Both pistols went off at the same instant, paired flashes and cracks from the hammers, followed by the deeper, heavier explosions of the main charges.

Hunter felt something snicker past his right ear, felt something hot pluck at his left sleeve. The man crumpled, torn knee to throat by a jagged line of bloody 9mm holes.

He approached cautiously. Hunter's burst had been triggered more by instinct than by decision. What if the man was not a time traveler?

Under his coat the dead man wore leather holsters designed for the pistols. One deep pocket held a flat mahogany box of the kind used to carry dueling pistols.

The radio tucked into a pocket of his waistcoat was the final proof, and Hunter let out a long, low whistle of relief. He found the Skorpion machine pistol a moment later, snugged away in a holster at the small of the man's back. One 7.63mm cartridge was solidly jammed in the weapon's chamber, explaining why the VBU agent had tried to use black powder pistols instead. Perhaps, too, Hunter thought, the Soviet had hoped to make him hesitate for a critical second. If so, it had almost worked.

A thunderous volley of gunfire roared across the field, making Hunter look up. He was in the Freeman's farm clearing, an open field over half a mile across filled now with ranks of soldiers and boiling clouds of blue-gray smoke.

The Americans, most dressed in rough, fringed hunting jackets, had come from the south, firing on the advance guard of a British column from cover. Then they'd surged into the open, charging past the farmhouse with wild cheers. In the woods at the north side of the clearing they'd met the full weight of the main British column. Red-coated infantrymen delivered a devastating volley, then advanced in lock step, bayonets gleaming in the early-afternoon sun.

As Hunter watched, the Americans wavered, many breaking and falling back toward the shelter of the woods. Flags bobbed above smoke and the faces of shouting men as the British swept past the house. More American troops appeared in the south, where mounted officers waved their swords and tried to rally fleeing men. Above the gunfire, Hunter heard a peculiar, lilting warble, a liquid gobbling sound repeated over and over. It took him a moment to decide what it was: a turkey call. American backwoodsmen were using turkey calls to rally their broken formations.

Hunter collected the Skorpion and the radio from the VBU man's body. It would not do for locals to find those. After a moment's hesitation he took the two pistols as well, tucking them away into the velvet-lined recesses for them in the mahogany box. The Russian didn't need those weapons anymore, and Hunter had a specific use for them.

The battle in the clearing was spreading. The Americans were making a stand south of the farmhouse, trading volley for volley with the advancing British regulars. Hunter could see the jerking movements of hands and ramrods above the drifting smoke as men reloaded each shot.

It was time to go.

Too late! More troops rushed from the trees: men in Tory green, and others wearing nothing but paint, breechclouts, and leggings pressing through the underbrush, half glimpsed through leaves and branches. Shrill, yipping whoops and screams wavered through the woods. Hunter dropped to his belly and froze, watching as loyalist militiamen and Indians burst from cover, stopping to fire, then rushing forward. They had cut him off from Walker and White.

The VBU presence here took on new meaning for Hunter. These Tories and Indians must be part of Fraser's column, sweeping down on the Continental's left flank. If that attack had been led by men with assault rifles, firing into packed ranks of Americans just as they were trying to rally in front of a British charge . . .

If the Americans broke once and for all, there would be nothing to stop the British from sweeping into Gates's fortifications at Bemis Heights. If Fraser's artillery could be planted on the hills to the west, if the VBU mortar attack from across the Hudson had been carried out . . . Hunter shuddered. He now knew exactly what the Russian plan had been. It had come so close to success.

The first ranks of Tories ran past, ignoring the two bodies lying at the edge of the clearing. Hunter got to his feet and started toward the woods and nearly collided with a half-naked Indian.

His face was painted black, not the smudgy, lusterless black of camo paint but a shiny, almost iridescent blue-black from which the man's teeth gleamed like jewels in a savage grin. The musket in his hands came up.

Hunter stepped past the muzzle of the long rifle, slapping it aside. The gun went off with the flat *ba-bang* of a flintlock, as his foot swept around in a sideswing targeted on the Indian's breechclout. As the savage folded up with a squeaking gasp, Hunter's hand came down on the base of his neck, driving him into the ground. Then the Ranger was sprinting through the woods. Several times he took cover as mixed bands of Tories and Indians hurried past, but it didn't take him long to get clear without being seen again.

Hunter had assumed White and Dark Walker had already exfiltrated the area and were on their way south. He was wrong. The tall British North American Indian materialized out of the brush and waved him on. A moment later the three of them were moving south together.

He carried vivid impressions of the battle with him as they made their way south toward Bemis Heights. He remembered the fighting in the woods, men loading and firing and loading again as sweat smeared their powder-blackened faces and their gun barrels grew hot . . . shafts of sunlight and shadow projected in bold streaks of dark and light across smoke clouds drifting among the trees . . . a boy still trying to tear his paper cartridge with his teeth and stuff the powder down the muzzle of his rifle, as blood and entrails spilled from his belly.

They arrived unchallenged at Bemis Tavern. The woods behind the fighting were filled with aimless, wandering men, many wounded, as well as mounted couriers and men carrying loads of powder and shot to their comrades. Bemis Heights appeared alive with men arrayed in close-packed ranks behind the fortifications raised by the Polish engineer, Colonel Kosciuszko. Their weapons shouldered, they anxiously awaited the order to advance.

Gates would not give that order, Hunter knew. The American commander was too cautious, too fearful of making the one mistake that might cost him his army. The battle would seesaw back and forth past Freeman's Farm for the rest of the day. Time after time, the British advanced across the field and into the woods to the south, only to be brought to a halt by the unerring fire of American sharpshooters. Time after time the broken redcoat lines fell back to the north, pursued by their eager foes. The battle ended in the early evening, when a third British column that had been proceeding down the Albany Road arrived just in time to stop the final American attack.

They walked unnoticed through the American camp.

Hunter saw lines of bloodied wounded waiting their turns with the surgeon and noted the nervous young faces of boys waiting to be committed to battle.

It was ironic, he decided. The Continentals could have won a clear-cut victory at any of several times during the afternoon, but General Gates seemed reluctant to commit more than a handful of men at a time. Most of his troops remained on Bemis Heights throughout the fight. Hunter could not help but imagine the bloody horror that would have been sown among those standing ranks if the Russian mortars had opened fire.

For now, at least, they seemed to have stopped the VBU.

Rachel pushed a lock of dank, black hair back from her eyes. All around her lay men with shattered bodies, their moans and screams mingling in a hellish montage of suffering.

It was early evening. Wounded were still being found and brought in from the thickets and brush of the heavily wooded ravines around Freeman's Farm where they had fallen. Earlier that afternoon, as the battle thundered and boomed off toward the southwest, Rachel had approached Lady Harriet Acland and asked her new friend if she could help with the wounded. The offer was graciously accepted, and Rachel found herself working through an afternoon as long as any she had known.

The battle must have been a disaster, Rachel thought. Burgoyne had lost at least six hundred men—insignificant compared to the bloodbath slaughters of the wars of a later day, but terrible by the standards of an eighteenth-century European army. Hundreds of wounded men crowded onto the grounds around the Sword Farm headquarters, overwhelming the efforts of a handful of army surgeons and orderlies who, in any case, could do little to relieve the men's suffering.

Medical treatment in this age was more brutal and deadly than combat. Rachel had seen one orderly leaving a hut carrying a bundle of legs and arms partly wrapped in bloody canvas. Few surgeons had more than a cursory knowledge of their craft, and laudanum and rum were the only painkillers. Rachel had spent most of the past twenty hours carrying water and bandages and simply talking with sweating, glassy-eyed boys as they waited for their turn with the doctors.

"You look exhausted, dear," Lady Harriet said. Her face was streaked with dried blood where a dying soldier had touched her. "You should get some rest."

"That's all right," Rachel said. She helped the soldier between them take a sip of water from a wooden canteen. "I can go for a while yet."

"Perhaps you should do as Lady Harriet suggests," a deep voice said behind her. Rachel turned and looked up. Burgoyne was there, immaculate as always in scarlet and lace but looking very tired.

"Oh! General! I didn't hear you."

Burgoyne's mouth moved in the shadow of a smile. "I am grateful for what you have done here, Mistress Rachel. And you, Lady Harriet. All of you women have been splendid amidst this . . . this horror."

Harriet wiped the soldier's face with a cloth. "There are so many of them, General."

"Yes." The word was whispered, almost inaudible. "My poor, poor boys . . ."

Rachel stood and impulsively took Burgoyne's hand. "General? What *happened*?"

"We didn't lose. God help us, we didn't lose. But neither did we win . . . and to suffer such losses so far from our supply bases in Canada . . . in this wilderness . . ."

Travis must be here! The thought sang joy in the back of her mind. *The British lost, which means the VBU lost. Travis did it!*

Burgoyne seemed to shake himself, to draw himself up straighter. "The army is intact, and we may yet be able to push through. Our position is still strong."

He looked down at Rachel as if seeing her for the first time. "Ah, my dear. I have not forgotten my promise. I will still see to it that you are sent across to the American lines. I fear it cannot be today, however. Perhaps Monday."

Rachel nodded. Behind her, someone shrieked in agony. "I . . . I understand, General. In the meantime there's a lot I can do here."

Lieutenant Rudolph Stepanovich Chernysh did not question the orders that had brought him and most of Selby's Rangers from Burgoyne's camp by the Hudson to southeastern Pennsylvania. He knew there were tensions between his superiors, between the KGB Andryanov and the GRU Yakushenko, especially. As a former officer of the KGB, he felt a certain loyalty to Captain Andryanov, of course, but the first commandment for the lower-ranking officers of the VBU—as for any other military organization—was obey orders and don't attract attention.

His orders directed him to flush the American time commandos known to be hiding in the Continental camp and capture or kill them. That should be easy enough to carry out. The Ranger numbers were not known but could not be more than a handful. Chernysh had twenty men . . . and an unexpected advantage.

Andryanov had explained at the *yavka*, the safehouse they'd set up in Philadelphia the day before. According to the history book the VBU was using to determine its strategies in this period, there was going to be a battle this night, a surprise attack by the British against an unsuspecting American camp. The VBU team would use the British attack as cover, drawing the Rangers out and trapping them, then break into small groups and exfiltrate on foot back to Philadelphia and the safehouse. Obviously the American Rangers didn't even realize the British attack was due tonight or they would have left Wayne's camp before this. It was perfect, the target unsuspecting of both the British approach and the Russian ambush masked by the larger battle.

"You . . . you . . ." He spoke in an urgent whisper, pointing out two of his men. He indicated a clearing a few meters ahead. "Take position there. Wait for my order."

The soldiers acknowledged their orders. Green-coated Russians crawled into position, careful to remain out of sight within the blackness of the woods. It was dark, though innumerable bonfires in the meadow cast shifting, dancing shadows across the American camp.

The battle that would be fought this evening would go down in the history books as the Paoli Massacre, a disaster for the Continentals.

But it would be more than that. It would be a massacre of the U.S. Rangers as well. Chernysh chambered a round into his AKM and smiled.

Thirteen

Greg King came awake to the shouts and the wet, splashing sounds of running men close by the wagon. He was wrapped in his sleeping bag, lying between the wheels of their wagon to avoid the steady drizzle that had been falling all evening.

Gomez was already up, stooping by the wagon and kicking King's leg. "Come on, Greg! Reveille!"

King fumbled for his leather-wrapped FAL. Ben Taylor struggled clear of his sleeping bag. "God . . . what is it now?"

"Nothin' much, Lieutenant," Gomez replied. "Just a British attack."

Taylor's eyes widened. King frowned but said nothing. The lieutenant had been acting strange ever since that first firefight at Saratoga. What was the matter with him?

King checked to make sure he had a fresh magazine of 7.62mm cartridges in his rifle and chambered a round. Beyond the wagon was a Dantean scene, chaos and noise everywhere. Sentry fires glared in the night, illuminating men carrying haversacks, muskets, even clothing, all dangling from their arms as they scattered. A sergeant stood in the open, waving the long polearm that was his badge of rank, trying to rally fleeing men.

"Redcoats!" Gomez pointed toward the northeast. "Through there! They must have sneaked up quiet, then rushed in with bayonets!"

There was gunfire in the night, scattered and isolated. The British were overrunning the American camp. King glanced at Taylor. The man was gaping at the running soldiers. "Orders, sir?"

Taylor looked as though he'd been struck. "I don't know. E and E, I guess."

The indecision in the man's voice was chilling. Taylor was an experienced Ranger, had been in combat many times before, but there was something wrong now.

"Get the horses, Eddie," King said with quiet authority. "Hitch up the wagon." He stared into the darkness beyond the fires. He'd heard shots fired . . . but not the sharp crack of muskets. The rattle of automatic fire was unmistakable.

"Oh, shit!" Gomez said. "Nothing else like an AK!"

"So the British have some help," King said. He wondered why the VBU was striking here. Washington was still miles away somewhere. Anderson had not yet returned, so King didn't know where the main body of the Continental army was, but the VBU certainly had no reason to attack Wayne's small detachment.

"C'mon!" he snapped. "Lieutenant! Move!"

"What . . . ?"

"Let's see where those shots are coming from!"

"Yes. Yes! Let's go, men!"

British regulars crowded into the camp, disciplined, moving silently, using their bayonets with ruthless efficiency. The defenders managed one ragged volley before dwindling away as groups of two and three broke and ran.

King, Taylor, and Gomez managed to avoid the tangled masses of fleeing Continentals, as well as the parade-ground movements of the advancing British. They reached the sheltering darkness of the woods. Ahead, they heard the clatter of autofire once again, much closer now. There appeared to be a clearing not far away. The autofire sounded again, and King saw the stab of muzzle flash flickering against the night.

"Who the hell are they shooting at?" Taylor asked. He shifted his H&K uncomfortably in his hands. "There's nobody there."

"Except us!" King said, driven by sudden realization. "Down!"

The three dived for cover as the woods around them opened up in a wall of stabbing, rippling flashes. King clutched at the ground behind a fallen tree trunk as bullets chunked and thudded into the wet wood, showering him with chips.

He remembered the radio conversation with Anderson the day before. *They tracked us! They used a radio direction finder and tracked us!*

The VBU wasn't here to kill Washington. They were here to ambush the Rangers.

And they'd managed to pull it off.

Roy Anderson knew the old military axiom about marching to the sound of the guns. In his case, he'd marched not to the guns but to the movement of a great many men. He'd returned from his scouting trip well after dark. General Washington, he now knew, was twelve miles away, north of the Schuylkill River, positioned to block the British army from marching on Philadelphia. Near Paoli, though, Anderson had seen redcoats moving with an eerie silence along muddy roads through the darkness. It wasn't hard to guess their destination. Wayne's camp lay only four miles away. For some reason the American commander seemed convinced that the British didn't know he was there, despite campfires and the habitual noise of the un-disciplined Continentals.

By the time he was close enough to use his radio to warn the others, the attack was under way. From two miles away, the sky was lit by the glare of bonfires spreading out of con-trol, and he could hear the scattered firing of men panicked by the silent and deadly redcoat assault.

Then he heard the rattle of AK fire.

He spurred his horse forward. There were British troops everywhere, but none paid him any attention in the dark and confusion. He was wearing his period costume, which looked enough like an officer's coat and hat in the darkness to let him pass.

The first, furious burst of automatic fire had died away, but the rattle of subguns continued to spit and snarl from the woods ahead. He dismounted when he could take his horse no farther. He'd left his machine gun with the wagon, but his M-16 was carefully bundled in leather against the wet and prying eyes, strapped to the back of his saddle. He unhitched it, jacked a round into the chamber, and started forward.

The patch of woods was alive with gunfire. He saw a man briefly illuminated ten yards ahead by the flicker of his muzzle flash. Anderson had only a glimpse of the man's Tory uniform . . . and the curved magazine of his AKM.

It was enough. He brought the M-16 to his shoulder and snicked the selector switch to single-shot. When the man fired again, Anderson squeezed the trigger.

In the darkness he didn't see the target go down, but he found the body a moment later. By the dim light of the fires consuming the American camp in the distance, he saw the bizarre, bug-eyed monster's face of Soviet infrared goggles.

"'Scuse me, son, but I need these more than you do," he said. He stripped off the goggles and settled them over his face. The landscape around him became clear, green-tinted, and artificial. Yellow shapes moved among the crisscrossing tangle of branches, glimpsed through foliage by their body heat.

He identified another Russian by the shape of his AK and fired another single shot. He crept forward, spotting another VBU soldier just as the man swung his bug-eyed, goggled head around to face Anderson. The M-16 round drilled a neat hole through the mask. The spray of hot blood looked white against shimmering green.

Silently the Texan advanced toward the center of the fight.

Taylor raised his head above the splintered log. The gunfire was dying away, and shouts and confusion sounded from the darkness.

"Something's got 'em spooked," King said. "I think they're falling back! Anybody hurt?"

"Just my pride," Gomez said. "Where the hell did they come from?"

"Offhand, I'd day Russia," King replied. "I don't think the British are using AKMs."

"Some of them could be British," Taylor said. "God, Greg. I don't like shooting in the dark at targets we can't identify! If there are locals mixed in with the Russians, we could—"

The rush caught them all by surprise. Taylor looked up in time to catch a glimpse of a green uniform . . . a goggled face under the cocked hat.

King triggered his FAL, punching the masked figure backward. Another attacker appeared . . . and another. Gomez snapped his rifle up, pumping three quick rounds into the closest shape.

"No!" Taylor screamed, his face white in the unsteady light. "Don't shoot!"

Things were happening too fast. The woods were full of running men, some with AKMs, but it was impossible to check them all. A green-coated soldier sprang over the log, sending Gomez sprawling. Taylor didn't see an AK, but King brought his FAL up. Taylor snapped his hand out, slapping the barrel down. *"I said don't shoot!"*

The Soviet attacker's lower jaw exploded in blood and chunks of flesh and bone.

Roy Anderson strode out of the darkness, firing at the attackers. A half-glimpsed figure swung his AK like a club, striking King across the head. Taylor triggered a burst from his H&K, kicking the VBU agent back. Other Soviets ran into the woods, scattering in all directions.

The silence that followed was startling. Gunfire continued to crackle from the burning American camp, but the firefight here was over as suddenly as it had begun. "Hello, Roy," Gomez said. "Glad you could make it."

King staggered to his feet, dabbing gingerly at the trickle of blood on the side of his head. He looked at Taylor as though he couldn't quite believe what had happened. "What the bloody hell . . . ?"

"I'm sorry, Greg," Taylor said. He gestured toward the body of the man Anderson had killed. Taylor had not seen a weapon in the man's hand when he'd knocked King's FAL aside. Now he could see the small, deadly Skorpion clutched in the Russian's fist. "I thought . . . I thought—"

"You damned bloody idiot!"

Taylor was shaking. He folded his arms, ashamed of the physical reaction that was setting in. It was the responsibility, he realized, and the not knowing. Firefights with Russian soldiers he could handle, but this kind of blind guesswork, the endless need always to be right was paralyzing him, rendering him helpless.

King turned away sharply. "Eddie! Check those bodies! Get the AKs."

"C'mere, Greg," Anderson said. "Let me see your head."

"Shit, Roy," Gomez said. "You oughta know by now how hard his head is!"

Taylor turned away, feeling alone, isolated. The three were

bantering about something that had happened before he'd joined the team. He knew the story; a bullet had grazed King's head during a previous encounter with the VBU, and his survival continued to generate endless comments about the thickness of his skull.

The joke excluded Taylor from their circle, leaving him on the outside. Mechanically he began going through the pockets of one of the dead Russians. Inside one coat pocket he found a sheet of folded paper. It was too dark to see what was on it, but it could be important.

He looked up and caught King's eyes on him, hard and thoughtful.

"I've got to get to Pennsylvania," Hunter said.

"I would say so," Wycliff replied. He exchanged glances with Buchanan, propped up in the bed beside him. "Sorry we can't go with you, but we'd just slow you down."

"Mrs. Parson doesn't seem to mind us staying as... boarders for a time," Buchanan said. "She and her son have been taking good care of us."

"Captain..." Hunter searched for the right words. "I'll want to take some of your boys with me. I don't know what my people are facing in Pennsylvania, but..."

Wycliff held up one hand. "They're yours, Leftenant. Buchanan and I can hold the fort here." He looked away, uncomfortable. "I... I owe you an apology, Lieutenant. You carried out the raid well, smashed the VBU op here. Where I put my boot in it..."

Hunter stood up, embarrassed. He paced across the narrow room to an untidy pile of equipment, satchels of clothing and the SAS recall beacon recovered a week before from their first camp. He found his own rucksack, opened it, and extracted the mahogany case. Candlelight gleamed from the polished surface and brass fixtures.

"We... found this yesterday, Captain," he said, returning to the bed. "At the battle. Your VBU friend from the tavern was carrying it. I thought you might like it."

Wycliff took the case and snapped open the catch. The pair of matched flintlock pistols lay inside, together with various accoutrements Hunter did not recognize.

"You said you wanted a real one," Hunter continued. "I thought these might serve."

Wycliff looked up from the pistols. "They might indeed. Thank you, Travis." Animation returned to his eyes. "Look at this . . . Hawkins of London! Silver chasing . . . nine-inch hexagonal barrels. What the devil was a VBU man doing with them?"

"We're not sure," Hunter replied. "They look like they're in perfect condition. He might have taken them off a British officer . . . maybe as loot to sell in the future. I imagine they would be valuable in 2007."

"Valuable? Yes. Yes, indeed!" His finger traced one silver barrel. "Thousands of pounds, at the least. Interesting concept, what? Looting the past of treasures priceless in the future . . ."

Hunter stood up. "Well, I'd better be going." He nodded toward the recall beacon. "I'll have the men bury all your extra gear . . . out of sight."

"I'd appreciate that."

"I'd like to take five men with me. I'll leave Fuller and Callaghan to look after things while we're gone."

"That will be fine."

Hunter wanted to say more, but further words would be wasted. He felt a nagging torture at the thought of leaving Rachel.

The Russian we questioned was telling the truth about five VBU agents with Fraser. Maybe he was telling the truth about Rachel!

Not knowing tormented him. But if Rachel had escaped from the Russians, she must still be with Burgoyne. She would be safe there, he reasoned. There were a number of women with the British force, wives of soldiers, camp followers, even mistresses. And Rachel could handle herself.

In any case, there was nothing he could do about her now, not with only a handful of men and the knowledge that he had to rendezvous with Taylor.

Once they were sure the Russian threat was ended, there would be time and opportunity to find Rachel.

But now they had a long, hard journey ahead of them.

• • •

King unfolded the paper taken from the dead VBU agent.

"A map," Gomez said. "Has to be."

"I can't think what else it would be," King agreed.

Taylor peered over King's shoulder. It was several hours after dawn on the morning of the twentieth. Wayne's force, savaged at Paoli, had fled west and north through the night and was drawn up now on the north side of the Schuylkill River. The Rangers had followed and sat now in their wagon, planning.

"Yeah." Gomez studied the paper. Straight, intersecting lines were drawn on it in pencil, several with Cyrillic notations. "Hey! I bet these are street names."

Taylor squinted at a name. "Mapket?"

"Cyrillic alphabet," King said softly. "That *P* is an *R*."

"Market Street," Taylor said with unexpected decision. "That's Philadelphia."

"How do you know that, sir?" Gomez asked. "There's nothing here but straight lines and a few names."

"Gotta be," Taylor insisted. "I'm from Pennsylvania originally, remember?" He reached across King's shoulder and pointed at a rough crosshatching of lines. "These streets here. That'll be Society Hill, south of Market Street. Uh... Delancey... Lombard... wait. What's this number?"

"A house number," Gomez suggested. "An address on Lombard."

"What would the Russians want with an address in Philadelphia?" King asked.

"Travis ought to be told," Taylor said. "This could be something important."

"It'll have to keep, Lieutenant. But if things went right at Saratoga yesterday, they ought to keep the first rendezvous. That'll be on the twenty-fifth."

"Damn," Taylor said. His voice was bright... artificially so. He was covering some inner struggle. King could hear it behind the man's words. "This could be hot... maybe another VBU headquarters. Maybe their base! We've got to do something about it!"

"We will, Lieutenant," King said slowly. "But we're not going to jump in half cocked, are we?"

"Of course not. I just hope this keeps until Travis gets here."

Right you are, Lieutenant, King thought. *I just wonder if you're going to keep . . . or if you're going to screw this whole bloody op!*

Fourteen

"We tried it your way, Comrade Andryanov." Yakushenko's eyes were cold and deadly. "Note the result. Complete failure . . . nine more men dead."

"The idea to send Chernysh and his men to Pennsylvania—"

"It was not the decision I was criticizing, Major! It was the tactics! This . . . this sneaking around in costumes, playacting, *that* is the problem!"

Andryanov stifled his anger. Yakushenko was a posturing GRU ass, but that made him no less dangerous. Best to let the idiot's rage play itself out. "*Da*, Comrade Colonel."

"Now we will do it *my* way . . . the way it should have been done from the beginning! Remember! It was my plan to ambush the Americans when I first discovered they were in the area. Overwhelming force at the right place and the right time!"

When Vadim Grigorevich discovered them at the tavern, you mean, Andryanov thought. *And he did it by "playacting," as you put it*.

He kept the thought to himself. Yakushenko would not appreciate being reminded of Salekhov's accomplishments now. There had been no further word from Saratoga since the nineteenth. There was no doubt now. Salekhov's force had been wiped out.

The question was how to get back on the offensive, before it was too late.

"We still have a sizable contingent, Comrade Colonel." Andryanov chose his words with care. "Both spetsnaz and KGB . . . plus the helicopters. Chernysh is on his way here with

133

what is left of his team. There is still the safehouse in Philadelphia. How do you intend to apply this . . . this overwhelming force now?"

"By striking decisively at our original targets."

"Sir?"

"Yes." The colonel stood suddenly and paced from behind his desk. He rubbed his hands together. "The action at Paoli last night will have the Americans off-balance. They will believe that we are pursuing them, rather than their history, and so will prepare for our next attack . . . against them. Instead we will continue with the original plan to kill their George Washington."

Very good, Andryanov thought. *With an artist's skill, you transform failure into the perfect execution of a carefully laid plan! They will appreciate that, back at Uralskiy.* He kept his face neutral. "How will you do that, Colonel?"

A don't-bother-me-with-details expression twisted Yakushenko's mouth. "We will work that out. This next major battle coming up soon . . . the one outside Philadelphia."

"*Da.* Germantown."

"Whatever. Inform the Philadelphia *yavka* that they must begin planning for that action. There must be something in the histories about where Washington was during that battle . . . and when. We will kill him. And, Comrade Major, it will not be by sneaking around in disguise, trying to avoid attention!"

"Eh?" Andryanov felt a moment's panic.

"Be bold, Major! We create a new history here . . . a new future!"

Andryanov closed his eyes. Yakushenko didn't even know the name of the battle he wanted to change! He treated the re-ordering of history like a game. "You don't understand, Colonel. To rush in blind . . . What you suggest is incredibly dangerous."

"Do not lecture me, Comrade Major! The key here is the destruction of the United States. Washington will die at . . . at . . ."

"Germantown."

"*Da.* Meanwhile we will prepare here for the second battle at Saratoga. We will send Chernysh there at once. He can report on enemy activities there." He looked thoughtful. "We should tell our people at Uralskiy. Perhaps we can rearm

Sasha. A rocket barrage against Bemis Heights would be quite effective, don't you agree?"

"Comrade Colonel, if the Mi-24 is *seen* . . ."

"Bah! What does it matter?" He dismissed the protest with a wave. "You will inform our agents in Philadelphia. Once we plan the Germantown operation, we will need them to scout the area for us."

"*Da*, Comrade Colonel." Andryanov struggled to control his own disquiet. He was beginning to doubt the colonel's sanity.

Gentleman Johnny is as good as his word, Rachel thought. It was early in the evening of Monday, September 22, and she was being conveyed into the American camp by Continental officers.

Her journey had begun that afternoon at the Sword Farm landing, where a chaplain with Burgoyne's army, the Reverend Edward Burdenell, had helped her aboard a low skiff. Two seamen in striped shirts under the command of a painfully young naval midshipman named Pellew raised a white flag and set off at a leisurely pace down the broad gray waters of the Hudson with gentle strokes of the oars.

Rachel was surprised to find seamen with Burgoyne's army but was glad to be going by water instead of overland. The woods seemed darker now, and terrifying, after giving up so many dead and maimed. She'd heard nothing more about Selby or his Loyalists. Were they still out there, waiting for her? Or were they working on some other, more sinister plan?

She shivered and hoped for the thousandth time that Travis was at the American camp. Burgoyne had lost at Freeman's Farm . . . and that could only mean that someone had stopped the VBU.

Travis must be here!

The skiff was challenged by a sentry on shore not far from the bridge where Rachel had left Buchanan. Rachel's letter of introduction from Burgoyne won her the attention of a militia officer, Captain Blake, who gravely accepted responsibility for her from the chaplain. With four men as escort, he walked her past sentry posts and a great barrier of logs and earthworks thrown up across the Albany Road, past lines of cannon glowering down from Bemis Heights, and all the way to the headquarters of General Horatio Gates, a tiny log cabin belonging to a farmer named Nielson.

The American encampment reminded her of the Sword Farm. The soldiers here wore blue coats instead of red, but the activities were the same. Men gamed with cards or with dice beaten from lead musket balls; smoked clay pipes; patched clothes; laughed, talked, and attended to the endless chores and tasks of camp life. Everywhere tough, lean men leaned on their rifles, swapping stories with animated expressions. Spirits were high . . . in stark contrast to the shock and gloom of the British camp after Freeman's Farm.

"Please wait here, ma'am," Blake said. "I'll announce you to the general."

He left her with the soldiers of the escort and walked onto the porch between two sentries who brought their rifles up in a clumsy salute. He opened the door and almost closed it again as a bellowing roar burst from inside the building. "No, sir! By heaven, I shall not—I *cannot*—stand for that!"

Somewhat gingerly the captain stepped through the door and closed it gently behind him. Even with the door shut, Rachel could hear the torrent of angry words continue to pour from the building.

"Sounds t' me like ol' Granny's got his hands full," one of the soldiers said.

Rachel turned to face the soldiers. "Granny?"

The youngster looked embarrassed. "Uh . . . it's just what some of us call him, Mum. Don't mean no harm. General Gates, he's a good soldier, he is. Looks after us right well."

"Mebbe," an older soldier said. He leaned against his flint-lock and stared toward the cabin. "Mebbe. But Granny Gates nearly lost us that scrap Friday. An' it seems a mite mean-spirited that he won't recognize the man who won it!"

Rachel felt a thrill of excitement. One man won the battle? Could that be Travis? "What do you mean?" she asked. "Who won the battle?"

"Why, Gen'rul Arnold, of course, ma'am! By God . . . uh . . . your pardon, ma'am . . . but if'n anyone deserves the credit for the victory, Gen'rul Arnold does!"

"Arnold?" The name tickled at Rachel's memory. Recognition flared. "Wait . . . *Benedict* Arnold?"

"None other. Why, him an' Colonel Morgan fought the

battle at Freeman's Farm single-handed practically . . . damn near threw the redcoats back into the Hudson! He woulda, too, if ol' Granny had sent in somethin' more'n dribs and drabs of reinforcements!"

"That's right," a third soldier added. "Someone oughta tell Granny off . . . an' it sounds like Gen'rul Arnold's the man t'do it!"

The men continued their good-natured grumbling. Rachel stared at the hut, thinking furiously. Benedict Arnold! She wasn't the historian Travis was, but she certainly knew the name of America's most infamous traitor!

She remembered her earlier questions about further VBU plots. Might this be one? The thought that Benedict Arnold himself might be a Soviet agent was appalling, but the Russians had tried similar tactics before. In 1923 Munich, Adolf Hitler's right-hand man, Max von Scheubner-Richter, had been a VBU plant.

Or the Russians might be manipulating Arnold for their own ends.

"Good God, man!" the voice thundered again. "I shall return to Philadelphia! General Washington, at least, appreciates my talents!"

"Then do so!" a thin, reedy voice replied heatedly. "I'm not so sure you have authority here in any case! I certainly have no place for you in the Northern Army! What are you doing here, anyway?"

"You okay, Mum?" one of the soldiers asked.

"Yes," she managed to say. She felt cold, weak. "I'm just a little unsteady, after being aboard that skiff."

The door to the hut crashed open. A short, powerfully built man in a blue officer's coat stomped onto the porch. A green sash was visible under the coat, and he carried a black-and-white plumed hat in one hand. His round, swarthy face was purple with rage. "I will not brook such usage, sir!" he shouted, then banged the door shut. As he turned, his eyes met Rachel's for an instant. They were pale and filled with a raging, bottomless anger. Then he jammed his hat over his black hair, straightened his coat, and stormed past Rachel into the gathering twilight.

Captain Blake came through the door a moment later, followed by several officers. One, wearing a uniform like Arnold's, had a pinched and wizened face, with spectacles perched on the end of his nose and a sour expression. This, Rachel decided, must be "Granny" Gates, so perfectly did the nickname fit the face.

Blake cleared his throat. "This is the young lady I spoke of, General. General Burgoyne sent her down the river to us."

"The letter," Gates snapped. "Let's see it."

The captain handed Burgoyne's letter to Gates, who squinted at it through the spectacles with suspicious eyes. "This says you were mistakenly abducted by Tories under Burgoyne's command? That he secured your release and is granting you safe conduct to our lines, where you have relatives."

"Yes, General." Rachel had told Burgoyne of her "brother," picking up on the story Wycliff had invented for Jotham Bemis. It was easier to explain than the truth.

Those suspicious eyes looked up from the letter and found hers. He looked as if he did not believe her. "How did you find the British camp, Miss Wycliff?"

"S-sir?"

"What is the situation in Burgoyne's camp? Are the men happy . . . excited . . . depressed? We have heard conflicting rumors here, even a rumor that Burgoyne is dead. What can you tell us?"

Rachel fought to still her inner turmoil, a surge of competing thoughts. She had already noted the emotional difference between the American soldiers and those in the British camp. That was what Gates wanted to hear about.

But Burgoyne had been good to her; she still thought of him as a gallant rescuer, the man who'd delivered her from torture and death. He'd refused to believe that she was a spy . . . so how could she act the part of a spy now, after her release?

Thoughts of Benedict Arnold clamored for attention. What was the relationship between these two men? Did the VBU plan to use Arnold to guarantee a British victory?

An answer appeared with dazzling, elegant clarity. What if she told Gates that she'd seen Arnold in the British camp? It was clear the two hated one another. Such an accusation might get Arnold hung as the traitor he was . . . might at least expose his treason and block his plans, whatever they were. Gates wanted information of the British camp. *That* would satisfy him . . . without betraying Burgoyne's trust.

It was perfect.

Or was it?

No. No . . . perhaps it was not so clear, after all. She knew little about Arnold. How had he betrayed his country? When? What had he been before that treason? So many questions. Her helplessness without the answers was infuriating.

Damn it all! I'm starting to sound just like Travis now . . . without enough information to act on! Now she knew what he meant. *Anything* she said could change history.

"Speak up, miss," an officer standing at Gates's side snapped. "Tell us what you saw over there!"

She looked up. "General Burgoyne *is* alive," she said. "I can't tell you any more than that. He treated me kindly. He . . . he saved my life. I can't betray him."

The officer next to Gates glowered and opened his mouth to say something more, but the general laid a hand on his arm. "Never mind, Wilkinson."

"But, sir . . ."

"It doesn't matter. The lady is quite correct." He peered over his glasses at her. He sounded tired, as though the fight with Arnold had drained him. "I shall arrange to have you escorted wherever you wish to go."

"Thank you, General." But she was looking off into the woods as Gates perfunctorily kissed her hand. She was thinking of her mistake with the Polish engineer.

Benedict Arnold! Have I done the right thing?

Wycliff hitched himself farther up in the bed. "My God, Rachel," he said. He was surprised at his own pleasure. "I thought you were dead!"

Rachel's arrival had come as a complete surprise. Callaghan had seen her on the Albany Road, coming from Bemis Heights. He'd brought her to the house, introducing her to the Parsons as Wycliff's sister.

"Saved . . . by an English officer, no less!" she said. Her laugh sounded forced.

"You *are* a sight, luv," Buchanan said from his side of the bed. "Been shopping for new clothes?"

She looked down at the long blue dress. Bloodstains darkened the sleeves. "Sort of . . ."

With great care Wycliff put the flintlock pistol he'd been cleaning back in its felt-lined case, closed the lid, and set it aside. He hesitated. "Travis isn't here."

"I know. Callaghan told me. They're all gone?"

"There's just us four left now," Buchanan said. "Five, countin' you. All the rest are off to Pennsylvania."

Wycliff saw something in the girl's eyes. Pain? Or was it worry? "Are you well?"

"Fine. It's just . . ." She rubbed her hand over her eyes. "Dammit, Captain. I may have the bare bones of a VBU plot here, and I don't know what to do with it!"

"Tell me."

She proceeded to tell the two commandos about her experiences after her capture, and particularly of her brief encounter with Benedict Arnold. Wycliff listened carefully.

"I saw Arnold three hours ago," she said at last. "I've been wondering ever since if I did right not saying anything! I was hoping Travis could tell me." The worry showed in her eyes, in her smile. "What do you think?"

Wycliff studied her. "You know . . . I've been doing a lot of thinking, laid up in this bed. A couple of weeks ago I'd have told you not to worry, that one man couldn't hurt all that much. I don't believe that anymore."

"You don't?"

He didn't reply for a long moment as he tried to sort out his own feelings toward the girl. He had blamed Rachel once for her carelessness in the tavern for giving them away. But he was looking at things differently now. Rachel was not to blame . . . *he* was. It was his own arrogance that had discounted the possibility the VBU might have an observer at Bemis Tavern in the first place. It was his unwillingness to believe the enemy might be ready for them that had led all of them into the trap.

And one man, Travis Hunter, had turned the situation around again.

"Seeing the past like this . . . it gives you a new perspective on how things work. On how *history* works. Hunter was right. People, individual people, count."

"Are you saying I should do something about Benedict

Arnold? That he *does* count somehow in all this?"

"No . . . that *you* do." He picked up the pistol case once more and opened it. The light from a nearby candle gleamed along the polished, hexagonal barrels. He'd not been able to express to Hunter what the gift had meant to him. He looked up into Rachel's dark eyes. "I'm saying that I don't know your history . . . the history you're trying to rebuild. This Benedict Arnold must have been in my world's history, but he didn't make enough of a splash for me to have heard of him. So I'm the wrong person to ask."

Rachel closed her eyes for a long moment. "I think I knew all along it was my decision," she said at last. "I think . . . I think I was right the first time. Arnold will have to wait until we can learn more."

"Sounds wisest, luv," Buchanan said. "Leave well enough alone or it's liable to turn around and bite you."

There was a knock on the bedroom door. Rachel opened it, and Mrs. Parson entered with a tray set for tea. Wycliff watched Rachel and sighed. She reminded him of Julie. Her hair was black instead of gold . . . but her intelligence and sharp wits made her one of a kind with Julie MacGregor.

Julie . . . God, why did she have to die?

His hands closed on the pistol case so tightly that they trembled, the knuckles white against the dark wood.

Lieutenant Chernysh watched from the woods across the road from the Parson house. It had been sheer luck that he'd spotted the girl in the American camp. He'd thought she was still with Burgoyne.

By following her, he'd found the enemy headquarters. There appeared to be two soldiers, wearing civilian clothes and patrolling the area, plus the girl and whoever was inside the house.

The discovery could erase the sting of defeat at Paoli. His superiors would be pleased.

Fifteen

Hunter pressed his back against the rough bricks of the house. The street appeared deserted, and there was no sign of alarm from the target.

He was sore and tired, still suffering from the aches and blisters of his five-day ride from Saratoga. Hunter, with the five SAS men trailing on horses stolen from Gates's camp, had rendezvoused with King, Gomez, Anderson, and Taylor at Leicester House the evening before. The map the Rangers found at Paoli had led here, to a two-story brick house on Lombard Street, six blocks south of Carpenter's Hall and the center of Philadelphia. The church tower of St. Peter's speared into the night sky nearby.

One window showed the soft and wavering glow of candles within. Moving with slow, precisely planted steps, Hunter edged closer. Through the glass he heard laughter and a low mumble of conversation.

Dark Walker's sharp eyes had spotted what might be a radio aerial on the roof, and that was the confirmation Hunter needed to identify this house as a VBU command post. Legitimate citizens of 1777 Philadelphia might have Ben Franklin's lightning rods on their chimneys . . . but not shortwave radio antennas.

Hunter ducked under the window as Anderson positioned himself on the other side with Taylor's H&K in his hands.

What am I going to do about Ben? Taylor had been posted across the street with a British L85A1, with orders to watch the front of the house while Dark Walker covered the rear. His friend had not been happy at that, but until he had a chance to talk with Taylor, Hunter did not want to risk the operation by placing an unreliable man in a crucial slot on an assault team. King had given Hunter no specifics yet . . . only the fear that Taylor was a coward. *Something* had happened to his old friend at Paoli . . . but what?

He checked the street again. It was still empty.

September 26, 1777. I'd forgotten that date.

The timing was perfect. A few hours before, the streets had been filled with Tory citizens watching an endless parade of British troops marching into Philadelphia. The excitement and confusion had given the team the cover it needed to slip unnoticed into town. Fortunately any British soldiers still wandering the streets were staying out of the Society Hill area. A burst of raucous singing from the direction of a tavern called the "Man Full of Trouble" a few blocks away suggested where some of His Majesty's troops must be at the moment, and several times they heard a far-off bang as some enthusiastic Tory fired off a celebratory musket.

He nodded to Anderson, who slipped a wooden canteen off his shoulder, then reached high up along the edge of the window frame, looping the strap over the corner of a brick so that it dangled next to the glass. A short fuse hung from the canteen's neck.

Hunter checked his watch. Gomez and King would be going through the same maneuver on the other side of the house, while the SAS men gathered by the door on the front porch. Those canteens were stuffed with black powder taken from one of the casks left in the wagon after the confusion at Paoli. There was no way to make Eddie's three black powder bombs explode simultaneously, but with careful timing, the blasts would be close enough to do the job.

Ten seconds to go. . . .

He signaled with his finger. Anderson struck a match and set it to the short fuse. The two men backed away to opposite corners of the building, crouching against the wall and covering their eyes.

A loud boom sounded from the far side of the house. A second later the night lit up as Gomez's improvised entry charge smashed the window in thunder and hurtling glass.

The two commandos raced back to the window, now a gaping hole against fire-blackened bricks. Flames raced up curtains on either side. Anderson dropped to one knee to give

Hunter a boost through the window. He sailed through the opening, landing on the glass-powdered floor, rolling on his shoulder, and coming up on one knee.

There was only an instant to sort targets from chaos. A man thrashed on the floor near the window, flames licking from his clothing. Another man in frontier garb rose from behind a table across the room, reaching for a weapon among disordered papers. A third gaped surprise from a door.

Hunter's Uzi bucked in his hands, punching 9mm slugs into the VBU agent behind the table. He shifted aim . . . but the man in the doorway was gone. He heard the rapid-fire stutter of Anderson's H&K behind him, saw the burning man pitch back against an ornately carved chair and slump to the floor.

A third boom echoed through the house from the direction of the front door. Hunter heard shouts, a flurry of shots. . . .

Lieutenant Ben Taylor brought the optical sight of the borrowed rifle to his eye. Through the scope he could make out the front door of the house where the four SAS commandos had just lit the fuse to their gunpowder bomb.

He tried to control the bitter thoughts that crowded around the edges of his awareness, tried to focus on the house and nothing else. No matter how hard he tried, though, the same thought kept returning, causing his aim to waver and his vision to blur.

They think I'm a coward.

Taylor knew that Master Sergeant King didn't like him. Their relationship had been stiff and formal ever since Paoli, and he was certain that King's feelings would color any report he made to Travis.

Travis doesn't trust me now. That's why he stuck me out here.

The explosions came one-two-three. He saw the orange flash from the front porch through his scope, saw the SAS men slam against the shattered door and crowd in through the smoke. The shots inside were muffled.

I should be in there.

He glimpsed movement, a shadow against the light of a fire burning inside, beyond the gaping doorway. A man in period civilian dress staggered onto the porch, hatless, wear-

ing breeches and a leather vest. He looked exactly like any of
the hundreds of ordinary citizens of Philadelphia Taylor had
seen that day. Was he VBU in disguise . . . or could there be
some mistake? Taylor hesitated.

The wall through which they'd entered was ablaze now, as
flames raced up curtains and wallpaper. Hunter moved toward
the table, checking to see that the man he'd shot was dead.
There were maps spread out there, with Cyrillic notations
penciled in. A thick, hardcover book of American history was
open to a chapter on the American Revolution.

"Watch it . . . !" Anderson yelled. Fire roared behind him.

Hunter ducked and spun as the H&K spat again. A man in
Tory green collapsed in blood and splattered gore, his AKM
clattering onto the floor.

"Thanks, Roy!"

"Hey, no problem, LT. Not bad for a damn popgun, eh?"

Hunter grinned. Anderson's liking for full-size machine
guns instead of smaller weapons was well known. "Let's
move it, Roy! This old house is going up fast!" He held his
hand up, shielding his face against the heat as he pulled out
his radio. "All units! All units! Front room secure!"

"Main floor secure," Mason's voice echoed a moment
later.

"Upstairs secure," King added.

The smoke was growing thicker. "All units . . . get out! The
fire's spreading!" He glanced at the flames consuming the
wall. "Get the maps, Roy . . . everything you can grab! We'll
go out the front!"

They had only seconds now.

Through his sights Taylor watched the man sag against the
doorway, obviously wounded. One of the SAS must have shot
him, but was he VBU or an innocent Philadelphian caught in
the crossfire?

Bracing himself upright, with one arm dangling bloody and
limp, the man groped inside his vest, then pulled out a small,
round object. Through the scope, in the uncertain light, the
object looked apple-green. The target fumbled with a pull ring.

Taylor's finger closed on the trigger, and the British rifle
barked once. The man jerked convulsively and spun back

through the doorway, flopping spread-eagled on the floor. The Soviet RGD grenade rolled harmlessly across the porch.

Hunter and Anderson appeared. The Texan stooped to check the body, then looked up into Taylor's sight. His thumb and forefinger touched in a silent okay.

I'm not a coward!

"I didn't say you were a coward, Ben," Hunter said. "But I'd like to know what the hell is going on."

Hunter studied Taylor's angry face. *Damn, I don't believe you are. But Greg wouldn't make a thing like that up! I can't disregard what I've heard.*

"Look . . . I'm sorry for what happened at Paoli," Taylor said. He appeared to be struggling to control his voice, his breathing. "I thought King was about to shoot one of the locals. That's why I grabbed his FAL."

"That's piss-poor judgment, Ben."

"Dammit, don't you think I know that? But, God! One stray round in a firefight and we could kill someone important! Maybe a future president! Maybe the father of someone famous!"

"Is that what's bothering you, Ben? That we might screw up history?"

"Doesn't it bother you?"

"Every minute of every day!"

Taylor studied his hands. "I don't think I can take it anymore, Trav."

"What the hell are we supposed to do? Sit and do nothing? Let the VBU take over? Good God, Ben . . . we've got to do *something*!"

That sounds damned familiar, Hunter thought. *I sound like Raye now.*

"It's no good, Trav!" Tears were streaming down his face now. Anguish tore his voice. "I just can't take the responsibility for the whole damned world!"

Hunter looked away, embarrassed. The low, rolling Pennsylvania countryside stretched away from them, with visibility reaching for miles from their camp on the banks of the Schuylkill. Their escape from Philadelphia had brought them here, south of Washington's camp on Perkiomen Creek.

He turned to the wagon and rummaged in the back for his

rucksack. He pulled out a book, the book he'd taken from the VBU headquarters in Philadelphia. Its title was *Birth of the United States*.

His United States.

Hunter ran his fingers over the binding, knowing again the thrill he'd felt when he'd first seen that title. This book was from his own universe and recorded the history he knew . . . a history where the Colonies had won their Revolution with the surrender of General Cornwallis at Yorktown in 1781, and the Peace of Paris two years later. The Russians must have brought it back to 1777 with them as research.

For the first time Hunter felt confident. Together with the captured maps, this book was the key to what the Russians were doing next.

"We've got a big op coming up, Ben," Hunter said at last. "Maybe the end of this whole mission. Those maps we picked up in Philly showed us exactly where the VBU is going to hit next. We're going to give them one hell of a surprise."

"It's just no good, Trav."

He set one hand on Taylor's shoulder. "I'm relieving you, Ben."

Taylor's head snapped up. "What?"

"I'm pulling you out of action . . . at least until you can get your head together."

The decision hurt Hunter as much as any decision he'd made in his career, but there was no alternative. With only ten men in his little command, he had to know that he could trust every single one. If Taylor fell apart during a firefight, it would mean disaster.

"I'm sorry, Ben."

"*Sasha* is not yet ready, Comrade Colonel." Andryanov gestured over his shoulder toward the tent where VBU technicians were working on the assault helicopter. "They estimate the weapons pods can be reconnected within another hour."

"It is not necessary, Comrade Major." Yakushenko inhaled deeply, savoring the chilly predawn air. "*Misha* will be quite enough. Ah! A splendid day for a battle, wouldn't you agree?"

Andryanov handed the colonel a flight helmet. Spetsnaz in camo gear filed up the ramp and through the clamshell doors of the Mi-8 transport parked nearby. The rotor blades were already turning lazily as the pilot warmed up the helicopter's double turbines. "The histories mention a heavy fog over Germantown. Nasty flying for a helicopter."

"Volnov is our best pilot. Besides, our people in Philadelphia have thoroughly surveyed the area. The landing beacon is transmitting. All has been anticipated."

"Indeed, Comrade Colonel? And what of the *yavka*? We have not heard from them in over a week. If they have been caught, our entire operation could be compromised."

Andryanov, expecting Yakushenko's temper to flare, was surprised when the man merely smiled. "Sergei Sergeivich, I'll tell you the truth," the colonel said. His tone was patronizing. "I hope the Americans *have* discovered our Germantown operation. Our deployment should present them with an exquisite surprise."

"It's a dangerous gamble, Comrade. I really must protest your taking so many of my KGB troops with you. Surely you have sufficient spetsnaz for—"

"Enough!" Yakushenko exploded. "I remind you, Major, that the VBU is a joint enterprise of the KGB and the GRU! I am in command!"

He kept his face an expressionless mask. "*Da*, Comrade Colonel." He would not tell him of Chernysh's report. Not yet.

Yakushenko placed the helmet over his head. "This will not take long. Maintain radio silence! I shall return well before noon."

"We will be waiting, Comrade Colonel."

Yakushenko turned, striding toward the helicopter and up the ramp. A moment later Andryanov saw the colonel in the cockpit, squeezing himself into the copilot's seat. The rotors began turning faster, raising dust from the landing area hacked out of the wilderness where the Soviet main base was located.

He doesn't trust me, Andryanov thought. *That is why he's taking eight of my best KGB troops with him. He fears I will shoot him down when he returns!*

The thought was a pleasant one, though not something Andryanov actually would have considered. *The Americans are the enemy*, he reminded himself. *No matter how complete an idiot Yakushenko is!*

He stepped back out of the way as the Mi8's rotors came up to speed and the heavily loaded helicopter lifted into the night sky. He watched the transport vanish into the darkness, then turned and hurried across to the tent, where mechanics were in the process of remounting the heavy weapons pods on the stubby wings of the Mi-24.

There would be time enough to arm the helicopter later. If he worked quickly, Andryanov would have a chance to spring an exquisite surprise of his own.

Sixteen

An impenetrable fog clung to the landscape like a blanket. The air was chilly, the ground soggy underfoot. It was not yet dawn.

Hunter and King looked up into the mist. "So now we wait and see if you were right," the master sergeant said.

"I'm right," Hunter said. "They'll be here."

He had given the matter considerable thought. The map captured in their raid the week before was of the area around Germantown, a village five miles north of Philadelphia. Several prominent features were noted in Russian: the Skippack Road; a square marked "Clivedon," which the history book they'd taken described as belonging to a Justice Benjamin Chew; a low ridge two hundred yards west of the Chew House; and a broad meadow several hundred yards west of the ridge. The meadow was circled on the map and marked with the Cyrillic peh, which looked like the Greek letter pi. After several hours of discussion they finally concluded that the notation might stand for *posadochnaya ploshadkah* . . . Russian for "landing field."

Lines and ranges described what might be arcs of fire from the ridge. It was easy enough to guess what those VBU agents at the Lombard Street house had been planning. The Continental Army would be coming down the Skippack Road later that morning.

And General Washington would be with them.

The team had arrived at Germantown on October 1. Careful to play the part of local farmers, they surveyed the land thoroughly. Gomez found the small Russian transponder buried in the meadow, sending out radio pulses with a metronome's tick-tock regularity.

Now it was October 4. The team had arrived at 0400 to take up position on the ridge. The Chew House was invisible, shrouded in fog and darkness.

"Hey!" King said, looking up. "Hear that?"

Hunter listened. He heard the dull throbbing sound growing louder in the north.

"That's it," Anderson said. "Gotta be."

"Heads up!" Hunter warned. "Company's coming!"

The men spread along the top of the ridge sought cover.

"Remember," Hunter called to them. "No radio until we've sprung the trap. Hold your fire until you're sure of the target. I don't want you firing at each other. And don't shoot at all until you hear Roy's MG."

One by one the commandos faded into the darkness. Anderson found his spot behind a fog-soggy, moss-covered log and began setting up his L7. Hunter lay down beside him. Both men pulled out infrared goggles and slipped them over their faces. They'd taken the IR gear from the dead Russians at Paoli. In the fog they offered only slightly better visibility . . . but even that small margin would help.

If Hunter had read the Russian plans correctly, the helicopter would land on a low hill on the far side of the meadow. The fog was thinner on the hills, thickest over low ground. Guided by the beacon, the Soviet helo would have no trouble landing in the murk. The troops would debark, coming up the ridge straight toward Hunter's position on their way toward the Chew House.

They would catch them here. Once Anderson opened up, the rest of the commandos would fire, crisscrossing the west slope of the ridge with death. White would have the second L7 set up to provide a sweeping crossfire from a copse of woods below the crest of the ridge and to the left.

The ambush would be as complete and as deadly as the trap that had caught Wycliff on the ridge above the Hudson.

The helicopter sounded nearer. Somewhere off to the north, the flat bang of a musket exploded in the early-morning air . . . followed by another . . . and a third. Then there was a steady, rattling clatter of massed musketry, swelling in volume, mingling with the startled shouts and calls of soldiers in the Chew House yard.

"Sounds like things are off and running," Anderson said.

"Washington's started his attack," Hunter replied. He strained to hear over the gunfire. "I can't hear the chopper now. They must've planned it this way, to approach without being heard."

Anderson didn't answer. He lowered his cheek against the stock of the machine gun. The muzzle described short, deadly arcs above the bipod as it searched the mist ahead.

"Wait!" Hunter said a moment later. "Listen!"

The rotor sounds were clearer now, this time well to the west, approaching.

"Maybe they swung way around," Gomez said. "Or else both helos are up."

"God, I hope not. This fog ought to work in our favor, though. Their gunship won't find us in this soup."

The heavy *whup-whup-whup* of the helicopter was much closer. Hunter could close his eyes and picture it landing close by the beacon. If it was the Mi-8, there would be about twenty-four men on board, swarming out the rear doors and down the ramp. Odds of twenty-four to nine were heavy, but the surprise set up by the SAS and Ranger team would more than balance them.

Minutes dragged by, an agony of waiting punctuated by the growing thunder of the battle nearby. Anderson saw them first. *"There . . ."*

Glowing IR images wavered as a line of Russians advanced up the slope out of the fog. Hunter could make out five . . . six . . .

He slapped Anderson's shoulder and the L7 erupted into chattering, flaming death. Instantly gunfire burst from across the top of the ridge and from the trees down the hill to the left. Hunter watched the glowing shapes slump and crumple as autofire raked the slope. Answering fire burst from the kill zone, the muzzle flashes providing targets for the American and BNA gunners. A long, quavering scream rose from the mist, was chopped short as the machine guns continued to probe the fog.

Hunter brought up his radio. "Cease fire! All units, cease fire!" The gunfire died, leaving an eerie stillness on the ridge. Musketry banged away to the north, and Hunter could still hear the slow turning of a helicopter's rotors somewhere ahead.

"What do you think?" Anderson asked. He smoothed out a kink in a hundred-round belt. The goggles gave him a bizarre, insectlike appearance.

"I don't know." Hunter wiped at the condensation forming on his own goggles, trying to penetrate the fog. "Seemed too easy."

At Hunter's order, Dark Walker slipped down off the ridge and began moving among the bodies. His report made Hunter frown.

"Eight bodies . . ." he said.

"Must be their Hind," Anderson said. "Those things carry eight troops."

"Yeah . . ." The rotor noise tantalized from the fog. Was it a Hind gunship, just big enough for the eight men now lying dead on the hillside, or the larger Hip transport, which carried twenty-four?

The situation bothered him. That invisible helicopter held irresistible temptation. It was perfectly logical for the Soviets to send only eight men to ambush General Washington when he arrived at the Chew House later that morning. But if they had a Hip available, why not send more? The Russians must be suspicious about the loss of their base in Philadelphia. And Hunter remembered the ambush Wycliff had walked into . . . with a helicopter as bait.

He didn't dare give orders over the radio, not when the enemy might be listening. Instead Hunter moved silently along the ridge, gathering his men and passing whispered instructions. If there was a trap, he didn't want the entire unit stepping in it.

King and Trooper Fitzroy moved slowly down the slope, directly toward the sound of the slow-turning rotors. Gomez and Mason looped far out to the right, while Walker and Shute swung to the left. Hunter hung back, Anderson and White at his side. Three columns converging on the helicopter should flush any remaining hidden Russians. With the two machine gunners as a mobile reserve, they might manage to trap the trappers.

Hunter resisted the urge to check his watch. The sky was brighter now, but visibility remained almost nil.

Damn this fog, anyway, Hunter thought. The VBU were out there, he was certain.

But where?

Yakushenko was pleased. His ambush promised to solve several problems with one sharp blow. He'd sent Andryanov's eight KGB troops ahead toward the ridge. If the Americans were not there, well and good. The spetsnaz could follow, set up the machine gun, and wait for General Washington to ride into its sights. If the Americans did know about the German-town operation, if they were waiting, it would be Andryanov's men who triggered the ambush . . . and Yakushenko had reasons for wanting to undercut the KGB major's power base. The Americans, believing the Russian patrol wiped out, would come forward, homing in on the sound of the helicopter's engines.

And the Americans *were* there. He'd been certain of it even before the savage rattle of autofire burst from the direction of the ridge. From the sound of it, the KGB troops hadn't lasted long. Pity . . .

A spetsnaz commando touched his arm and pointed. Two men materialized out of the mist a hundred meters away. Yakushenko hesitated. Only two? His lack of solid intelligence on the enemy bothered him. Only three Americans had been spotted at Paoli, but there might well be more. He was certain he'd heard the characteristic, deep-throated bellow of at least one general-purpose machine gun a moment before.

No matter. Kill these two, and the rest would follow to find out what had happened. *"Fire!"*

The PKM machine gun roared. One of the figures flailed at the air, twisting wildly as bullets hammered into its torso. The other pitched forward to the ground and was still.

Two up . . . two down. Yakushenko gave a cold smile. If there were more Americans, they would be along shortly.

• • •

Corporal Dark Walker peered around the fence post. The thinning fog still masked all but shapes and shadows, but the flash in his IR goggles had pinpointed the PKM on a low, rocky knoll at the south end of the meadow. He signaled. Trooper Shute came up beside him and nodded as the Dakota warrior pointed out the Soviet position.

Walker pulled out his radio. "Left," he said. The transmission was too brief to let the enemy pinpoint it, but it would tell Hunter where the Russians were.

"You stay here," he told Shute. "Give me thirty seconds, then open fire."

"Sure, Corp. But what . . ."

Walker was already under the fence and sliding forward through the tall, fog-wet grass. He arrived at the base of the knoll and paused, counting to himself. Above him, he could hear excited comments in Russian, could hear an authoritarian voice order silence.

Thirty two . . . thirty-three . . .

Shute's assault rifle opened up thirty yards behind him, the rounds whispering overhead and shrieking off rock. The Russians dived for cover. Then he heard the heavier thunder of the PKM and hoped that Shute was keeping his head down.

His hand went to his combat harness. The SAS troopers each carried two small antipersonnel grenades, but there was a certain bloody justice in using the heavy, green-painted RGD he'd picked up at the house in Philadelphia. He hefted the grenade's weight, grabbed the pull ring, and with a hard twist yanked the cotter pin free. Aiming at the thunder of the Russian machine gun, he let fly, then buried his head under crossed arms.

Hunter led Anderson and White through the fog, circling well to the south of the meadow. The ground was rolling here, broken by a line of split-rail fences and a narrow, twisting brook. Ahead, a shallow rise was silhouetted against the eastern sky. The fog was still so thick that no details were visible, but black shadows moved against the pearly glow.

The grenade explosion drove all three men to the ground. Chunks of muddy earth hurtled through the air, and shrill screams rose above the fading roar.

"Now!"

Anderson and White stood side by side, their L7s slung from leather straps across their shoulders. With no loaders to serve their guns, each man carried several hundred-round belts draped across his shoulders. Their fire was restricted to short, precise bursts, conserving limited ammo.

But those bursts were deadly, chewing into ground already raked by the grenade, cutting down VBU men as they fled or rose to fire. Hunter added the hammer of his Uzi to the chorus, the fire rolling on and on as Russian soldiers screamed and died.

Gomez began circling toward the south as the firefight broke out in the distance. There were no signs of Russians on this side of the meadow. He and Sergeant Mason began moving toward the sound of the guns.

The helicopter seemed to jump out of the fog in front of him, huge and gray, the five rotor blades still turning lazily. The rear of the Hip transport faced him, the clamshell doors invitingly open, the ramp extended.

An explosion roared beyond the fog. Four soldiers in camo uniforms pounded down the ramp, AKMs at port arms, and began running toward the fighting. Mason dropped to one knee and opened fire with his L85, knocking down one VBU soldier and tracking after the others with a long, rattling burst.

Gomez guessed at the range . . . fifty yards, far enough for a 40mm grenade to arm itself. He brought his hand up to the trigger of the M-203 ahead of his rifle's magazine. The grenade launched itself with a dull thump.

The explosion shredded one of the running soldiers and brought the other two down in kicking, writhing heaps. Mason fired two quick bursts, silencing the screams. "Cover me!" Gomez said, and he was sprinting forward before Mason could reply. The helicopter's rear doors hung open on blackness.

The gunfire was dwindling across the meadow. Whoever was still aboard the Hip must have realized something was wrong, for the rotors were speeding up as the turbine whine climbed in pitch.

Gomez chambered another grenade and brought the M-203 to his shoulder. One round squarely up the tail of the transport and . . .

He lowered the M-16. The inside of the Hip looked empty. "Aw, what the hell . . ."

Ilya Ilych Yakushenko limped down the eastern slope of the knoll and into the grassy meadow. He dragged his foot with each step, though there was no pain. The AKM he'd picked up was slick with blood . . . his blood.

The bodies of the two Americans cut down by the ambush lay sprawled nearby, one torn from crotch to throat, the other in a silent, crumpled heap.

He shook his head. He had to admire the American commander, willing to sacrifice two men to turn the ambush back on the ambushers. The American had outthought him at nearly every turn. He almost wished he could meet the man.

He turned, dropping into a crouch, the AKM raised. Three black silhouettes appeared along the skyline above the knoll, two carrying light machine guns, the third with a stubby SMG. He'd left only dead men on that ridge. The enemy was presenting him with a clear shot . . . an easy kill.

One good burst would take out all three.

King moved slowly to avoid attracting attention. The plan had been for him and Fitzroy to drop and play dead at the first Russian shot. He grimaced. Unfortunately that first shot had been too accurate.

Fitzroy wasn't playing.

It sounded as though the battle was nearly over. After the machine guns raked the knoll, survivors had scattered down the slope. One crouched twenty yards away, raising an AKM to bear on the trio of commandos coming over the crest of the knoll.

King rolled, scooping up his FAL and swinging it around, triggering a long, stuttering burst in an instinct-aimed shot that blasted small geysers of dirt and grass around the crouching figure. The Russian spun and fired, and autofire snapped a foot above King's head. The Ranger fired again, this time fighting for control and squeezing off a perfect three-round grouping into the VBU man's chest.

Eddie Gomez covered the last yards to the Hip's ramp in long, bounding strides. The cargo bay was cluttered with crates and stray articles of clothing. A Russian gaped at him from the doorway leading to the flight deck, then dived for a tanker's AKMS, leaning next to a firing port. This time Gomez triggered the assault rifle portion of his M-203 combo. Autofire smashed the Russian against the forward bulkhead. The Ranger was racing forward before the VBU agent completed his bloody slide to the deck. Gomez caught a glimpse of the pilot, reaching for a microphone on the console. Gomez fired again, a sharp, three-round burst.

The helicopter was quivering now on its tripod landing gear as the rotors thundered overhead. He pulled the pilot's body back from the controls.

"Son of a bitch," he said quietly. "This oughta make the sarge happy. Why ride when you can fly?"

"Looks like we caught us a colonel," Hunter said. He rose from the still body in the grass. "Nice shooting, Greg."

"No problem, Lieutenant. I'd rather not have to break in a new boss."

"Me too. Okay . . . start rounding up our people. Let's collect the AKs."

His radio beeped. "Yankee Leader."

"Hey, Chief! You know anyone who can fly a helicopter?"

Hunter looked across the meadow. The fog was distinctly thinner now. He could make out the Hip as a gray shape, its props turning. "I'll be . . ."

Anderson grinned beside him. "Crazy Eddie strikes again!"

"How about it, Roy?" The Texan claimed to be able to fly anything, but this . . . "Up to piloting a Hip?"

He scowled at the fog. "Can't say I like the weather much, but I reckon we can give it a try."

"It beats walking," King said.

"Right." He thought about his rides to and from Bemis Heights. "Beats riding too. C'mon. Let's check it out."

They trotted toward the helicopter. If there was enough fuel aboard, they might fly back to New York. Rachel must still be at Burgoyne's camp, and the Second Battle of Saratoga— Bemis Heights—was due in three days. The Russian Hip would let him get to her before the fighting began.

He raised the radio to his lips again as he ran. "Ben! Ben, this is Yankee Leader."

"I hear you." Taylor had been left behind with the team's equipment. He had said little since Hunter relieved him, his inner pain a weight on Hunter's conscience.

"Bring the wagon," he said. "Follow the sound of the helicopter. We're traveling first-class now."

"I'm on my way."

Hunter ran faster. *I'm coming, Raye. . . .*

Seventeen

Wycliff stepped off the porch. Dawn lit the Hudson Valley, spilling gold across the ridge line east of the river and touching the autumn-hued trees with fire. He waved at Callaghan and Fuller, who were leaning against the barn behind the Parson house where they'd set up their camp.

It was good to be up and around. His broken ribs were not completely healed, and movement still cost him pain, but almost anything was worth the chance to get out of the bed and into the open air. He scratched a fleabite on his neck. There were some aspects of eighteenth-century life best appreciated through the pages of a history book, rather than at first hand.

He saw Rachel by the trees, two hundred feet down the Albany Road. Wycliff was used to rising by dawn, a legacy of army life, but Rachel's restlessness was due to something else. He knew she was worried about her decision not to warn Gates about Benedict Arnold.

Wycliff felt a tug of affection . . . and something more. Beginning with her new interest in history, their friendship and mutual respect had grown until she meant a great deal to him. He didn't like to see her hurting.

Rachel was staring at something small in her hand, a locket attached to a slender chain around her neck. She tucked it back down into the bodice of her blue gown as he came up beside her. "You're up early," he said.

She turned, faint light glistening from the moistness on her cheeks.

"You have a problem. Can I help?"

"No." She shook her head. "No . . . I just keep wondering if I made the right decision."

"About Arnold? I think you did." He reached out and gently squeezed her shoulder, wishing he could offer more than words.

"It's been two weeks since Travis left," Rachel said. The words came in a rush. "He should have been back by now. What if Arnold is working with the VBU? Oh, God, David, anything could happen!" She turned suddenly, clenched fists hammering her pain against his chest. "Dammit! I feel so *helpless!*"

His arms closed around her. For a long moment he held her, drawing her close. His eyes met hers. She was so beautiful.

He lowered his head and their lips touched. They kissed, and for a moment he felt her melting against him.

Suddenly she broke from the circle of his arms. "*No!* I'm sorry . . . no . . ." She turned and fled toward the river.

Rachel stood above the waters of the Hudson, breathing hard. Her thoughts were jumbled, a confusion of impressions and emotions.

Two weeks of nursing the wounded SAS commandos had brought her closer to David Wycliff than she'd ever imagined possible. It would be very easy to fall in love with him. He was like Travis in so many ways . . . especially in his love of the past. And he was the first man she'd ever known who respected her for herself, who told her to make her own decisions according to what she knew was right.

If only Travis could be more like that.

But it was the thought of Travis that had broken that moment's spell in Wycliff's arms. Rachel thought she understood Hunter and his concern with historical detail better now . . . thanks to Benedict Arnold.

Now, more than ever, she knew she loved Travis Hunter. *Where is he? Why has he been gone so long?*

Movement caught her eye, two black objects halfway across the river several hundred yards downstream. For a breathless moment she thought it might be Travis.

No! She glimpsed the unmistakable shapes of Soviet AKMs. Sunlight flashed on wet paddles dipping into the water.

"*David!*"

She ran toward the road. Wycliff turned at her shout. "David! VBU!"

"What! Where?"

"In the river. Eight . . . maybe ten men! Rubber boats! I saw their guns."

He grabbed her elbow and spun her onto the road. "Back to the house!"

Rachel's thoughts raced as they ran. There'd been no sign of the VBU in the area for weeks. What were they doing here now? Were they here to interfere with history again, or . . .

Or was the VBU after them?

Andryanov rolled out of the raft and splashed up onto the west bank of the river. "Hide the rafts!" he ordered, scanning the woods around them. These forests were filled with Americans, backwoodsmen and militia mostly, gathering to surround the beleaguered British army. He'd taken his team well south of the main concentration of Americans before crossing the river, in order to avoid being challenged by their sentries. So far, all was going well.

Lieutenant Chernysh pointed up the slope. "That way, Comrade Major. The house is up there."

"Excellent." Chernysh had done well, finding the house where the Americans were hiding and leading Andryanov's team there. He turned to the GRU lieutenant, Morozov. "Assemble your men, Lieutenant. Bring the radio with the rest of the gear."

"*Da*, Comrade Major."

Andryanov watched him give the orders. Morozov was Yakushenko's man, but he and his commando team took orders well enough. *As they should,* he thought angrily. *The KGB should be in charge of our time operations, not these Army pigs.*

A success here would give him political ammunition against Yakushenko when Double Storm was over and they returned to Uralskiy. That would settle the issue of VBU leadership once and for all.

If he could just take his prisoners and be back at Double Storm base before the colonel returned from Germantown.

"Quickly! Quickly!" Andryanov was suddenly impatient.

The Russian spetsnaz team began scrambling up the slope into the woods.

Wycliff stumbled, clutching at his side.

"David! What is it?"

"Side . . ." Pain tore the word from him. "God . . . it hurts . . ."

She touched his side where the broken ribs were still snugged tight under a makeshift bandage. Her fingers came away wet. "Your wound's opened again."

The two SAS troopers were there. "We've got him, miss," Fuller said.

"Never mind me!" Wycliff said. "Russians . . . back there!" He grimaced against the pain. "You two . . . set up out here. Try to draw them away from the house . . . the civilians . . ."

"Yes, sir!"

"We'll hole up inside, try to hold them off."

Fuller and Callaghan saluted and hurried off toward the woods. Rachel and Wycliff reached the Parson house moments later, banging through the front door.

Both Judith Parson and her son were up, bustling about with the morning chores. The woman dropped the log she was holding on the floor. "What's happened?"

"Tories," Wycliff said. The word startled Rachel, but she immediately understood. To the Parsons, staunch supporters of the rebel cause, the word carried a sense of immediate danger that "Russians" or "VBU" most certainly would not. "I'm afraid they've come for us."

Rachel struggled to support Wycliff. The two injured men had been staying in a small bedroom up the stairs behind the fireplace chimney, but there was no way Wycliff would make it up that twisting passage like this. His face was chalk-white, his breath coming in sharp, pain-stabbed gasps. Blood trickled through the fingers pressed against his left side.

"Help me, Mrs. Parson!" she said. "We can't get him upstairs like this!"

Mrs. Parson pointed toward the door to a small room on the northwest corner of the house "Put him in my bed. Ephraim! Fetch the guns! Shot and powder too. Quickly!"

Rachel helped Wycliff into the tiny, windowless bedroom, easing him back onto a thick patchwork quilt on the bed. She turned to go, but Wycliff caught at her sleeve. "Wait," he said. "You'll need this." He handed her his Browning HP-35.

"But you might—"

"Take it. Not sure I could hit anything now. You'll need it to cover the windows."

She took the weapon, pressed the magazine release, and checked that it had a full load of thirteen rounds. "There's one up the spout," Wycliff added, and she nodded.

Rachel longed for one of the weapons buried in the cache outside, but there was no time to recover them now.

What's the VBU doing here? A second thought followed close on the heels of the first, chilling her; *Maybe Travis is dead! Now they've come here mopping up!*

The Parson boy stood in the open door. "Thought you might be wanting these, sir," he said, extending the mahogany pistol case. Wycliff had kept the flintlock weapons by his bed upstairs, where he'd shown them to an admiring Ephraim several times.

"Thank you, Ephraim." Wycliff managed a pained smile.

"They're loaded. I . . . I just thought y'might want 'em." The boy's eyes flicked to Rachel. "Ma says she needs some help barricadin' the door, ma'am."

"Coming, Ephraim." She hesitated as the boy went out, then went to Wycliff's side, bent over, and kissed him. He gave her a wink and a weak thumbs-up, and she hurried back out to the main room.

She helped slide the heavy dining table in front of the door, then hung massive, interior wooden shutters cut with loopholes across the windows. Did the Russians know they were here, or were they simply landing close by . . . by chance? Her eyes went to the massive logs of the house walls, layered with chinking dried to the consistency of concrete. They looked like they would withstand anything. Houses in the Hudson Valley in this period were often built like small fortresses. The threat of Indian attack on the frontier was still a very real possibility.

"Don't see nothin' yet," Ephraim said, his eye pressed against a loophole.

"I'm awfully sorry to get you and your ma caught up in all this, Ephraim," Rachel said. She felt a small agony of guilt. There was no way this family could understand what was really happening . . . or what they actually faced. "This isn't your fight."

"Shoot, ma'am, you just bet it is! I hope I can pot me a couple a' them Tories!"

Rachel glanced at the boy. He looked excited, his face flushed in pale candlelight, his fingers moving nervously over the rich brown wood of his musket. She'd talked frequently with Ephraim during the past weeks and learned much about him. He was fiercely proud of two brothers already in the American Army. He would have joined, too, he'd insisted with passion on more than one occasion, if it weren't that his mother needed him here. He'd spent hours recounting his "adventure," as he called it, guiding the engineers and being rescued by Travis Hunter. His eagerness to come to grips with the hated enemy contrasted sharply with Rachel's own fear.

She turned at a sound from the stairs by the fireplace. Buchanan was there, leaning against the doorframe, his splinted leg held awkwardly in the air and his HP-35 clenched in one hand. He grinned at Rachel's surprise. "You don't think I'm gonna lay up there like a rat in a trap, do you, luv?"

There was a sudden burst of firing, muffled by distance. That would be the two SAS men trying to draw the Russians away from the house. The firing went on for several seconds, then fell silent.

Fear clutched at Rachel's throat. What was going on out there?

Mrs. Parson turned from the shuttered window near the southeast corner of the house, her musket steady in her hands as she poured a cartridge down the muzzle. "Ephraim! Over here, I think—"

The wall behind her exploded in flame and smoke and whirling splinters. The woman was flung across the room like a bloody rag doll. The blast caught Rachel and slapped her down, head ringing, the Browning skittering out of her hand and across the polished wood floor.

The VBU had arrived.

Lieutenant Yevgenni Prokopevich Morozov strode through the smoking ruin of the cabin's wall. Nilov's RPG had struck the building squarely on the southeast corner, smashing in the heavy logs and opening a gaping hole between the gray stone fireplace chimney and the window to the right of the front door. Smoke boiled from inside as he leapt across splintered debris. A shrill voice screamed, *"Ma! Ma!"*

A boy crouched above the shattered body of a woman, obviously dead. Close by, a man with a splinted leg lay sprawled facedown, while across the room a slender girl in a blue dress was trying to get to her knees.

"Skaryehyeh!" he snapped as his men crowded into the room behind him. "Hurry!"

The boy rose, clutching at his pathetic, primitive flintlock.

Morozov's orders were specific. There were American time travelers at this house, and he was to take them prisoner. For Morozov, identification of the Rangers seemed an easy enough task; those with black powder weapons were obviously locals. Major Andryanov had stressed that locals were not to be involved in this operation if possible, but neither were they to be allowed to interfere. The look of shock on the boy's powder-smudged face changed to a snarl of rage as he brought the musket up, tugging the hammer back to full cock.

The Russian's AKM was set for single shot. The weapon spat flame and shattered glass across the room at the boy's back. The youngster's rage transformed to a fiend's grimace of pure delight, his muzzle loader swinging up to his shoulder.

Morozov triggered the AKM again, and half of the boy's face vanished in blood and chips of bone in the unexpected second shot. The musket went off with a sharp double flash and a two-syllable *ka-bam*, the ball burying itself in a ceiling beam over the Russian's head.

Baykov had already reached the man with the splinted right leg. "This is one, Comrade Lieutenant!" He held up an automatic pistol.

The lieutenant gestured with his rifle. "You! You! You! Search the house! Chernysh! With me!"

The girl at the other end of the room was groping for a pistol on the floor, her small hand closing over its grip. Chernysh's AKM came up, but Morozov raised his hand. "No! Take her!" He moved toward her and was surprised as she rose to her knees, the Browning tightly gripped in both hands. The handgun barked, and Morozov felt the force of the blast brush his arm. Chernysh, close beside him, twisted and stumbled. The Browning fired again, and Chernysh dropped. Morozov was on the girl in the same instant, smashing the pistol out of her hands with a vicious sweep of his AKM's barrel. She lunged past him, but he grabbed her arm with one hand, swinging her around to face him.

Captain Sir David Wycliff lay flat on his back, his eyes on the door three feet from the foot of his bed. He had recognized the boom of an exploding Soviet rocket-propelled grenade, heard the gunshots and the orders shouted in Russian. Now he waited, the sleek, warm grips of the two nine-inch flintlock pistols comfortably nested in his hands.

He'd not expected to put Hunter's gift to practical use.

The door burst inward, yanking free of its upper hinge. A heavy shape filled the doorway, and Wycliff caught a glimpse of the deadly curve of an AKM's magazine.

He squeezed the trigger on his right-hand pistol, the flash and smoke momentarily blocking his view of the door. The ball struck the Russian just below his left eye, knocking him back with the force of a swinging club.

Another Russian stood behind the first. Wycliff's second pistol spoke, the recoil snapping the gleaming hexagonal barrel up. The VBU trooper clawed at his throat and stumbled forward over the crumpling body of his comrade.

Wycliff didn't even have time to register the fact that both flintlocks were now empty before the third VBU trooper sprayed the bedroom with a wild, back-and-forth rattle of autofire slugs. The bullets driving through his arms and chest and legs struck like sledgehammer blows, smashing him over and off the bed.

Rachel struggled in the Russian officer's grip. The burst of autofire snapped the man's head around. He bellowed something in Russian, was answered by a soldier emerging from David's room, stepping across the bodies of two dead comrades.

She knew sick horror but took advantage of the officer's distraction. Rachel brought her knee up hard, catching him between the legs and doubling him over with a shocked grunt. She was off-balance and the blow was not a crippling one, but she was able to twist away and run for the front door.

Two men were there: another Russian soldier in camouflage fatigues and an officer speaking into a radio handset.

Then a hand clamped down on the back collar of her dress. Something metallic dug into her throat, twisting and choking . . . her mother's locket. Then the pressure around her neck was gone and she was free. She ran.

And sprawled on the ground as the officer with the machine pistol caught the billowing folds of her blue gown and wrestled her down. Rough hands yanked her wrists to the small of her back, and she felt the cool slickness of metal cuffs click into place.

Someone flipped her over onto her back and jerked her up by the hair. She wiggled, but strong arms supported her under her arms, hauled her bodily off the porch. Rachel saw Buchanan's limp form being dragged from the house, heard the dull whack as his splinted leg struck the doorframe.

The officer who had been speaking on the radio gestured at the house "Burn it," he said in precise English. One of the soldiers pulled a ring from the top of a dull gray canister and tossed it through the door. A burst of dazzling white light illuminated the interior for an instant, then was replaced by the greedy lick of spreading flames. Smoke curled up under the eaves of the porch.

One of her captors hoisted her to his shoulder. Her hair spilled across her face and down the man's back as he carried her at a jarring trot down the road.

A dull, thuttering sound brought new horror . . . the familiar *whup-whup-whup* of an approaching helicopter. Dust swirled as the turbine whine shrilled close by.

This time there would be no General Burgoyne to rescue her.

Eighteen

Smoke still smudged the sky above the ruin of the Parson house. Hunter looked at the scene and fought back the sour bile rising in his throat. After landing the Hip in a clearing in the woods a few miles away, they'd made their way to the Albany Road, south of Bemis Heights. He'd wanted to talk with Wycliff and Buchanan about the possibilities of getting Rachel free from the British camp.

They were two hours too late.

He turned to the others. King and Anderson stared at the ashes with tense, white faces. Mason rubbed at his chin nervously. "Found Callaghan and Fuller down there," the SAS sergeant said. "Dead."

"Spread out," Hunter said. The words came with difficulty. "Stay out of sight. Keep watch."

A small knot of locals was gathered by a still form. Hunter approached, wincing at the sight of David Wycliff's blistered face. The skin was blackened in places, cracked to reveal bright red blood. Breath hissed and bubbled as the captain fought for air.

"Found him at the front door," one of the locals said. He wore a Continental Army uniform. "We heard shootin' and figured it might be a Tory raid. Got here to find the house afire, and . . ." He completed the sentence with a soundless gesture.

Wycliff's eyes fluttered open. "You came . . ." The words were a flame-seared croak. One burned hand groped for the front of Hunter's vest. "VBU . . ."

"What's that?" someone asked. "What did he say?"

"Like you said," Hunter replied softly. "Tories."

"They got...Rachel." Wycliff said. "Tried to stop 'em...."

Hunter felt light-headed. Pain knifed at his stomach. "Rachel...here?"

"Managed to...to crawl. Had to get out." The mangled body twisted, trembled. "Burning...burning..."

"Easy, David."

"Found this...in the doorway." A bloody fist wavered in front of Hunter's face. It opened, and a gold locket dropped into Hunter's hand. He turned it between his fingers, tears blurring his eyes.

"She got here right...right after you left. Couldn't tell you." The charred lips dragged in a harsh, noisy breath. "Wonderful girl, Travis."

"Yes."

"She's alive. They...took her and Jimmy."

"How many were there?" There was no response. "David! How many were there?"

The eyes snapped open, staring unseeingly at the blue sky. Wycliff began shaking, a scream tearing at his throat. *"Julie!"*

He died.

Hunter stood slowly, looking at the locket. So close and yet...

Angrily he turned on his heel and strode back to his waiting men.

The door banged open and the soldier flung Rachel inside. The walls of the cell were corrugated steel, the floor concrete. She lay in one corner, chest heaving, as two more soldiers dragged Buchanan in and dumped him on a folding cot.

Slowly she rose, rubbing her wrists where the handcuffs had chafed. She wore nothing but her cotton shift. They'd taken the dress and petticoat when they searched her.

One of the soldiers gave Rachel an appreciative leer. Then they were gone, slamming the door behind them. She heard the rattle of keys in a lock, and her breath caught in a sob.

She'd only glimpsed the buildings around the bare dirt landing field. This building was a Quonset hut, a low, prefab structure separated by thin partitions into a work area crammed with map tables and radios, and a row of small rooms at the far end, used for storage. Their cell had obviously been a storeroom cleaned out to accommodate prisoners.

Buchanan moaned and tried to sit up. "I don't care for their bedside manner."

"Are you all right?" she asked, kneeling beside the cot. Except for that one piece of furniture, the room was completely bare. Light came from an incandescent bulb dangling far out of reach overhead. Somewhere outside, she heard the rumble of an engine. A generator, she thought.

"I think so. They slapped me around some, searching me." He eyed their surroundings. "Not much for interior decor, eh?"

She managed a smile. "No. Do you know where we are?"

"Couldn't see much from the helicopter, not lying on the deck with those fellows' boots on me. Judging from the angle of the sun, I'd guess we're south of Bemis Heights. Travel time . . . say an hour. Puts us maybe a hundred and fifty miles from where we started."

"Looked to me like we're out in the woods someplace," Rachel said.

"Four prefab buildings," Buchanan added, his voice a whisper. "Fuel dump. And God knows what that mess was on the far side of the heliport. I think we can safely say that we've found their main base."

"That mess looked to me like field generators for a downtime link," Rachel said.

"How's that?"

"It's the near end of a Russian time portal," she explained. "We ran into one once before. It's what they use instead of a recall beacon . . . but I never thought they could make them that big!"

Buchanan grunted. "They'd need something big enough to handle their helos. Wonder if they just flew 'em through the portal or brought 'em back piece by piece?"

"I don't know." Rachel stood and padded barefoot to the door. By pressing her ear to the wood she could hear conversation from the radio room and caught a scrape that might have been the scruff of a sentry's boot just outside.

"Anything?" Buchanan asked.

Rachel nodded. "Something," she whispered. "But they're speaking Russian."

She sagged down to the concrete at Buchanan's side, her suppressed terror and exhaustion dragging her like the surging, outgoing tide of an ocean. *Travis! Travis . . . are you alive?*

The roar of the Hip's rotors made conversation almost impossible. In the copilot's seat, Hunter studied the map of New York spread out before him, then gestured to Anderson. They were nearly fifty miles away from Bemis Heights and the rest of the team. Anderson nodded, then pulled back on the transport's stick. They'd been flying nape-of-the-earth to avoid curious eyes, but they needed altitude for what Hunter had in mind.

He was certain that Rachel and Buchanan were alive. The purpose of the VBU raid could only have been to take prisoners . . . presumably for interrogation, either at the local Russian base or back at their time-travel center in 2007. If Rachel had already been taken up to the Soviet portal base, she was lost, but there was at least a chance that she was still in 1777. It was unlikely that they would attempt to evacuate prisoners to 2007 before they knew the fate of the Germantown mission. Hunter remembered the dead colonel in the meadow. If he was the local VBU commander, the Soviets would be in confusion for some time to come. Russians tended to rely on higher authority to do *anything*, a weakness that Hunter intended to exploit.

The radio should already be tuned to the base frequency. Hunter reached out and unclipped a microphone from the console in front of him. He flicked on the transmitter and began speaking in Russian.

"Come in, base! This is Colonel Yakushenko!" He kept his voice rough and was thankful for the roar of the helicopter's engine. With enough noise and a brusque manner, he hoped to bluff his way past the guard or whoever was manning the radio at the Soviet base. It was a gamble, certainly. But Petrov had mentioned a Colonel Yakushenko, and there'd been a dead Soviet colonel at Germantown. Hunter doubted very much that there was more than one VBU colonel on this op.

"Come in, base!" he continued "This is Yakushenko! Do you read me?"

There was a long pause. Hunter signaled Anderson to go higher and tried again. And again. Finally, against the crackle of static, he heard a faint reply. *"Allo! Allo! Gahvareet Andryanov! Slooshayu!"*

Hunter grinned. He had them! He thought for a moment, then continued speaking in Russian. "This is Yakushenko! The Germantown mission was a complete success!"

There was a pause. *"Did you say a complete success, Comrade Colonel?"*

Was he being tested? Hunter decided to gamble further. It was fairly obvious from the captured maps and history book what the Soviet plan had been. They would know that George Washington had been in the area of the Chew House for some time during the battle in the fog. A machine gun or a sniper's rifle fired from that ridge would have cut down Washington and his staff, just as the VBU had planned to do at Brandywine.

"Washington is dead," he declared. "The American Army was routed. We have succeeded in changing history!"

Germantown had indeed been a defeat for the Continentals, ending in confusion when separate attacking columns blundered into one another in the fog, and the main advance was delayed by a British force holed up inside the Chew House. Washington had finally ordered a retreat at eleven that morning, but even the British would admit that the fight had been a close-run thing. There had been no rout in the real battle . . . and Washington had not been a casualty.

"That is excellent news, Comrade Colonel," Andryanov said. *"What are your orders now?"*

Anderson gave Hunter a thumbs-up and pointed. He had a line on the Russian base. If King was picking up the signal as well, they would be able to triangulate on the Soviet transmitter. Even if there was only one line, it would be possible now to follow it to the source.

But was Rachel still alive . . . or had she been taken out through the Soviet portal? Hunter had to know. How he mounted an assault on the VBU base would depend on whether or not she was there.

He decided to risk pressing for the additional information.

"Tell me, Andryanov," he said. "How went your raid? Did you get the prisoners?"

There was a long, long silence from the speaker.

Andryanov smiled. The radio operator had been right to call him. That Yakushenko should break his own order to maintain radio silence was merely strange, but the question about the prisoners proved that the call was from the Americans. The colonel knew nothing about the raid. It could only mean that the Germantown operation had failed, that the helicopter had been captured. The enemy was using the radio to locate the Soviet base.

Very well, he thought. *Let them! What better way to recover our helicopter and dispose of the American Rangers than to believe their little charade?*

"*Da*, Comrade Colonel!" he said cheerfully. "The raid went exactly as planned! We have the prisoners here, as you ordered!"

"*That is good, Comrade Andryanov,*" the voice said from the speaker above his head "*We shall return to base shortly. Yakushenko out!*"

"We shall be waiting for you, Comrade Colonel. Out!"

He replaced the microphone "You were right, Valery," he said. The radio operator was one of his own KGB men, placed there to keep news of the prisoner raid from leaking to Yakushenko. "That was not the colonel."

"What does it mean, Comrade Major?"

"It means that the Americans are about to pay us a visit. Continue to monitor . . . and send for me if they call again. I will be outside."

"*Da*, Comrade Major."

"We must arrange a special welcome for our American friends."

Twenty feet away, Rachel's eyes grew wide as Buchanan translated the Russian major's words. Her Russian lessons with Travis had not even begun to allow her to understand the language when it was spoken by native speakers, but she'd had no trouble picking out such phrases as *Amerikahnski drooghya*—"American friends." When the radio operator had summoned the Soviet major, she'd helped Buchanan get out of the cot and hobble the few steps to the door. Now his ear was pressed to the smooth wood with hers, and he whispered a running translation.

"Travis . . . alive!" she said softly. *Alive!*

"Sounds like they're plotting something nasty for them, though," Buchanan said. He grimaced and returned to the cot, gripping his splinted leg. "Damn! I wish we could bust out of here. Maybe we could warn him."

Rachel's eyes strayed to Buchanan's leg. "Maybe we can."

"They believed us!" Hunter said exultantly. "They took it hook, line, and sinker!"

"Back to Saratoga, then?" Anderson asked.

"Right you are, Roy. Let's see if Greg picked up that second line for us!"

The helicopter swung in a broad curve, descending back to treetop level for the return flight to the Hudson Valley.

Trading glances with Buchanan, Rachel squeezed up against the wall opposite the cot, three feet from the door. The SAS trooper smiled and gave her a thumbs-up.

His leg was wrapped again after a half hour's feverish work. By unwrapping the yards of cloth strips that bound up his right leg from ankle to thigh, they'd been able to remove one of the pieces of broom handle that served Buchanan as splints. The two-foot length of wood was jagged on one end where it had been broken. She held it behind her now, pressed between the steel wall and her buttocks.

Careful listening had satisfied them that there were only two men in the building: a sentry just outside the door, and another man named Valery at the radio. They would have to take out both men at the same time, or Travis would fly into the trap.

Rachel returned Buchanan's smile, took a deep breath, and screamed at the top of her lungs. *"Help! Help! He's bleeding! He's bleeding to death!"*

She was not certain either of the Russians spoke English, but she threw enough emotion into her performance to overcome any language barrier. Only a moment after her first shriek, she heard the rattle of keys, saw the door swing open.

Both Soviets were there, the radio operator holding the keys and the sentry just behind him, pointing an AKM into the room. The first Russian glanced at Rachel. She pressed her back against the wall and her hidden weapon, keeping both fists crammed against her mouth. "His leg is bleeding real bad!" she said. Her acting had her on the brink of hysteria, and her breath came in sharp gasps. "I think they hurt him when they dragged him in here!"

There was a rapid exchange in Russian. The unarmed soldier walked across the narrow room to Buchanan's side. He stooped by the cot, reaching down to examine the prisoner's leg. The guard with the AKM remained outside, his rifle covering Rachel.

Buchanan's arm snapped up, grabbing the VBU man by the neck and dragging him facedown against his chest. The Russian kicked, trying to break free, but the trooper's powerful grip pinned him for a thrashing, helpless moment. The soldier in the hall lunged forward, his rifle coming up to aim past his struggling comrade at the injured prisoner.

Rachel grasped the rod, took two quick paces forward, and whipped the broom-handle thickness of wood down on the soldier's head. He shouted pain and dropped to his knees, the rifle clattering forward out of his hand. Rachel recovered from her swing and jabbed the splintered end of her weapon into the man's face, then raised the club above her head and swung again.

The tortured wood broke across the Russian's head. He slumped, face bloody from a gouge in his cheek and a split in his scalp. Rachel wasted no more time on him but bent and picked up the fallen rifle with both hands, grasping the muzzle like a baseball bat.

The man struggling with Buchanan tried to pull back. "*Nyet! Pahzhahl'stah! Nyet!*" The improvised club lashed through the air in a short, vicious half circle, the butt smashing into the other soldier's head just as he twisted free from Buchanan's grip. He jerked and crumpled, his neck twisted at an odd angle.

Buchanan sat up and looked at Rachel. "Remind me never to make you mad!" He repeated his thumbs-up. "Luck, luv!"

She grinned but did not trust herself to reply. The fight had left her shaking inside, and she was afraid to do anything that might make her give in to the hysteria she felt. She reversed the AKM and hurried through the open door, into the main room.

Rachel had discussed her next move with Buchanan for some time. It might be possible, they both knew, for her to slip out the door and escape. Through windows on either side of the building's lone door, she could see other Russians off on the far side of the helipad. The Hind was off the landing area, on the far side of the compound. A number of soldiers clustered there, engaged in some unidentifiable activity at the aircraft's side.

No one was looking in her direction, and there appeared to be no sentries outside the building. If she chose, she could escape.

But that choice meant death for Hunter. He had to be warned that the Russians knew he was coming . . . that they were pretending to be fooled only to lure him into a trap.

The radio was still on, a soft hum coming from the open speaker. She picked up the microphone, stole a last glance toward the windows, then pressed the transmit switch.

"Travis . . . this is Rachel! It's a trap! Don't come! Travis . . . this is Rachel! It's a trap! Don't come!"

She squeezed her eyes shut to stop their burning. She repeated the message over and over, until the words rasped in her throat and sounded hollow in her ears. Rachel was gambling that Hunter's radio call earlier was intended to get a directional line on the VBU base. It seemed unlikely that he would simply turn the radio off. A further communication from the base might give him the opportunity to get more intelligence. As long as he knew the Soviet's frequency, he would keep listening.

"Travis . . . this is Rachel! It's a trap! Don't come!"

She heard the voices of men talking outside, coming closer.

"Travis . . . this is Rachel . . . !"

Nineteen

"Are we still goin' in, LT?"

Hunter looked across at Anderson as the Hip rushed low across the treetops. Saratoga still lay several minutes ahead. "I don't know, Roy," he said. Rachel's warning continued to hammer through the earphones. *"Damn!* I must have given it away!"

"Don't blame yourself. You had to know."

If the VBU knew they were coming, everything was changed. To even approach their base, not knowing what was waiting for them, would be suicide. His fists closed on the maps still spread out before him, where a penciled line angled southwest across southern New York and into New Jersey. So much could go wrong, but what was it Rachel had said once? *"Worrying about what might go wrong doesn't get us anywhere."*

Delay would only make matters worse. Rachel was in 1777 now, but for how long? The Russians would be in confusion after Yakushenko's death. *We've got to act!*

"Okay," he said. "We're going in. I thought we might just fly in, pretending to be nice, harmless VBU, but it looks like we're going to have to play it sneaky."

"Travis . . . this is Rachel . . . !"

The conversation outside halted the unbroken stream of words. If the Russians entered and found her transmitting, they would know Travis had been warned. Rachel replaced the microphone, then snatched the AKM and raced for the door. It opened as she approached, revealing a pair of Russian soldiers in camouflage fatigues.

"Astarozhnah!" one yelled, fumbling for his holstered pistol. The other lashed out with his foot, the side of his boot striking Rachel's arm before she could turn aside. The AKM spun away as the flat of the soldier's hand whipped into Rachel's jaw. The blow stunned her, knocking her to the concrete. A rough hand closed around her chin, forcing her head up until her left eye was one inch away from the muzzle of an automatic pistol.

The soldier smiled. "Going somewhere, *devoshka*?"

They'd pinpointed the Russian base.

It squatted in a clearing on the eastern side of the Kittatiny Mountains, just across the ridge line from the scenic depths of the Delaware Valley. British-occupied Manhattan lay only fifty miles to the southeast. This entire corner of New Jersey was heavily wooded, with only rare clearings marking homesteads and isolated farms. Much of this area was swamp, but the Soviet base was on dry land. The nearest sign of human habitation was a dirt road a mile down the slope, wending through the woods toward New York.

Hunter lay on his belly studying the base through binoculars. There were four prefab buildings, a fuel dump, and something that might be a very large VBU time-travel portal raised outdoors not far from what might be a generator station. The base seemed deserted. From his vantage point he could see no guards, no workers . . . not even the occasional off-duty soldier strolling between two buildings.

Had the Soviets evacuated? Where was the trap Rachel had warned him about?

Motion stirred at his side. He rolled over and nodded at the SAS trooper, Dark Walker. "Anything?"

The Indian pointed, guiding Hunter's attention to one of the buildings. "That appears to be a barracks," he said in his slow, precise voice. "I got close enough to see that they've set up a machine gun behind the doors covering the helipad."

"Ah!"

Walker pointed again. "That building is a storehouse. Food. Weapons. Spare parts. They've set up a machine gun there as well."

"Also covering the helipad."

Walker nodded.

"So they're waiting for us to land," he continued. "We come in pretending to be the bunch flying in from Germantown...jump out...and get mowed down in the crossfire from two MGs. Anything else?"

"The building close to the electronic apparatus is a generator station and control area of some sort. There are people inside."

"Portal controls?"

"Perhaps. Another thing..." He hesitated. "Just behind that building is a stable. I saw a wagon and several teams of horses. When I first approached, I saw men there in Tory dress. Then an officer came out of the generator building and ordered them inside. I suspect that it's part of their operation for inserting disguised agents into the period."

Hunter nodded. "Did you see Buchanan or...or the girl?"

"No, Lieutenant. They are not in the barracks or supply areas." The ghost of a smile played at his lips. "I got quite close. Do you see the building with the radio antenna?"

"I see it."

"That is their headquarters. There are small rooms inside but no windows. I could not get inside without being seen. But if our people are anywhere, they are there."

Our people... "Did you see the Hind?"

The Indian shook his head. "That tent near the helipad may be where they service aircraft. I saw tools...and a small electric winch. But there is no helicopter."

"Okay. Thank you, Walker."

Teeth flashed in the swarthy face. "Anytime, Lieutenant."

Hunter took a last look at the base. Where was the helicopter? On patrol, perhaps...or they might be checking on their people at Germantown, since they knew now that the op there had gone sour. It was probably just as well they didn't have the gunship to tangle with as well as two machine guns.

Now, for the approach...

Taylor was angry. He jerked his thumb at the Hip, resting now on its tripod gear in a small, woods-enclosed glade. The other men, SAS and Rangers, looked on curiously from across the field. "Dammit, King! I can fly those things blindfolded."

"I didn't say you couldn't, sir," King replied. His voice

was soft and carefully controlled. "All I said was what Lieutenant Hunter told me: that Anderson is the pilot."

Four years in the Army . . . two in Rangers! I don't have to take this shit!

"I know you don't approve of me, King." His fists clenched at his sides. "But you damn well know why . . . why I had that trouble at Paoli. We're not looking at a screwup of history here. We're looking at Russians! I can kill Russians."

"Yes, sir." King was maddeningly polite. He looked away. "Here comes Walker and the lieutenant. If you want to kill Russkies, you'd best check your weapon. But . . ." King's eyes were hard as he faced Taylor again. "It's decided. Roy's flying the op."

It had taken over an hour to get in position. The paths discovered by Walker during his recce were nearly invisible traces through forest and swampy ground, and their staging area in the glade was on the far side of a rugged, wooded ridge.

Hunter looked back over his shoulder. Gomez grinned and hefted his M-203. All of them were wearing full combat gear and harness, with their faces painted green and black. Their approach to the VBU base had been made in complete silence. Two Russian sentries posted at the camp perimeter heard nothing at all until hands clamped across their faces and knives sliced through red-blossoming jugulars.

Ten yards ahead Trooper Shute signaled. Hunter gestured to the others. His eyes met John Mason's, bleak behind the mask of camo paint. The trooper was taking Wycliff's death hard, but shock and pain seemed to be giving way to a dull, burning hatred of the VBU. Will the man function, or does he hate too much? Hunter dismissed the thought. He wasn't sure how much he trusted Ben, either, but they needed every man.

According to plan, the team split at the edge of the woods —King working his way with Mason, Walker, and White around to the supply building while Hunter, Shute, Gomez, and Taylor got ready to hit the barracks. The waiting dragged through endless minutes. There was still no sign of alarm from the camp.

Hunter heard a distant stir in the autumn air and checked his watch: 1115 hours. That would be Anderson in the Hip, right on time. The four men tensed, scanning the VBU compound.

The front door of the HQ building banged open and a camo-garbed soldier stepped out, an AKM slung over his shoulder. He took a long, hard look toward the approaching Hip, then began a casual stroll toward the barracks. *Making it look good,* Hunter thought.

The Hip approached with a roar, stirring up dust from the dirt surface of the LZ, the nose lifting up as it flared in for a landing. The lone Soviet soldier turned to watch. Inside those buildings, every eye would be on the helicopter.

Hunter gave the signal. Like shadows, they flitted across open ground, racing for the curving steel wall of the barracks. The Hip settled to the ground.

Hunter and Shute took one window, Gomez and Taylor another. With choreographed precision Shute and Taylor smashed in the window screens with their rifle butts. Then Hunter and Gomez flipped grenades through. The blasts were deafening inside the steel cavern of the building. The door blew out into the yard, closely followed by a somersaulting VBU trooper and the wooden stock of a PKM.

An instant later another blast ripped from the supply hut across the compound. Inky smoke gathered above the gaping door. The lone VBU soldier whirled, shouting an alarm, and was cut down by a burst from Hunter's Uzi.

Hunter jerked his fist up and down, signaling. *"Go! Go! Go!"*

Rangers dashed from cover. Their first targets were the ruined ambush sites. Autofire chopped into Russians groggily crawling out from under smashed furniture and fallen interior partitions. More grenades followed. Russians burst from the generator building, then went to ground as White's machine gun chopped into them. A moment later Gomez's M-203 thumped, and a spin-stabilized, 40mm parcel of high-explosive death landed among the VBU troops, scattering them in limp, bloody heaps.

Hunter fired at a running spetsnaz trooper, missed, fired again, and watched him fall. The compound was clear for the moment. He oriented himself on the HQ building, slapped a fresh magazine into his SMG, and broke into a run.

• • •

Andryanov leaned over the shoulder of a VBU time-travel technician. The control station was crowded, a cramped room of stainless steel and snaking power conduits, engulfed by the humming throb of the generator plant. Several technicians sat at the console, watching as energies were channeled through to the downtime link outside. In the back of the room, a number of spetsnaz troopers cradled their AKs, listening to the approaching sounds of battle.

The Americans were showing unexpected resourcefulness, using the Hip as a diversion while mounting an attack by foot. Their destruction of the two machine gun nests was uncanny. How had they known?

No matter. The second part of the trap was about to fall. He picked up a microphone. "Shepelev!" he said. "Patch me through to Fomenko!"

"Da, Comrade Major. Contact established!"

"This is Fomenko," another voice said, relayed through to the control station from the radio at headquarters.

"Fomenko, this is Andryanov. Launch your attack!"

"At once, Comrade Major!"

"Base . . . out."

The technician turned to look at Andryanov. "The gate is open, Comrade Major. We have full power."

"Excellent! Keep it open for as long as possible. I will return to Uralskiy and get help."

Lieutenant Morozov clutched at Andryanov's arm. "What are you doing, Comrade?" The spetsnaz officer was intense, his eyes fiery. "You cannot leave us."

Andryanov's lip curled in a sneer. "Do not worry, Comrade Lieutenant. Fomenko and *Sasha* will keep the Americans amused until I return with reinforcements."

"Nyet, you KGB dog! You only wish to save your own ass while we—"

The Skorpion was in Andryanov's hand, spitting before Morozov could finish.

Andryanov turned mild eyes on the technicians and soldiers. "He panicked . . . as you all saw."

"Da, Comrade Major," one said. "The strain must have been too much."

He faced the spetsnaz troopers, watching from the back of the room. "KGB or GRU, it does not matter," he said. "We are VBU, and we have our duty. Do any of you question my authority?"

A sergeant shook his head, his eyes on the dead lieutenant. "*Nyet*, Comrade Major. You are senior in command."

"Exactly." He holstered the weapon and turned to leave. A thought struck him, and he reached past the technician to pick up the microphone again. "Comrade Shepelev," he said. "This is Andryanov."

"*Shepelev here, Comrade Major.*"

"How many men have you?"

"*Myself and one another, Comrade Major.*"

"I want you to deal with the prisoners. The wounded man will be unable to walk. Kill him. Then bring the girl to the downlink gate. I want you to take her through to 2007."

"*At once, Comrade Major!*"

He handed the mike back to the technician. Gunfire chattered from the far side of the compound. "I am going. You have your orders, should the Americans get this far."

"*D-da*, Comrade Major."

He laid his hand on the man's shoulder. "It won't come to that, Pyotr. The gunship will be here at any moment. I will return soon."

Outside, the battle seemed to be breaking up into isolated firefights between survivors of the Russian ambush and the shifting, darting forms of the Americans. None were close to the control station. Close by, a loose metal scaffolding enclosed a broad, level space. An eerie blue glow pulsated between power nodes and field generators, holding open the 230-year corridor across spacetime.

He rubbed at a fleck of blood staining his cuff, straightened his tunic, and squared his shoulders. He was not worried. There could be no doubt that Double Storm's failure was Yakushenko's fault. No doubt at all.

He walked forward into the glow and vanished.

Rachel spun as the cell door burst open. Two Russians appeared, one with an AKM, the other with an unholstered Skorpion.

Slowly she got up from beside Buchanan's cot. "What do you bastards want now?" Defiance tore the words from her.

They hadn't hurt her after her recapture . . . they'd made

her watch while they hurt Jimmy. The one called Andryanov ordered one VBU trooper to hold her while another unwrapped Buchanan's leg, took the remaining length of wood splint, and used it to beat the helpless man. They were careful not to cripple him, but the thrashing left Buchanan bruised and semiconscious. After ten minutes Andryanov called a halt, promised more personal attention for them both at Uralskiy, and left.

It seemed like hours later when explosions echoed across the compound, followed by the sounds of battle. Her first irrational surge of hope faded almost at once. As the gunfire died away she found that tears were streaming down her cheeks. The escape . . . the beating . . . all for nothing. Travis had come, after all, and fallen into the trap.

Oh, Travis! Why did you come?

The soldier with the Skorpion gestured with his head. His eyes were cold and deadly. "Out. We have orders."

Her shaking increased. "Orders" could only mean a trip to 2007 Russia . . . or death. Desperately she found herself hoping for death.

As the VBU agent led her into the main room, the soldier with the AKM drew the bolt on his weapon and stepped into the doorway.

"Wait!" she said. "What are you doing?"

She tried to grab the man with the AKM, but the other Soviet grabbed the neck of her shift and pulled her away. The first man aimed at Buchanan . . .

Hunter hit the HQ door with his shoulder, smashing through with his Uzi leveled. He saw Rachel, her white undergarment torn, struggling with a Russian holding a Skorpion. Another soldier had an AKM.

Hunter's first burst caught the rifleman, smashing him against the doorframe and splattering the partition with blood. His Uzi tracked across to the man by Rachel . . . *no!*

He froze. The VBU agent stood behind Rachel, his arm tight under her breasts, his Skorpion against her head. "No move, American!" the VBU soldier yelled. "No move!"

"Let her go!" Hunter snapped in Russian, whiplash command in the words.

"*Nyet!* You will put your weapons down . . . slowly."

"No, Travis!" Rachel screamed as Hunter gently set the Uzi on the concrete. "Travis...no! He'll kill me, anyway! Don't do it!"

"The pistol too!" the Russian said. Carefully Hunter unsnapped the holster of his .45 and drew the weapon by its grip, between thumb and forefinger.

"Travis! No!"

"It's okay, Rachel," he said. His heart pounded in his chest. "It's okay! You were right, remember? Sometimes we have to stop and think things over carefully, instead of acting!"

The Russian smiled as Hunter put the colt on the floor. The Skorpion moved away from Rachel's head, shifting to aim at Hunter.

Rachel slumped forward against the man's arm, then snapped her head up and back with a convulsive jerk. The back of her head smashed into her captor's nose.

Hunter was already rolling across the floor, scooping up his pistol. Rachel broke free, leaving the Soviet in the open, one hand clawing at the blood streaming from his nose. A .45-caliber slug passed between his fingers, ending his attempts to stop the bleeding. Two more rounds entered his body as it flopped back, but the VBU agent was already dead.

Hunter enfolded Rachel in his arms as she ran to him. "Travis!"

"It's okay, hon. It's okay."

But there was no time to enjoy the embrace. The roar of a helicopter low overhead shook the building, followed by the stuttering yammer of heavy-caliber machine guns.

Hunter dragged Rachel to the floor, sheltering her as a thunderclap of noise shook the building.

The Hind was back!

Twenty

Anderson peered through the Plexiglas canopy of the Hip, trying to spot the attacker. The Hind's shadow swept across the compound like the specter of some vast bird of prey. The Texan gunned the Hip's engines, preparing to take off. Airborne, he might distract the Soviet gunship . . . perhaps lead it away so that Travis and the others could escape.

Machine-gun fire geysered across the compound, kicking up dust and clots of earth. Trooper Shute sprinted for cover as tracers flickered past his legs, tangling them, tripping him. The SAS soldier pitched forward and rolled over and over, coming to rest in front of the grenade-shattered storage building. Anderson cursed and reached for the control stick. Bullets struck the Hip's cockpit, splintering glass and pocking holes through the thin metal hull. Searing flame lanced his right shoulder, punching him back against the pilot's seat. He felt dizzy. Blood spilled over his left hand as he grabbed at the pain, coating both arms and trickling onto his lap.

Anderson looked up in time to see a puff of white smoke appear along the Hind's flank. A moment later the Hip lurched violently, and he heard shrapnel rattle off the hull. Rockets! They'd armed the Hind with rocket pods! Hind-As normally carried sixty-four of the deadly missiles on each pylon, but there'd been no sign that this one mounted them.

Another blast rocked the Hip. It did now.

Roger White rose from the wreckage near the storage hut, his L7 cradled. The massive weapon thundered at the armored helicopter passing low overhead. The Hind slipped sideways, its downdraft swirling smoke and dust into a billowing, impenetrable cloud. For a moment Anderson saw the SAS machine gunner standing in the open, his MG kicking and bucking as he poured round after round at the enemy gunship.

Then smoke puffed from the Hind's weapons pods again, and White vanished in a roar of smoke and hurtling earth, his body shredded by a 57mm rocket.

Anderson tried to rise . . . failed. Agony radiated from his broken shoulder.

Ben Taylor saw the Hind's machine-gun fire tear into the grounded Hip. He turned to Gomez, crouched beside him. "Eddie, I'd say now's when we need a big bang!"

Gomez patted his M-203. "Yeah . . . but I don't have a chopper hunting license, man! Thumpers ain't no good against Hinds!"

Taylor's eyes narrowed as he watched the Soviet helicopter. It was hovering now, eighty yards away, sweeping the compound with machine-gun and rocket fire.

"You got smoke?"

"Yeah," Gomez said. He fished a 40mm round out of his bandolier. "I been tryin' to quit for years, but . . ."

Taylor pointed. "Then drop some smoke there . . . and there. Build me a wall."

"Sure. Hey, man!" Gomez grabbed Taylor's arm as he started to rise. "Where you goin'?"

"Just give me cover, Eddie." He grinned. "Lots of small, smoky bangs!"

Gomez's love of things that went bang was a running joke among the Rangers. Taylor clapped him on the back, then sprinted from cover toward the Hip. The thump of the M-203 sounded behind him. White smoke boiled into the air across the compound.

Taylor ran, crouching low. The rotor wash from two helicopters would clear Eddie's smoke quickly, but it provided the cover he needed to reach the Hip. The transport's rotors chittered overhead as Taylor jogged the pilot's access hatch on the right side of the aircraft, twisted the handle, and pulled it open. Anderson was slumped in the pilot's seat, eyes glazed with pain, blood soaking his fatigues. Working quickly, Taylor unfastened the harness and hauled the man from the cockpit.

"What . . . ?" Anderson blinked up at him as Taylor probed the injured shoulder. Then the Ranger lieutenant pulled off his cap, wadded it up, and jammed it into the wound. There was no time for elaborate first aid.

He climbed into the open hatch.

Anderson lay on the ground, mouthing something lost in the roar of the engines. Taylor grinned at the Texan and raised his thumb. He *belonged* now. Anderson yelled another unheard protest as Taylor slammed the hatch shut and checked the console.

The cockpit was a mess of broken glass, but the vital instruments were intact. Blackness fell as the Hind swept past the sun. *There's the bastard!*

The seat was wet with Anderson's blood. Taylor grasped the control stick and eased it back, his feet delicately directing the floor pedals.

The Hip rose, airborne now. The Hind skittered sideways, its machine gun tracking this new menace. Taylor felt the aircraft shudder as 12.7mm rounds sliced through the hull aft. One Cyrillic-letter gauge warned of a drop in oil pressure. Another warned of leaking fuel.

The Hind fired again.

Hunter watched from the doorway of the HQ building, Buchanan's limp weight draped across his shoulders in a fireman's carry. Rachel pressed up close beside him, his Uzi in her hands. They had seen Taylor's sprint to the Hip, seen the wounded Anderson sprawled beneath the cockpit. The Hind hovered to the south, hammering at the sluggish transport with machine-gun fire.

"Ben, no!" The words were a prayer, but they went unheard. The Hip swayed for a moment under the autofire fusillade. The starboard landing pylon tore away, falling. Smoke billowed from an exhaust vent. The turbine whine faltered, suddenly rough.

Then the Hip lunged forward, homing on the gunship like a whale turning on a hungry shark. The Hind pilot saw his danger at the last moment, began to swerve away...

The two aircraft merged, coalescing in a flash of exploding fuel. Wreckage twisted out of the sky, writhing in white flame. One intact five-bladed rotor spun lazily through the sky and slashed into the squat gray tanks of the base fuel dump. Avgas sprayed under the impact as fiery debris rained from the sky. The second explosion swallowed the first in a deafening fireball, boiling into the sky like an erupting volcano.

Hunter picked himself up off the ground, unaware of having been knocked down by the blast. The sky burned as flame-shot, black mountains of oily smoke blotted out the sun. *"Ben!"*

Gomez looked up in the blinding flare of the midair collision. He'd not realized, could not have realized, that this was Ben's plan. Tears streaked his paint-blackened face. *"¡Madre de Dios!"*

King lay next to Dark Walker, a hundred yards across the compound. He'd seen Taylor pull Anderson from the Hip, seen him climb into the cockpit. For one terrible moment he'd thought Taylor was running. King started to rise. Roy needed help.

Then the Hip slashed into the Hind, lighting the sky. "Oh, God! I thought he was a coward."

Walker's face was hard. "No. He is a warrior."

"C'mon." Shock numbed Hunter's mind. "Let's move."

Hellfire seared the sky. Hunched under Buchanan's bulk, Hunter moved as quickly as his aching legs could carry him. The heat seemed overwhelming as the Russian tank farm burned.

"Where are we going?" Rachel asked.

"We've got an RP. Over there . . . in the trees. That's where we regroup."

"Over there" was on the far side of the generator building near the stable. Hunter's breath came in short gasps, his legs and shoulders burning. He wanted to stop, to rest, but not here. Not here . . .

As they moved past the generator building Rachel touched him. "Travis!" She pointed at the tangle of busbars and power cables of the downlink gate. "It's running!"

Hunter could see the blue glow even against the glare of burning avgas. The unstable wavering of auroras shifted and moved in the interplay of complex energy fields.

The Russians had opened a time portal.

• • •

First Technician Pyotr Petrovich Polyakov screamed at the others in the control room. Outside, thunder rolled among the flames. The help Andryanov had promised counted for nothing now. The generator building and portal were intact for the moment, but the Americans would be here in minutes.

Through the open door he saw figures, silhouetted against orange fire . . . one man carrying another, and a girl with an SMG.

Polyakov touched the shoulder of a spetsnaz trooper beside him, pointing. "Americans!" he shouted over the roar. "Stop them! We need time to get to the gate!"

"*Da*, Comrade Technician!" The soldier signaled his men. Six spetsnaz brushed past Polyakov and out the door, AKMs ready.

It was all over now. There was nothing left but to carry out Andryanov's last orders and evacuate . . . if they could. He returned to the console and brought his thumb down on a large red button. A siren shrieked warning. "One minute!" he yelled. "Everybody out! All personnel to the gate! *Hurry!*"

John Mason crouched in the glare of the flames near the stable. He'd been separated from Walker and King earlier, had seen Rog White take on the Hind one-on-one and die. He shuddered at the memory.

Across the compound, Hunter and the girl hurried across his line of sight. The lieutenant was carrying . . .

Jimmy!

Wycliff's death was a throbbing pain behind his eyes, driving him to kill and kill, and kill again. The sight of the Ranger with Jimmy Buchanan slung over his back caught him like a slap across the face.

He'd been willing to concede Dark Walker's point that Hunter knew what he was doing . . . until that morning. If Hunter had not taken the SAS team south, Sir David might still be alive.

But now Hunter was making his way painfully across the fire-swept compound, burdened by Jimmy. He cared. . . .

A commotion nearby caught Mason's attention. Men were spilling from the generator building, some in white technician's coats, some carrying AKMs. Spetsnaz troopers were spreading out to attack Hunter and the girl, while the scientists fled toward the looming complexity of the time portal.

The Russians were behind the two, out of their line of vision. Mason saw the VBU troops raise their weapons.

But he was behind the Soviets. He snatched up his L85 and charged, his weapon blazing. One Russian screamed and pitched forward. A second clawed at his back as bloody holes stitched up his spine.

The other four spetsnaz commandos spun, their AKMs blasting wildly. Mason felt something smack into his side. He kept firing, cutting down a third Russian. His Individual Weapon clicked empty as his legs gave way and he dropped to his knees.

A white-hot wire seared through his bowels, and pile-driver blows hammered his arm and chest. He snapped a fresh magazine into the bullpup receiver, chambered a round, and cut loose again. Another Soviet spun aside, his face a bloody pulp.

He was still firing as flame and thunder were swallowed up by night.

The burst of autofire from behind caught Hunter by surprise. He turned in time to see three Russians already down, a fourth toppling as bullets smashed into his head.

Mason was on his knees, fifty yards away, still shooting as a pair of VBU troops continued to pump fire into him.

Rachel brought the Uzi up to her face and squeezed off a burst. One spetsnaz twisted and collapsed. The other threw down his AKM and bolted for the portal, following the last of the technicians into the shifting glow and vanishing.

Mason was dead.

Explosions ripped through the interior of the generator building. *They're destroying everything so we can't get at Uralskiy,* Hunter thought. The Rangers knew nothing about the VBU's counterpart to the Chronos Complex except the name. *Not that we have enough men to do anything about it.*

They found the others at the RP, just beyond the base perimeter and not far from the stables. King and Dark Walker were giving first aid to Anderson. Gomez mounted guard.

Hunter lowered Buchanan to the ground. "God, am I glad to see you," King said. "We thought you'd bought it. Did you see . . . ?"

"Ben," he said. "I saw."

"I . . . didn't know him very well," Rachel said.

"Maybe none of us did."

King nodded. "I wish—" He bit off the words, then bent again over Anderson.

Rachel shivered. Dark Walker stood, pulling off his camo fatigue jacket and draping it over her shoulders.

Fresh explosions rolled across the compound as the flames found new stores of fuel. Horses stamped and snorted inside the stable, terrified of the fire.

"Eddie?" Hunter said, watching the spectacle.

"Right here, Chief."

"You and Walker hitch up the wagon. Get all the horses. I think it's time to leave."

An hour later the wagon lurched onto the dirt road a mile from the base. Gomez drove the team while the others slumped in the back. Extra horses trailed along on a lead behind the wagon. By changing horses when they got tired, they'd be able to push on farther, travel longer. Hunter wanted to reach their destination in three days.

Rachel snuggled beside him. "Where are we going?"

"Back to Saratoga. All our gear is there, our recall beacon . . ." He rubbed his face. He was so tired. "Home, Raye. We're going home."

"Saratoga . . ." Her eyes widened. "Travis! I have to tell you something!"

"What?"

"Benedict Arnold! I saw him!" Exhaustion slurred her words as she spilled out the story of her encounter with the American traitor and her decision to do nothing. "I've been terrified," she admitted finally. "I was afraid he might be part of the VBU plot!"

Hunter smiled but said nothing.

"Travis, say something!" Her head sank against his knee. "If I screwed everything up . . ."

"Don't worry." He stroked her hair gently. "It'll be fine."

Rachel pushed away from him. "Travis! This is important! You're the one always worried about historical details! Don't you think . . . ?"

Hunter laughed.

"*Travis!*"

"Trust me, Raye. This is one time when it was best not to act!"

The wagon bumped and creaked. Behind them, smoke palled in the sky above the forest. Those fires would rage for days. Swamp would reclaim burned-over ground. Soon there would be nothing left at all to show that time travelers had built there.

Nothing . . . except for the life of a man named Washington and an American victory at a place called Saratoga.

Epilogue

From the ridge top across the Hudson River from Bemis Heights, the little party watched smoke rise from the battle ground as the far-off crackle of musket fire drifted across the valley. It was October 7, 1777, three days after Germantown and the destruction of the VBU base. The second battle at Saratoga was unfolding among the woods almost three miles away, and they were watching it through binoculars.

"See there . . . toward the center?" Hunter pointed. "Those are the British redoubts: earthworks thrown up after the Freeman's Farm battle. The Americans have thrown the first British advance back and are closing in on them now."

"The Americans win, huh?" Buchanan asked. He was recovered from the beating now, his leg once more splinted and bandaged. He could get around fairly well now on a pair of crutches Anderson had carved for him. "I'm not sure I see how."

"They'll win. After this fight Burgoyne will realize he's trapped. He'll be forced to ask for terms."

"I feel sorry for him," Rachel said. She wore her black nightsuit, recovered with the rest of their gear from the cache near the ruined Parson house.

"Don't, Raye," Hunter said after a moment. "This campaign was the turning point for the American Revolution." He'd been reading the history text they'd taken during the Philadelphia raid. "There were two key points, you see . . . here and in Pennsylvania."

"Saratoga was one," Anderson said. His arm was in a sling, but he was recovering well from his wound.

"And Washington's fights at Brandywine and Germantown

were the other," Hunter said. He was feeling more like an expert on the period now. There'd been plenty of time to study *Birth of the United States* during the trip from New Jersey.

Gomez looked puzzled. "But he lost both battles!"

Hunter nodded. "Yeah, but he didn't lose his army. And at Germantown he almost won . . . caught the British by surprise and damn near whipped them. Here in New York, a ragtag army with a divided leadership *did* whip them . . . forced a British army in the field to surrender. It impressed the hell out of the French. They sent an army and a fleet. That led to the British surrender at Yorktown three years later." He nodded toward the rising smoke across the river. "And it wouldn't have happened without that battle over there."

Rachel raised the binoculars to her eyes, and Hunter joined her. After a moment he took Rachel's arm. "There! Look at the redoubt by Freeman's Farm! See the man waving his sword?"

"Yes . . . oh!"

"'Oh' is right. I think that's Arnold."

"It is! I recognize him! You say he *belongs* here?"

"Benedict Arnold was the hero of Saratoga. I guess it's not well known anymore, but he fought the British to a standstill at Freeman's Farm and would have won the battle if it hadn't been for Gates's stupidity. After the first battle they quarreled. He was a bit of an egotist, but Gates was jealous and refused to mention him in the official dispatches. By the time of the second battle, Arnold didn't even have a command."

"Then what's he doing there?"

"Fighting. He had to do something, so he charged out onto the battlefield and went to the head of his troops, even though he wasn't their commander anymore. The book says he was all over the field, rallying, charging. Finally he led the assault on that redoubt personally. He was wounded in the leg, but the victory was already won by then."

"And he's not part of a VBU plot."

"Not at all. You know . . . it's ironic. If his wound had been fatal, Benedict Arnold probably would be remembered as one of America's greatest heroes."

"What happened?" Walker asked.

Hunter shook his head. "That's another story. Right now . . . today . . . he's a hero. Let's leave it at that."

Rachel turned to look at the backpack beacon set up behind them. A familiar blue glow danced and wavered in the air above it. "Look! The portal's open!"

Hunter looked. Home lay just beyond that glow.

He hoped. Rachel had assured him that with the changes introduced by VBU intervention undone, the universe of Brigadier Carruthers and the Dominion of British North America was gone, wiped away by the transformation wave traveling uptime to 2007. Now the recall beacon should allow them to contact Time Square and the Chronos Project.

At least that was the way it was supposed to work.

"Jimmy?" Hunter said. "Dark Walker? Time to go. What's it going to be?"

Buchanan looked across the valley. "I've been giving it a lot of thought, Leftenant," he said. "I appreciate the offer. But I think I'll stay here."

"Are you afraid you won't make it through?"

There were details of time-travel physics that no one yet understood completely. One aspect of that physics, though, seemed to dictate that time travelers from one universe could not enter a present where they already existed. A few months before, a number of commandos from one universe had vanished upon returning to 2007, apparently because analogues of themselves already existed there.

He looked at Buchanan and Dark Walker, the only survivors of Wycliff's SAS team. Their universe, and their history, were gone . . . hopefully replaced by the past Hunter and his people remembered. Would they vanish when they stepped through the blue glow, or were the two universes different enough that their own analogues did not exist in Hunter's world?

"No, it's not that," Buchanan said. "I . . . wouldn't be at home in your world, mate. The lads and I talked about it a lot. We all knew we couldn't go back to British North America. Some of 'em wanted to try goin' through with your lot. Others figured this wasn't such a bad place here." He nodded toward the panorama across the river. "A man could make a life for himself here." He shot Hunter a look. "And not to worry. I won't go tampering, if that's what's worrying you."

"Not at all. Where will you go?"

"Oh . . . I'll probably hang around at Bemis Tavern until the leg heals up. You know, I had family in Pennsylvania." He smiled suddenly. "I *will* have family in Pennsylvania? I don't think I can handle time travel anymore, Leftenant. The language gets too confusing. Anyway, maybe I'll head down there. I could marry, raise a family. . ."

"I understand." Hunter turned to Dark Walker. "How about you?"

White teeth showed against dark skin. "I think I'll come with you, Leftenant. If the offer's still open."

Hunter nodded gravely. "I can't promise you'll make it. We told you what happened to other people who tried it."

"Sure," Buchanan said. "You could come with me. Your own people are out there. There are Indians with Burgoyne's army!"

Dark Walker shook his head "My people are the Dakota, out in the west. And in this time they are savages, Jimmy. They take scalps . . . torture their prisoners." He made a sour face. "I have far more in common with the Rangers."

"Then I wish you well, Dark Walker." He extended a hand, and the Indian took it. "You're a good mate."

"And you."

"You sure you'll be okay?" Hunter asked Buchanan.

"Sure. Don't worry about me. I've got the wagon. That'll get me back to the tavern."

"Good luck." Hunter shook the sergeant's hand, then looked at his team. "Okay, people. Take a last look at 1777, and let's go. Thompson must be beside himself by now."

Dark Walker smiled. "At least we know *I* won't be beside myself."

One by one they filed through the blue glow, vanishing from sight. Hunter watched them go, then turned to wave at James Buchanan, standing now by the wagon.

Something nagged at Hunter's memory. Buchanan? That name . . .

There had been a president of the United States named Buchanan. That had been just before the Civil War. Hunter didn't remember much about him, except that he was the only president to be born in Pennsylvania . . .

. . . and the only U.S. president to have the same name as his father.

President James Buchanan must have been born sometime in the late 1700s. His father . . .

Hunter looked again at the SAS man leaning on his crutches. Was it possible?

"Nah . . . ! Couldn't be!"

Hunter stepped into the shifting blue light.